NEWFOUNDLAND
NES
ELITE SECURITY

NES * SERIES

Risky Extraction

RHONDA BREWER

Dedication

I've dedicated this book to all the people who have stuck by me in my struggle to get this book completed. To my family, I love you all. To my friends, you give me the strength to push through. Last but not least, to all of my wonderful readers who have waited patiently for this book. I appreciate all of you more than I can say.

I love you all.

Acknowledgments

So many people have made my writing and publishing journey possible. A simple thank you never seems enough to convey my gratitude.

To the extraordinary ladies Michelle Eriksen and Abbie Zanders, who helped me improve my stories, I don't know what I would do without your advice, suggestions, keen eyes, and encouragement.

Thank you for always being there when I need you, Jackie Dawe Ford, Nancy Arnold-Holloway, and Karie Deegan, as my dedicated betas and dear friends.

Thank you, Corey Majeau of Majeau Designs and Golden Czermak of Furious Fotog, for making my covers stunning.

Prologue

Nineteen years ago…

His pulse pounded in his ears and muted the guard's conversation as Brent Adams crouched near the stone building. Not that he'd understand them anyway; he didn't speak the language. Camouflaged by the shadows, it would be difficult for anyone to see him, but unease made his body rigid.

In the four years since he enlisted, this was his first deployment. He'd expected it at some point in his military career when he'd decided at eighteen this was what he wanted. Brent was proud to serve Canada, and at twenty-two, he was the youngest on Ghost Team. He was well-trained and confident in his abilities, but things could go to hell with one wrong move.

When Lieutenant-Colonel Titus Gibson called the team's seven members, Brent was surprised. He never expected to join a specialized group sent to the Middle East, especially such a classified mission where he wasn't permitted to divulge information outside the team and Gibson. Everything about the mission, including their location and travel details, was confidential.

The critical extraction was the team's first mission together. The seven-member group consisted of Captain Otto Fudge, Brent, Dale Eubanks, Virgil Boone, Wyatt Christopher, the spotter, Perry Brown, and the team sniper, Axel Wright.

Brent grew up with Axel and Wyatt in Newfoundland. Both men were older by a year, but the three of them joined the military together. That's why it surprised everyone when Titus put them on the same team. Titus insisted it was because they knew each other so well that they would be compatible.

Brent got the call less than seventy-two hours earlier and arrived in Syria six hours ago. Damascus was one of the most dangerous parts of the country; one wrong move could mean being captured or worse. He didn't want to be another body sent home in a box.

Titus sent Ghost team to rescue a woman and her daughter, abducted by a cruel, abusive man. The situation could turn unstable in the blink of an eye because they were in a country that was a virtual war zone.

With his back pressed against the mud bricks, he remained motionless until the team leader gave the word. His body didn't like the uncomfortable position, but he was a statue until a quiet voice crackled in his ear.

"Ghost one, to ghost three, do you have visual," Otto asked.

Otto was a highly decorated and the most focused soldier Brent ever met. He was the oldest on the team, and if anyone could get them in and out safely, it would be Otto.

"Ghost three, to ghost one, no visual yet, but another tango just stepped inside," Perry informed Otto.

Perry and Axel set up to remove anyone considered a threat to the team or the mission. They had intelligence on individuals associated with Nasir Hasan, so there were no surprises, and they could get in and out quickly.

"Ghost one to ghost seven, do you have a visual on Tango?" Otto asked Brent.

Brent and Wyatt were the closest to the building's entrance, ready to move the second Otto gave the word, but the plan would change if someone unknown were in the building. He leaned forward to peer through the small window and spotted a man beside the door. Brent backed away and held up an arm to Wyatt.

"Ghost seven to ghost one, two inside with an unknown." Brent locked eyes with Wyatt when Otto let out a string of curses.

They had one chance to get the woman before Nasir moved her and the child. According to Titus's information, Nasir didn't want her to return to Canada and kept her against her will.

Dale and Virgil were on the other side of the building, trying to get a visual of the woman and little girl. Nasir probably kept them close for fear she would escape. He'd moved them several times over the last few weeks, so Brent and his team needed to get in fast. Ghost team was Halima's last chance to get away from the man.

"Ghost one to Ghost four, do you have eyes on target?" Otto sounded frustrated.

There was about a minute of silence, but it seemed longer as they waited for confirmation. If they couldn't confirm the woman and child were inside the building, they'd need to abort the mission until Titus had an exact location.

"Ghost four to Ghost one, have visual. Rear south corner. Both targets in the same location." Dale informed them.

"Restrained?" Otto asked.

"Negative," Dale replied.

Brent relaxed a little. Restraints would make it harder to extract them, but there was no way Nasir didn't have them locked down. Getting through the small windows would be impossible, so there was no chance Dale and Virgil could retrieve them that way.

The muffled voices caused Brent and Wyatt to back up further into the shadows. Virgil was the only one who understood the language because his wife was Syrian, so he would remain close to the woman and her daughter.

"Tango leaving," Perry's voice crackled in his ear.

"Alone?" Otto asked.

"No, Hasan is leaving too." Perry sounded excited.

Titus had told Otto that if they had a chance to neutralize Nasir, they should take the opportunity. This meant that if the man was out in the open, that would be the end for him.

"Take him out," Otto snapped.

They didn't have time to think before all hell broke loose. Brent and Wyatt moved quickly around the building to join Virgil and Dale as they breached the structure. Bullets flew all around them, but none came from their team. They kept to the task of making it to the room and rescuing Halima and Aya.

A woman's scream and a little girl's shrieks mixed in with explosions, and the popping sound of automatic weapons made it almost impossible for Brent to hear the voices of his team through the earpiece.

"What is she screaming about?" Otto asked.

"She said she's safe," Virgil responded and said something in Syrian to the woman.

She shook her head as she kept pointing and looking over her shoulder. Before she could say another word, Virgil picked her up and ran from the chaos behind them. Brent didn't know why the woman was so distraught because she could see her daughter in Brent's arms. He hoped she needed rescue.

"Get out now," Perry ordered.

They headed quickly to the rendezvous point. The little girl looked barely three years old and clung to Brent as if he would disappear. Halima looked ready to jump out of her skin, and Virgil tried to reassure her, but she shook her head and tapped the flag on the shoulder of his uniform. Virgil nodded, but there was fear in her eyes.

Brent could see the finish line as they loaded the mother and daughter into the helicopter. Wyatt grabbed Brent's forearm and pulled him through the hangar door, but before he was inside, something hit

Brent on the back of the head. He turned to look behind him only to see a ball of fire, and then everything went black.

Chapter 1

Seventeen years ago…

He rolled off the woman he'd met at the bar and reached for the bottle of whiskey on the table next to him. After swallowing almost a third of the bottle, he held it out to the curvy brunette and tried to recall her name.

Another nameless girl he'd never see again once he left her place. He always made sure his casual fucks lived at least an hour from his apartment. It made it less likely to run into them again, and exchanging numbers was a hell no.

Settling back into civilian life wasn't easy after his injury. The memories of the hell he went through with Ghost Squad continuously played in his brain if he didn't have a distraction. The booze, pills, and women worked, but he couldn't escape it when he closed his eyes at night. Brent relived that day in his dreams.

Virgil and Dale never made it back. They rescued Halima and Aya, but it cost two good men their lives. That was bad enough, but to make matters worse, Lieutenant Colonel Gibson didn't seem to care about their deaths or the fact Brent and Axel were hurt.

They didn't know the truth until they returned home and pulled into a debriefing. Titus sent them into hostile territory to rescue a woman and child, but it was off-the-books. He'd not only taken it upon himself to send Ghost Team over there, but he also funded the entire thing. Since he came from family money, he could easily afford it.

After they'd returned and the whole thing was exposed, Titus Gibson was forced into retirement. He never contacted Brent or any of the remaining Ghost Team again, and as far as apologizing, all they got was a generic letter with no actual signature. Brent assumed it was probably sent from the office, not from Titus.

The higher-ups covered for Titus, though. Brent's and Axel's records stated they sustained injuries during a training exercise and were medically discharged. If anyone investigated, the group was in a helicopter that went down. According to documents, Virgil and Dale died in the crash. It was a load of bullshit, but the military couldn't allow anyone to know about the fuck up. Titus should be behind bars, but he was probably sitting pretty with his military pension.

At least Virgil and Dale got a proper military send-off, and their wives received death benefits. If the truth came out, none of that would've happened. Dale's wife was pregnant and almost lost the little girl after she heard of Dale's death. Thankfully, the sweet child survived.

The only thing Brent knew about Halima and Aya was they were safe. Axel inquired about it once but couldn't get any answers. Wyatt somehow learned the woman and child were in Newfoundland.

Constant nightmares plagued Brent's nights. Loud noises caused his heart to race and drag him back to that day. Back where he'd lost his innocence and the belief he could make a difference. There was a time when he thought Titus Gibson cared about the team. What a fucking joke. If Brent never saw the son of bitch again, it would be too soon.

He distanced himself from the remaining team members after they returned. Seeing them only made things worse because it reminded him of what they'd done together. He couldn't tell anyone the depths of the guilt he felt because he survived, but Dale and Virgil didn't.

When he returned to Alberta, he avoided communication with his family and would only contact them when one threatened to fly up to see him. They went through hell when they found out he'd gotten hurt, and he had to pull off some Oscar-award-winning acting to convince his parents, brother, and sister he was okay.

Brent didn't return home to Newfoundland as they wanted. Instead, he spent his time in dive bars, drinking too much and doing shit he never did before. It's where Brent met Snapper Horlick. The man was a mean son of a bitch when someone crossed him, but he treated Brent well. As far as he knew, Snapper was also a former soldier and knew what the horrors of war could do to a person.

Snapper wasn't a huge guy, but he had a lot of large friends. Brent saw the man beat a man senseless for not saying thank you when offered a drink. Brent could swear Snapper's eyes turned black, almost sadistic.

Brent's back injury put him on a bad road, with three broken vertebrae and a concussion. The doctor prescribed painkillers to help with his discomfort, but he didn't need them for his physical pain anymore. He used them to help him survive the emotional pain and mental anguish. Getting drunk out of his mind, popping a few pills, and having a random fuck with any woman who said she'd take him home was how he dealt with it.

All Brent had to do was flash a smile, show his muscles, say he was retired military, and women fell into his lap. If he didn't want to make the effort it took to get a girl into bed, Snapper would find a willing partner.

"Hey, do you have any blow?" Brandi asked, or was her name Randi?

"Don't do that shit." Brent sat up against the headboard and took a swig of whiskey.

He tried Cocaine once but didn't enjoy it. Plus, pills and booze were easier to get, and he didn't have to suck it up his nose. Although if he wanted it, Snapper had connections.

"I don't either, but I've always wanted to try it." She straddled his legs.

He had to admit the woman had a killer body, and she was attractive but not enough to keep him there all night. He grabbed her around the waist and flipped her onto her back. She giggled, probably thinking he was about to give her another pounding, but Brent got up and pulled on his cargo pants.

"Where are you going?" She cupped her breasts.

"Look, this was fun, but I gotta go." Brent tugged his t-shirt down over his head.

"Oh." She sat up. "When can I see…"

"You won't," Brent interrupted, then drained the whiskey bottle.

"I see."

She was disappointed, no doubt, but that didn't stop Brent. He yanked on his boots and stood up. It was an asshole move, but he wasn't looking for a relationship. He'd never leave a woman unsatisfied in bed, but he wasn't about to whisper forever in her ear when he didn't see his life past the next bottle.

His phone buzzed on the night table, and he picked it up. When he saw the number, he rolled his eyes. Snapper was always making sure he wasn't low on supplies. If only everyone gave that kind of customer service, although if Brent ever screwed him over, Snapper wouldn't be so accommodating.

"Yo," Brent grunted.

"B, my man," A gruff voice replied.

Snapper sometimes sounded like he had an accent and hid it well, but now and then, it slipped. Brent couldn't figure out why it sounded familiar. When anyone asked him, Snapper told people he was from all over, but his mother was French.

"I'm not your man," Brent grumbled.

"Fuck, did Brandi not give you an enjoyable ride?" Snapper chuckled.

Nobody knew Snapper's first name, but he kept Brent in pills and women for the right price. The women weren't prostitutes, they simply didn't mind opening their legs, and Brent wasn't about to turn down available pussy.

"She rode me like an Albertan cowgirl," Brent retorted.

"Excellent. I'm checking to see if you need any provisions."
Snapper was always willing to help.

"Nope, got lots."

The sad thing was that Snapper and his crew were snakes slithering around people at the lowest point in their lives, Brent included. Snapper tried to make it look as if he cared enough to give his fellow soldiers whatever they needed. Brent could see himself heading down a slippery slope but didn't want to admit it.

Snapper did seem to show Brent extra attention because he'd never known the guy to call any of his other clientele. One of Snapper's delivery guys asked Brent once what he had on Snapper because the guy bent over backward for him. Brent didn't know or care.

"Okay, my friend. Call me if you get low," Snapper said, and Brent ended the call without a response.

With a half-wave to Brandie, he pulled on his jacket and quickly exited her shabby apartment. He practically skipped half the steps down to the main floor to make sure he could escape without the girl causing a fuss. They usually didn't, but he wasn't taking any chances.

The icy wind was biting at his skin as he made his way to his car. He shouldn't get behind the wheel, considering he downed half a bottle of whiskey, and the beer he drank earlier had not left his system. He had better sense, especially knowing what happened to his father years earlier. The alcohol dulled the little voice in his head, and he jumped in the car to head back to his crap apartment in Calgary.

Pulling into his parking spot an hour later, he sighed in relief. He managed to get home without wrapping his car around a pole or getting nabbed by the police. Brent almost fell as he staggered into the apartment building. On the elevator ride to the second floor, he shuffled through his keys so he could get into his place quickly.

As he stepped off the elevator, he stopped. Someone he didn't want to see stood with his shoulder against the wall, and Brent cursed under his breath. This was the last thing he needed—Axel Wright's lecture on how Brent was screwing up his life.

Axel constantly harassed Brent about getting help for his post-traumatic stress. Brent did fine and didn't need anyone to tell him what he already knew. Rehashing it every damn day didn't help. The memories of seeing Dale blown to pieces not more than twenty feet away were etched in his brain.

"Where the hell have you been?" Axel questioned.

"Out," Brent snapped as he fumbled with the lock on his door.

"Out boozing again by the smell. Snapper keeping you high, too?" Axel pushed off the wall.

"Did you come here to bust my ass? If you did, you can leave." Brent threw open the door and blocked Axel from entering.

"You're killing yourself, B. This is not the way to deal…" Axel began.

"You should throw that broken record away, Ax. It's my life. Now fuck off." Brent slammed the door.

"You forget who your real friends are, B. You leave me no choice, man. I'm going to have to take drastic steps," Axel shouted through the door.

Brent rolled his eyes and flipped the bird to the closed door. Axel always threatened to "*take action*," but Brent didn't know or care what he meant. For over a month, Axel made that statement every time he dropped over. As far as Brent was concerned, Axel was blowing shit out of his ass.

He stripped off on his way through the apartment, leaving a trail of discarded clothes. He stepped into the bathroom completely naked, and before jumping into the shower, he zeroed in on the pills sitting on the counter. He ignored the warning to avoid alcohol when he took them because taking both helped him sleep.

The doctor limited the number of pills he prescribed, but Snapper always came through when Brent ran low. Vicodin wasn't something he took every day, but he needed to get through an entire night without waking up in a sheen of sweat.

After a quick shower, he tossed back a pill and then flopped down on the bed. His head fell to the side, and his eyes locked onto the picture on his nightstand. His team took it before they left that day, but nobody knew what they would face, or they wouldn't be grinning like fools. He flipped over onto his stomach and squeezed his eyes shut. It didn't take long before he fell into an alcohol and drug-induced sleep.

The loud banging had to be a dream because there was no way someone would be beating on his door and not expect a punch in the face. He tossed back the blankets and pulled on a pair of boxers. He stumbled and had to take a second to clear the cobwebs from his brain before continuing to see who was about to get pounded into the floor. When he yanked open the door, he cocked his fist but dropped it immediately.

"Dad?" Brent's brows furrowed.

"You look great," his father didn't bother to wait for an invitation and stomped into the apartment.

"Thanks, Dad." Brent pulled his hands down over his face to ensure he was awake.

"It wasn't a compliment," his father replied.

Brent's heart picked up as several scenarios ran through his muddled thoughts on what would cause his dad to fly across the country. Was someone sick? Dead?

"Yeah, I figured that out. Why are you here?" Brent asked.

"I flew in from Newfoundland an hour ago because I got a call from Axel." His father glared at him.

"You got here pretty fast." Brent was going to kick Axel's ass.

"He called me almost eighteen hours ago. After he left here yesterday," his dad said through gritted teeth.

If that was true, it meant Brent had slept for that long. He must have been out of it when he got home. He didn't miss how his father scanned the messy apartment with disappointment written all over his face. Brent couldn't blame him. The place was a shitty mess.

"Get dressed. We're going to a meeting," his dad ordered.

"Meeting?" Brent wasn't alert enough for this.

"An Alcoholics Anonymous meeting or a Narcotics Anonymous meeting. By the looks of you, we probably need to go to both. Get some clothes on." His father crossed his large arms over his chest.

"You came to Alberta to take me to a meeting? Pretty sure they still have them in Newfoundland," Brent grumbled.

"At least I'm taking you to a meeting and not planning your fucking funeral," his father snapped.

"You're out of your mind. I don't need..." Brent didn't get a chance to finish when Axel stepped into the apartment.

"I told you I'd take drastic steps." Axel leaned his shoulder against the doorframe.

"You called my dad? Had him fly across the country?" Brent stared at his friend.

"Yes, because you're one bottle away from killing yourself or someone else. I know about the pills, too," his father retorted.

Max Adams wasn't a small man, and Brent knew from experience his father wouldn't take no for an answer. Arguing would only give Brent a bigger headache than he already had.

"This is ridiculous." Brent threw his arms up in the air.

"Ridiculous or not, you're getting your ass dressed and coming with me." His dad picked up Brent's clothes scattered on the floor and tossed them at his son.

"You need to clean up too."

"I'm..." Brent didn't get a chance to argue.

"Get fucking dressed now, Brent. I didn't tell your mother why I had to come here but don't push me. Do you want her to see you this way?" His father knew Brent's weakness.

He didn't want his mom to know what a screw-up he was. He wouldn't be able to handle seeing that disappointment in her eyes. His mother had been through enough when his father almost drank himself into an early grave. It was the first time he'd seen his mom break down when they walked into the hospital, not knowing if his father would survive wrapping a car around a pole and nearly killing someone else.

"No," Brent grumbled.

"Well, get dressed, and for the love of God, brush your teeth. You stink." With that statement, his father turned and headed into the small kitchen.

An hour later, Brent sat in a large room with a pounding head, drinking shitty coffee and listening to people's struggles with addiction. With everything he heard, he realized the stories weren't much different from his. Then someone stood up and made him sit up straight. Axel stepped in front of the podium and locked eyes with Brent.

"My name is Axel, and I'm an alcoholic. It's been thirteen months since my last drink…"

Brent's mouth opened, and he almost dropped the paper cup. He hadn't known Axel drank. His friend spent most of his recovery from a leg injury in Ontario with his sister and only returned to Calgary six months earlier when his sister moved there for a job.

Axel's deep voice echoed in the room, and as Brent listened, he glanced to his left. His father gave up drinking ten years earlier after that accident almost took his life. It was a wake-up call for his dad.

Brent took his dad's hand, letting his emotions take over for the first time in months. Tears stung his eyes, and he dropped his head as Axel finished his story.

"I need help," he whispered.

"That's why I'm here, son." His father wrapped an arm around Brent's shoulder. "That's why I'm here."

If anyone could help him, it was the man next to him. His dad wouldn't give up until Brent was back on his feet, and that was precisely what he needed. He hoped he could do it.

Chapter 2

Four years ago…

Allyson Sullivan watched him slowly walk down the beach. His eyes were haunted but usually were after a bad night. In the three years she'd known him, his nightmares came and went.

Brent, or Crash as he was known by most, worked for Newfoundland Elite Security or NES. Most of the employees were referred to by nicknames. Some received the name because of something they did in the past, but she wasn't sure where Crash's came from.

Crash might project the appearance of a self-confident, muscular former military man, not to mention sexy beyond belief, but the demons that haunted him from his time in the Middle East were many.

Crash saw a therapist and went religiously. He told Allyson everything about his life, and she reciprocated, for the most part. There was one thing she didn't tell him or anyone. As a doctor, she knew it wasn't her fault, but as a woman, it wasn't easy to allow the words to come out of her mouth.

When he crouched and picked up some beach rocks, she approached him. He needed a friend, and she was there to lend an ear. She fell in love with him a long time ago, and if she could give in to her feelings for him, things would be easier, but he deserved someone who could give him everything a man wanted.

Brent stood up and began flinging stones into the crashing waves. He told her once it was something he did to help shake unpleasant feelings. The rocks represented everything that brought him down, and throwing them into the ocean symbolized getting rid of those emotions, if only for a short time.

"You know if you hit a seagull, you'll get a ticket," Allyson said as she walked closer.

"I won't tell if you don't," he replied with a smile.

His smile was forced, but it still made the lines at the corner of his eyes crinkle. The strain of the day showed on his handsome face, but it didn't matter to her. He could have mud from head to toe, and he'd still make her heart skip a beat.

"Your secret is safe with me." Allyson smirked.

"Thank God," he returned and then blew out a long breath.

She'd received a text from him at five that morning, and when she answered right away, he thought he'd woken her. She was due at the hospital early, so he'd caught her as she got ready for work.

Crash got news that one of the men he served with had died. She wasn't sure how and considering the about of mental health issues that former vets faced. He might have ended his own life.

Allyson couldn't imagine the things Crash and his team saw. At least Crash got help, but some didn't think they could or didn't feel they deserved it.

Another friend of Crash's returned from deployment a couple of weeks earlier and struggled with civilian life. Crash told her that he and Wyatt went to high school together and enlisted with Axel. Wyatt's wife was pregnant, and Crash helped him get on the right track, but now, Crash suffered because he relived his last deployment through nightmares. He wouldn't tell her exactly what happened, probably because her late husband died while deployed, or maybe he wasn't permitted to talk about it.

It was tough to think about Trent's last moments, even after four years. She was grateful Crash wanted to spare her the gory details of life in a war zone, but she wished she could help him.

"Bad day?" Allyson knew the answer.

"Yeah." He shoved his hands in his pockets.

"What was his name?" Allyson asked.

"Perry Brown." Crash sighed.

"Do you know what happened?" Allyson assumed he'd probably taken his own life.

"He died in a fire."

"Do you want to talk about him?" She wasn't sure if that was the right question, but it was all she could offer.

"It's not going to change anything." Crash choked out the words.

"I wish I could help," Allyson whispered.

"Me too." He gave her a forced smile. "Otto said the place was a fire hazard and begged Perry to find another place to live. Otto and Perry were close."

It was a cool day, but nothing was as relaxing as watching the beautiful dance of the waves as they crashed against the rocky shore and dragged the pebbles back into the Atlantic Ocean. The sound was a soothing melody. For several minutes, they stood in silence before she turned to him.

"I could use a piece of Alice's blueberry pie. How about you?" She nodded toward the combination pub and diner not far from the beach.

"I won't say no to that." Crash grinned.

Jack's Place was one of three restaurants in Hopedale. The owner, Alice O'Connor, prided herself on her traditional Newfoundland cuisine and homemade treats. One side of the building was the diner, and the other a pub. People could go to both places, catch up with friends, drink, and dance. All the residents of Hopedale ended up at the place at some point during the week.

They walked in comfortable silence along the road next to the beach and toward the diner. The mid-September wind had a fall chill, making her shiver. Allyson pulled her sweater tighter around her body as they rounded the corner into the parking lot.

"You should be wearing a coat," Brent chastised.

"It wasn't this cold when I left my house, Mom." Allyson poked his muscular arm.

"It's September in Newfoundland, and Hopedale is practically surrounded by water. Are you new here?" Brent teased.

Allyson rolled her eyes at his response and stepped through the diner door. Entering the cheery place, the aromas of fresh coffee and sweets filled her nostrils, and she sighed as they slid into a booth next to the window.

Glancing around, she waved and returned greetings to several familiar faces. Some she knew by name, others she saw around town. Hopedale was a typical small Newfoundland fishing community.

It's why she returned to Hopedale when she left Ontario after Trent's death. She hadn't grown up there, but her mom was from the tiny town, and Allyson lived there until she married. She would never have left if the military hadn't posted Trent to Ottawa.

It was different from living in Ontario, where some people didn't even know their next-door neighbors. Being around familiar people helped her through losing Trent and gave her the help she needed to raise her son. Cameron was growing up so fast, and she was proud of the young man he had become.

"Well, hello, you two," the owner of Jack's Place stepped next to the booth.

"Hi, Alice." Allyson smiled up at the woman.

"It's nice to see you." Crash kissed Alice's cheek before sitting down.

"I'm so sorry about your friend, Brent." Alice squeezed his arm gently.

"Thank you," Crash replied.

It didn't surprise Allyson that Alice knew about Crash's loss. Crash and his co-workers were close to the O'Connor family, much the same as Allyson's. Her sister married the youngest of Alice's nephews, and because of that, she spent lots of time with the family.

"You just missed Bethany and A.J." Alice placed the menus in front of them.

"Were they escaping the baby again?" Allyson knew her sister tried to get away at least once a week.

"I think so," Alice replied with a chuckle. "Now, what can I get you both?"

"I'll have some of your delicious blueberry pie and tea." Allyson smiled.

"Same for me, but I'll have coffee," Crash said.

"Coming right up."

Alice hurried off. For a woman who was sixty years old, she certainly didn't appear as if she would slow down anytime soon. Even though she owned the pub and diner, she still worked full-time during the day.

"Do you think someday she'll retire?" Allyson smiled.

"Not anytime soon. The O'Connor women don't seem to know the meaning of the word slow. Nanny Betty still volunteers more hours than most people work, and Kathleen is always babysitting at least a couple of her grandkids." Crash chuckled.

Kathleen O'Connor was married to Alice's brother-in-law, and they may have raised seven boys, but she hadn't slowed down either. She helped her daughters-in-law by babysitting her many grandchildren or helping with chores. Bethany told Allyson she didn't know what she would do without the woman.

Nanny Betty, the matriarch of the O'Connor family, was in her mid-eighties and volunteered at the hospital, animal shelter, and community center. She was also always ready to cook a feast when someone needed it. Allyson wasn't sure if the woman ever slept.

As if talking about the sweet woman made her appear, Nanny Betty stepped through the door with her companion, Tom Roberts. They were the cutest couple, with an interesting story. They'd been childhood sweethearts, but a series of events separated them. Betty married Jack O'Connor, and after he passed away, Tom came back into her life.

"Hello, me lovelies," Betty said as she walked to their table.

"Hi, Nan." Crash kissed her cheek.

"Hi, Nan," Allyson said with a smile.

Nobody was permitted to call Betty anything but Nan unless she didn't like them. To her, everyone was family.

"Are ya havin' a date?" Betty asked with an Irish lilt.

Newfoundland had a mix of dialects that sounded similar to Irish. Each community had its own unique accent, and even though Allyson grew up in the province, she still found some places challenging to understand the people. Betty was from what was known as the Southern Shore, where most of their ancestors were from Ireland.

Allyson hated to correct the woman, but she was not on a date with Crash. They were friends, and as much as she had to keep telling people that, she had to remind herself why that was all they could be.

"Just having coffee and chatting," Crash answered without a minute's hesitation.

"I see," Betty replied.

She narrowed her eyes as if waiting for one of them to admit she was right. Allyson's brother-in-law, Aaron, once revealed it was impossible to lie or hide anything from the women, especially when she gave what they called the "devil's glare."

"I was very sad to hear about yer friend. I'll keep 'em in me prayers." Betty laid her small hand on Crash's shoulder.

"Thanks, Nan." Crash nodded.

"Let's let the youngsters have their coffee, darling," Tom gently wrapped his arm around Nanny Betty.

For a minute, Allyson thought Betty would lecture them on the powers of Cora the Cupid and how she was never wrong. Betty's daughter, Cora, was also the resident matchmaker, and some people truly believed the woman knew when couples belonged together. Allyson thought it was all a bunch of bull, but to be fair, Cora Nightengale had never been wrong.

Betty gave them one last look before turning and allowing Tom to guide her toward the table Alice reserved for her mother-in-law. As she walked away, Allyson heard her mutter something to Tom.

"What's wrong wit da young ones today? Why can't dey see what's right in front of 'em?" Betty shook her head.

Crash closed his eyes, seemingly hearing her remark. Cora hadn't told Allyson directly, but she'd told everyone else. The woman was wrong this time.

"I love that woman," Crash whispered.

"You and everyone in Hopedale." Allyson smiled.

Crash took a deep breath and blew it out. He was obviously trying to hide his emotions, but his body tensed again when the distraction wore off. She hated that he had to go through anything so tragic.

"Want to talk about it?" Allyson asked after Alice brought their order.

"It's the same old stuff. Hearing about Perry brought it all on again." Crash poured cream into his coffee.

"The nightmares?" Allyson asked.

"Yeah, Axel called and said Wyatt took it hard, and he's afraid it will cause Wyatt to fall off the wagon." Crash sighed.

"Does he have help?" Allyson knew some of Crash's history with substance abuse after he left the military.

"He's trying to pull himself out. His wife is having a baby, and he wants to stay on the straight and narrow, but when something like this happens, it can send you spiraling again." Crash took a sip of his coffee. "I have my dad for support."

"I'm sure he'll reach out if things get too bad." Allyson knew people with addictions had a hard road ahead of them.

"Yeah, but this crowd he was involved with… let's just say I know what they're capable of. I was lucky not to get in deep because Axel and my dad had my back." Crash turned and gazed out at the harbor across the road. "Wyatt has no other family. He grew up in foster care. He was close to Lieutenant-Colonel Gibson, but that changed."

"He has you and your family, but make sure you take care of yourself too," Allyson warned.

"I will." Crash smiled.

Allyson still found it challenging to think of Crash as someone who'd associated with the type of people who sold drugs and committed crimes. The Crash she knew was dependable and law-abiding. Still, she'd seen some of her late husband's friends slide the slippery slope into drugs and depression once they returned from a harrowing tour overseas.

"Axel lives in New Brunswick, right?" Allyson asked.

"Yes. I've been trying to get him to move here because he has no family there. He says he can't leave because people need him there and his girlfriend won't move here. Wyatt is still in Alberta, so it makes it harder to be there for him." Crash stared down into his cup.

"I wish I could help more," Allyson whispered.

"You do. More than you know." Crash lifted his eyes, and they locked with hers.

She never knew what color she'd see when she looked into his eyes. Sometimes, they were hazel, and sometimes, green, but no matter what shade they were, when he looked at her, she wanted to forget everything and get lost in his gaze—to be alone and forget why they would never work out. She couldn't do that to him.

She turned her blue eyes away and finished the last of her tea. Crash dropped some money on the table before she could pull out her wallet. He stood up and waited for her to pull on her sweater before they left the diner.

They didn't talk as he walked her home, but when they arrived at her house, he made sure she was safe inside before leaving. When he did, she grabbed his hand.

"You shouldn't be alone right now." Allyson was worried about him.

"I know. That's why I'm going to a meeting with my dad." Crash gave her hand a gentle squeeze. "Thank you for being a friend."

He pulled her hand up and gently kissed her knuckles before he dropped it. Then he jogged down the front steps and was out of sight before she could respond. A friend was all she could be.

Her phone vibrated in her pocket, and when she pulled it out, she saw a message from one of the hospital nurses asking her to call. Getting a call from the hospital with questions about patients she'd treated during her shift wasn't unusual. Allyson called the emergency department as she stepped into her house. Someone answered on the second ring, which was remarkable because the place was always a hive of activity.

"This is Dr. Allyson Sullivan. I got a message from Leah Sellers asking me to call." She tossed her keys on the kitchen counter.

"One moment, Dr. Sullivan." The man put her on hold.

A few minutes passed, and she was getting ready to hang up. Messaging Leah would probably be easier, but someone answered before she could end the call.

"Ally?" Leah sounded frantic.

"Hey, Leah. What's up?"

"Dr. Davenport was looking for you. He's slightly bent out of shape because I wouldn't give him your home address." Leah snorted.

"What the hell does Witt want my address for?" Allyson asked.

Dr. Witt Davenport was a plastic surgeon with whom she'd gone to supper once and realized they had nothing in common. Luckily, she was smart enough to meet him at the restaurant and not have him pick her up. He bragged about all the people he worked with through his career but never dropped names. Witt was one of the top plastic surgeons, but he was arrogant.

"Guess he wanted to come to visit." Leah chuckled.

"Yeah, well, I get enough of him at the hospital. I don't want him dropping by here. If he asks again, tell him I don't want my home address given out." Allyson sighed.

"You know I wouldn't ever give him that, but I figured I'd give you a heads up. There are lots of ways to find where someone lives," Leah reminded her.

"I know. Thanks for the info." Allyson closed her eyes.

"You know I got your back, girl. I'll see you tomorrow." Leah ended the call.

She tossed her phone on the counter and sighed. She had no patience for Witt and his snobby attitude. She was worried about Crash and wished she could fix everything. Allyson's heart hurt for him and herself because she could never give him what he deserved.

Chapter 3

Present Day…

Crash propped his back against the bar, watching his newly married friend dance with his beautiful bride. Bruce 'Hulk' Steel gave new meaning to having two left feet, but nothing could wipe the smile off the man's face.

Hulk gazed at Caroline as if she hung the moon, and she smiled with the same lovesick grin. They were perfect for each other, but it was difficult not to feel a twinge of jealousy.

"Lucky bastard," Crash muttered under his breath.

"Another one down." Gage 'Smash' Hodder stepped next to the bar.

"They're falling fast," Crash remarked.

"The number of single residents in Hopedale seems to be dwindling fast," Smash said, motioning for the bartender.

After ordering a beer, Smash turned back to watch the crowd moving around the large venue. Most were like family to Crash, but Smash wasn't wrong. It seemed every year, someone was getting married or having a baby.

"Yeah, it must be wonderful to be that happy." Crash sighed.

As the words left his lips, she walked by, and Crash's heart thudded the way it always did when he saw her. Allyson was the only woman to bring him to his knees with a simple smile. It would be great if it weren't for the fact that she made it clear they could only ever have a platonic friendship.

At first, he thought it was his job as a security specialist with NES. The government contracted the accredited company for all the security needed for diplomats, politicians, or protection for private citizens. Over the last several years, some jobs were more dangerous than expected, and he had a bullet scar to prove it. Of course, that was the day he met Allyson; she had been the one to tend to his wound.

Crash met her when her sister needed protection after Bethany witnessed a murder. It was personal for his boss because the women were family friends. Keith 'Rusty' O'Connor didn't hesitate to assign Bethany security.

Crash spent several weeks in Allyson's company, and they discovered they had a lot in common. After Bethany's ordeal, he continued spending much of his free time with her. They talked about what he'd gone through after he left the military and why he rarely drank.

There was one thing he kept to himself but had planned to tell her if their relationship became romantic. He thought they might head in that direction until one night, about a year after they met, he leaned in to kiss her goodnight after they spent the day together. Allyson practically threw him out of the house once she made it clear they were only friends.

The next day, she called to apologize for overreacting but told him she couldn't have a romantic relationship with him. She enjoyed spending time together, but he'd be disappointed if he wanted more than friendship. He remained in the friend zone with the only woman he could see a future with.

As if she heard his thoughts, her eyes found his. Allyson stopped when he reached back to place his empty water glass on the bar without breaking their gaze. She was stunning in a gold dress that hung below her knees and dipped low enough to give a hint of cleavage. It was the sexiest damn thing he'd ever seen.

Allyson's smile slipped a little as he stalked toward her, and she tipped her head back to gaze up when he stepped in front of her. The twinkle lights around the hall looked flickered in her blue eyes. Her chestnut hair hung loosely over one shoulder, and her lips glistened with some gloss he would give his right arm to taste. She was so gorgeous it took his breath away.

"Well, don't you look handsome," Allyson shouted over the music.

"Thanks." Crash smiled. "You look… breathtaking."

"Thank you, Brent," Allyson folded her hands in front of her.

"Would you like to dance?" Crash asked.

The band slowed the tempo of the music, and he held out his hand with hopes she would accept his request. When she glanced back over her shoulder, he expected her to decline, but when she turned back, she timidly placed her hand on his, and he escorted her to the dance floor.

Crash's heart thudded as her hand rested on his shoulder. One of his hands slipped around her waist and lay flat against the small of her back. The open back of her dress made it easy for him to touch her silky skin, and he bit back with a groan.

"Bruce looks happy." Allyson nodded toward the newlyweds.

"Can't say I blame him. Caroline's an amazing lady, and those boys of hers love him." Crash kept his eyes on Allyson. "Love wins."

Caroline had two sons from a previous relationship who worshiped the ground Hulk walked on. The large man became a complete marshmallow when it came to those kids and would do anything for them and his new bride.

"Yeah, love wins," Allyson said, but sadness clouded her eyes.

"Won't be long before they pop out a few kids. I know Hulk loves those boys, but Caroline wants more. I think he would give her the moon if he could." Crash chuckled.

"It's nice they can have that kind of relationship." Allyson's eyes glistened as if she were holding back tears.

"Hey, what's with that face? It's a wedding. Happy thoughts." Crash crouched so he could look into her eyes when she dropped her gaze to the floor.

Crash stopped their dance and wrapped an arm around her shoulder. He guided her outside onto the club's patio. When the door closed behind them, he turned and placed his hands gently on her shoulders.

"Ally, what's wrong?" Crash asked.

Allyson shook her head and stepped back. She moved to the railing that encircled the deck of The Rock, a dance club on the main strip in Hopedale. Hulk rented the reception location because it was the only place large enough for the number of guests. Practically the whole town attended to see the happy couple start their life together.

"Sweetheart, talk to me," Crash turned her around and used his knuckles to lift her chin so he could see her face.

"I'm fine. Weddings… they just… too many memories." Allyson shrugged.

Crash pulled her into his arms, and she rested her cheek against his chest. He pressed his lips against her forehead as he embraced her. It was hard to think of friendship when the simple act of holding her made his heart pound.

"I'm sorry. I'm ruining this for you. You should go find your date and enjoy yourself." Allyson pulled back and smoothed her hands across the lapels of his suit.

"I didn't bring a date, Ally." Crash placed his hands over hers.

"Oh," Allyson whispered.

"There's only one woman I wanted to be my date, but that's not possible," Crash said.

"No, it isn't." Allyson sighed.

"Still not going to tell me why?" Crunch touched her cheek.

Allyson tipped her head back, and her gaze met his. In his heart, he knew she was it for him, but she was reluctant. He didn't know why. When her gaze dropped to his mouth, her tongue flicked out and licked her lower lip.

"Ally," Crash whispered as he lowered his head.

"Brent." Allyson breathed his name.

Crash swallowed as he brushed a kiss lightly against the corner of her mouth. She gasped as her eyes met his but didn't pull away. When she fisted the lapels of his tuxedo and tugged him closer, his mouth crashed against hers, and he slipped his hands around the back of her neck.

He'd dreamed of kissing her for eight years, but it was much better than he'd imagined. The scent of her jasmine perfume and the taste of champagne on her lips was intoxicating. As his mouth moved with hers, she pressed against his body and ran her tongue across his lower lip.

Allyson threaded her fingers through his hair as their mouths moved together in a desperate, passionate kiss. She moaned into his mouth, and his dick pressed against the zipper of his trousers, hard as steel. He knew she could feel what the kiss was doing to him, what she was doing.

"Oops." A voice squeaked.

Allyson abruptly ended the kiss, and Crash glanced over the top of her head. He bit back a curse when he saw the older woman a few feet away smiling.

"I'm right again," Cora Nightengale singsonged as she linked into her husband's arm.

"You're always right, my dear." Brian smiled as they made their way toward the parking lot.

Keith's aunt was a lovely person, and Brent adored her. Several years earlier, she told Crash to ask Allyson out. She reminded him every time he was in her company that he was wasting precious time.

Crash wanted to pursue a relationship with Allyson, but it never got close until tonight. Maybe they'd reached a point where she realized there was something between them. Not that he didn't value their friendship because he did. He could tell her anything, well, almost anything, but there was still one thing he kept to himself because only the woman he married would find out about it.

"Shit," Ally muttered under her breath.

Allyson stepped back and wrapped her arms around herself. Their moment had clearly ended, so Crash allowed her the space, but he knew being simply friends wouldn't work for him. He wanted a life with her and was about to say that when she spoke.

"That shouldn't have happened." Allyson shook her head.

"Why?" Crash stepped closer, but she lifted her hand to stop him.

"We can't… I can't… It won't work… I got to go," Allyson stammered.

She spun around before he could stop her and ran back into the club. Crash folded his hands and rested them on his head as he faced the parking lot.

"Fuck," Crash growled through his teeth.

He had no idea why things wouldn't work between them, but he wanted to know. He'd do anything for her; if it took some convincing, he'd make her see they belonged together. He was about to stomp inside and demand an answer, but something caught his attention in the corner of the parking lot.

He ran down the steps to the lot. Cora and her husband drove away several minutes earlier, which meant someone else was there, and if they were staying in the shadows, they were up to something.

He crouched down to look under some of the vehicles, but it was dark, and even if someone were there, it wouldn't be easy to see them. Crash made a note to talk to the club's owner about putting extra lighting in the area. Since Roman Young was also married to Keith's cousin, Isabelle, NES monitored their security.

He was about to pull out his phone to use the flashlight when two headlights blinded him. He barely had enough time to dive out of the way when the tires screeched, and a car sped out of the lot, leaving him on the asphalt, covered in dust.

"What the fuck?" Crash shouted.

He jumped to his feet but only saw the red taillights disappearing around the corner, headed toward the highway leading out of Hopedale. Even if he were next to his vehicle, he'd never catch them once they hit the highway. He would ask Smash to check the security cameras for safety; someone could be staking out the club.

"Crazy fucking people," Crash muttered under his breath as he brushed himself off.

He felt sick in the pit of his stomach as he returned to the wedding. With a last glance over the parking lot, he turned and headed back inside. That car was there for something, but what?

Chapter 4

Exhaustion set in as she walked around the emergency room to check on the patients still waiting for test results. She needed to move primarily to keep from falling asleep on her feet and the other small part to stop her thoughts of Crash.

She hadn't seen him since the night of the wedding, but that was because she'd been avoiding him. It was difficult enough for her to resist him before, but now that she knew how it felt to get lost in his kiss, she wanted more. Much more.

Allyson hadn't felt that alive in a long time, if ever. She couldn't remember a kiss affecting her so much, even with Trent. It wasn't that her late husband didn't know what he was doing, but he'd never made every part of her body buzz.

It added to her guilt over her late husband. After Trent died, she blamed herself for his death. She always wondered if he'd been distracted because before he'd left, they'd decided to divorce when he returned.

It wasn't anyone's fault. Allyson and Trent couldn't get past losing their second child and Allyson almost losing her life when she gave birth. They tried everything to work it out, but, in the end, they couldn't. She never told anyone about their issues after his death; regardless of their problems, part of her still loved and missed him.

Since his death, she tried dating. There were a couple of other doctors at the hospital and a pharmaceutical salesman she met when he came to tell her about some products, but she felt very uneasy with him. None of the men ever got a second date. Although Witt continued to ask for another night out, she always turned him down. If she was honest, it had nothing to do with Trent. None of the men she'd gone out with compared to Crash, but it was a relationship that couldn't happen—at least not a romantic one.

The problem was since they kissed, she couldn't forget how it felt. She was surprised Cora hadn't mentioned it. Her sister Bethany tried to talk Allyson into going out with Crash when Cora continued to insist she belonged with him, but as much as she wanted to, she couldn't.

Allyson walked into the small office off the emergency desk and scanned the patients on the whiteboard. Most of them were waiting on tests, and one was detoxing from too much alcohol consumption.

"Are you okay, Ally?" Leah asked.

Leah had been a wonderful friend since the young nurse moved to Hopedale. She had a son and bonded with Allyson over being single mothers, although Leah didn't talk much about her son's father.

Allyson loved working with her because she was efficient and fabulous with the patients. Thankfully, they worked most of her shifts together, and Leah was the first one Allyson went to when she thought about going into private practice because she wanted her to go with her.

Dr. Sean O'Connor was retiring and offered her his part of the practice. His son, Ian, worked at the clinic as well, and Allyson was glad to work with someone she knew. The fact she could walk to work and have regular hours was the icing on the cake.

"Yeah, I'm fine. Had a long shift," Allyson assured her friend.

"Well, Dad is taking Liam this weekend, and I know you're off. Want to hit Jack's Place for a few pints?" Leah asked.

"That sounds great, but I'll let you know for sure tomorrow." Allyson was about to leave the office when someone blocked her path.

"Hello, Dr. Sullivan," Witt said with a smile.

"Dr. Davenport," Allyson replied, trying to step around him.

"I hoped to run into you." Witt rested his shoulder against the doorjamb, blocking her exit.

"I'm busy, Witt." Allyson motioned for him to move.

"I see the board, Allyson. I wonder if you'd have supper with me on Saturday?" Witt asked.

Allyson tried not to roll her eyes. After four years of turning him down, he didn't seem to take the hint that she wasn't interested. The bastard even showed up at her door one evening with a bottle of wine. She lied, telling him her father was on the way to take her to supper.

That evening, she saw a side of Witt she never wanted to see again. He'd grabbed her arm and practically demanded another date. Luck was on her side because her father pulled into the driveway before

Witt could do anything. He didn't come by her house again but never gave up.

Leah had suggested she tell the asshole she was involved with someone, but she didn't want to lie. Besides, the only guy she could think of was Crash, and she wasn't about to involve him in a ploy.

"I don't know how to make it any clearer to you, Witt. I'm not interested in going out with you. I wish you would stop asking." Allyson looked him directly in the eyes.

"You'll say yes one day," Witt smirked as he chucked her under the chin with his knuckle. "I mean, who wouldn't want to date a successful plastic surgeon."

Before she could respond to the jerk, another trauma rushed into the ER. Witt moved, barely giving her enough room to pass him. Hopefully, he'd be gone after she dealt with the patient.

Three ambulances arrived over the last couple of hours of her shift. One patient didn't make it, and the other two admitted. She wanted to go home and fall into bed for a week, but Allyson didn't have that option.

The following day, she had a meeting with Sean and Ian. They wanted to go through all the paperwork and let her become familiar with Sean's patients because she would take them over when he retired.

The drive home was twice as long as usual. Typically, it took ten minutes to get from St. John's to Hopedale, but road construction seemed to be on every section of the highway. The province always pushed road work in the fall to complete it before winter, causing detours that she didn't have the energy to deal with.

When she finally pulled into her driveway, she wasn't sure she'd make it up the stairs to her bedroom. She dropped her stuff in the front hallway, shuffled into the living room, and flopped down on the sectional. She was about to close her eyes when she noticed the open patio door. Allyson was diligent about checking all the doors and windows before she left for work, so it struck her as odd that she didn't lock it.

The hair on the back of her neck prickled as she sat up and glanced around the room. Neither her father nor her son had dropped by because they would call first. Did she leave it open, or did someone break into her home?

Allyson slowly got to her feet and went to the sliding doors. She didn't touch it or the frame but looked up and down to see if someone had pried it open. She crouched down to look at the latch.

"As if you'd know if someone had jimmied the lock," Allyson grumbled to herself.

She reached into her pocket to pull out her phone, but it rang before she put her hand on it. Allyson startled at the sudden shrill tone and cursed herself for being jumpy.

"Hello," she answered as she slammed the patio door closed.

"Hey, Ally," her sister's voice sounded weird.

"What's up?" Allyson locked the door and jiggled it several times to ensure it was secure.

"I'm so bored," Bethany complained.

"You have three kids and a husband. How are you bored?" Allyson laughed.

"Because my mother-in-law kidnapped my kids for the night, and my husband is gone to his weekly guy's night with his brothers." Bethany sighed.

"So, you're calling your boring sister to see if we can be bored together?" Allyson dropped down on the couch.

"I'll bring wine," Bethany tempted.

"Deal." Allyson jumped to her feet. "Give me thirty minutes to shower."

"I'm getting dressed and grabbing the wine." Bethany hung up before Allyson could respond.

She may be tired, but it was nice to curl up on the couch and chat with her sister. They didn't get much time with each other because of their busy schedules. Bethany had recently taken over the only pharmacy in Hopedale because the owner wanted to retire. As a pharmacist, Bethany jumped at the opportunity to work close to home. It was also another reason why Allyson chose to take over for Sean. It meant she could stay in Hopedale and not drive back and forth to the city daily.

She saw her phone flash and realized it was about to die, then hurried to the kitchen to plug it into the charger she kept there. They were all over her house because she wanted to ensure the hospital could always contact her. Since her phone needed to always be on, she needed it charged all the time.

After a shower, she pulled on a pair of comfy leggings and an old T-shirt. She'd pulled her damp hair into a messy bun when her sister's voice echoed downstairs.

"I'm opening the wine and not waiting for you," Bethany shouted.

"I'm coming," Allyson replied with a chuckle.

As she reached the bottom of the stairs, Bethany walked out of the kitchen with an open bottle and two glasses. They made their way into the living room, and as she was about to sit on the couch, she felt a cold chill swirl around her legs.

"Shit, Ally, I know after forty you go through the change, but your living room is freezing," Bethany said as she placed the bottle and glasses on the coffee table.

"I am not going through the change," Allyson grumbled.

That already happened when she had the hysterectomy. The operation had forced her body into menopause, but her sister didn't know that.

"Then why do you have your patio door open in the middle of October?" Bethany asked as she closed the sliding door.

Allyson froze. The door she'd closed before her phone call was open again. Stepping next to the door, she checked the latch, but it didn't seem broken, and after she locked it again, she yanked on it several times.

"Do you think I don't know how to close a patio door?" Bethany asked as she poured the wine.

"No, the door was open when I got home, and I'm sure I locked it before I left—I know I did before I went to shower." Allyson closed the blinds.

"Did you leave it open before you went to work?" Bethany snuggled on the couch and pulled a blanket over her legs.

Allyson flicked the switch for the propane fireplace and then joined her sister on the couch. As they snuggled under the large blanket, she sipped the red wine and sighed.

"I'm not a hundred percent sure of that, but I know I did before I showered," Allyson said as she sipped her wine.

"Why don't you get Brent to look at the latch? There could be something wrong with it," Bethany suggested.

"I don't need Brent to check a lock. I can do it myself." Allyson sighed.

"Could be a reason to get him over here and…"

"Stop." Allyson put her hand over her sister's mouth.

Bethany did her best to push Allyson and Crash together. It was difficult enough to resist him because she wanted him so badly, but when they constantly pushed her, she sometimes wanted to scream at them.

"I'm just…" Bethany tried to say, but Allyson stopped her again.

"Brent and I can't be anything but friends. End of the story and end of the conversation." Allyson tipped her glass and took a large gulp of wine.

"Fine," Bethany huffed.

"How are the kids?" Allyson asked, hoping to get her sister on to another subject.

"They're good, but they're growing up too fast. Grayson is already five, and Katie is two." Bethany sighed. "Avery is five months old, but I want another before I get too old to have one."

"You're not too old," Allyson said with a chuckle.

"Okay, I don't want to be pregnant again, but I still want a baby." Bethany grinned.

"You and A.J. could adopt," Allyson suggested.

"No, I'll wait until another one of the women pops out a baby and go to their house to get my baby fix." Bethany snorted.

"Isn't Caroline having a baby?" Allyson remembered someone mentioned it at the wedding.

"Yes, and she's so excited. They knew before the wedding but didn't want to say anything until they returned from their honeymoon last week." Bethany put her glass to her lips.

"I bet Bruce is as well, but if it's a girl, she won't be allowed to date ever." Allyson laughed as Bethany nodded in agreement.

They were on the second bottle of wine when Bethany's phone chirped with a text message. She looked up from the screen and grinned.

"My hubby finished his guy's night, and he's coming to pick me up." Bethany drained the rest of the wine in her glass.

"And what are you two ever going to do tonight with no kids and an empty house?" Allyson smirked.

"I'm sure we'll find something to fill our boring night." Bethany winked.

Allyson walked her sister to the door and waved as Aaron strolled up the driveway. She almost choked on the wine she sipped when he picked Bethany up and tossed her over his shoulder as if she weighed nothing. It was at that moment she noticed the truck Aaron headed for.

Crash must have been dubbed the designated driver for the evening. Her heart picked up as she met his gaze through the passenger side window. She gave him a little wave, and he nodded to her.

Things were different since the wedding three weeks ago, but maybe that's the way it had to be. She had to make sure that line in the sand was clear because, as much as she hated the thought, Crash needed to find a woman who could give him the life he deserved.

"I'll see ya later, Ally," Bethany shouted before Aaron helped her into the vehicle.

"Okay, love you," Allyson returned.

"Love you too," Bethany called out through the window as they drove away.

Allyson sighed as she stepped back into the house—alone again. Selling the large house seemed like a better idea every day. Then, she could be lonely in a smaller place. Maybe she should get a dog.

She'd put the wine glasses in the dishwasher and tossed the empty bottles in the recycling bin when her doorbell rang. Glancing at her watch, she tried to think of someone who would be coming to her house so close to midnight. Maybe her sister had forgotten something.

When she opened the door, her breath caught. Crash stood there looking way too good for her slightly inebriated brain. She swallowed several times before she finally spoke.

"Brent. Um, what are you doing here?" She tried to sound casual.

"Beth said you're having issues with your patio door."

He stepped around her and headed toward her living room without hesitation. She stood holding the door for a few seconds before she realized he wasn't leaving until he checked the lock.

"I probably didn't lock it properly." Allyson followed him.

"Well, I'm going to make sure it's locked. I'll never sleep worrying about you here alone and a bum lock." Crash tried to open the door with the lock engaged.

When it didn't open, he unlocked it and crouched to look at the latch. Allyson's eyes immediately checked out how his jeans molded to his fine ass. Her distraction caused her to miss that he'd said something.

"Ally?" She jumped when he called out to her.

"Uh. What?" She tucked her hands into the pockets of her sweater.

"Pass me the broom," he said.

She hurried into the laundry room and returned a few seconds later with her broom. Crash was scanning outside the patio door as if looking for someone to pop out at him.

"Why do you want the broom?" Allyson asked, handing it to him.

He took the bristle part of the broom off and jammed the handle into the frame of the patio door after closing and locking it again.

"Nobody is opening this unless they're inside the house. I'll pick up a security bar for it tomorrow. These doors aren't always secure," Brent explained.

"You don't…" Allyson stopped when he put up his hand.

"I know I don't have to, but I'm doing it anyway." He took a step closer to her.

"Thanks," she whispered.

"Hopedale isn't exactly the city, but the idea of you here alone and having a door anyone could open doesn't sit right with me." Crash shoved his hands into his pockets.

"I appreciate it. Tell me how much…" Allyson stopped again when he raised an eyebrow.

"Just say thank you and move on, Ally." Crash sighed.

"Thank you, Brent," she replied.

She wanted to ask him to stay, but she had to keep a distance between them. Allyson wanted him to have the best life possible with a family and a wife who could give him everything. That would never be her.

"Okay, so now I can sleep." He walked around her and went to the front door.

Allyson followed him, trying to keep the lump in her throat from strangling her and the tears in her eyes from spilling down her cheeks. She felt lost without his friendship.

"Thanks again, Brent." Allyson's voice cracked.

"No problem." He headed down the steps, then stopped. "Goodnight, Ally."

He didn't turn around as he walked to his truck and hopped in, and Allyson was glad because he would see the tears in her eyes. Things were never going to be the same. Why was life so unfair?

Chapter 5

Cha-ching

Cha-ching

That was what Crash heard in his head when he walked through the three unfinished bedrooms with his father. The man rattled off a list of what was needed to complete the remainder of Crash's house. With the way his dad talked, he might need to double his budget. At least he could now live in the house while he finished the renovations.

The house had been vacant for years, and when the real estate agent showed Crash the place, it needed a lot of work. Abbie assured him the place had great bones and managed to get him the place for way under the asking price. This meant he had plenty left for renovations, and in the almost two years he owned the house, he'd made a massive dent in that money.

Abbie married his co-worker, Ben 'Trunk' Murphy, who lived near Crash's place. Some of the guys he worked with lived nearby, which worked out when he needed a few extra hands for cheap labor. He also got help from Keith since his boss owned NES and a construction company. In Hopedale there was always someone ready and willing to lend a hand.

It took a lot of blood, sweat, and tears to get the house he wanted because once done, it was where he planned to spend the rest of his life. Hard work wasn't a problem; he enjoyed working with his dad. His father built houses for a living before he retired, and the man didn't hesitate to put on a tool belt when Crash showed him the place. His father wasn't enjoying retirement, and according to Crash's mother, he was driving her crazy.

When Crash first returned to Newfoundland, he cut all ties with Snapper. The guy didn't seem upset when Crash explained he was getting help. Snapper simply wished him luck. It was a relief and much easier after he'd left Alberta.

"These rooms are not too bad. The floors are original and in decent shape. If we sand and refinish them, they'll be as good as new. We'll have to strip those bathrooms to the beams and put one of those multi-head showers like we did in the master bath." His father grinned.

"Dad, I do have a budget." Crash chuckled.

"You're looking at the king of budget crunching. Trust me. We can get all of that done and still be under budget." His father sounded confident.

His dad may be the king, but Crash had dipped deep into his savings with the kitchen and the living room renovations. Not to mention replacing all the electrical components because they were completely outdated. That little snag took a big bite out of his money.

He'd moved in once he had finished the lower level of the house. While Crash renovated, he'd lived with another co-worker, Hunter 'Crunch' Crawford. After Crunch's fiancé moved in with her daughter,

Crash decided it was time for him to reside in his place. He slept in the living room until they finished the master bedroom and bathroom. Thankfully, he finally got to sleep in his new bed, and his nightmares subsided again.

They were close to the final touches, and he was happy with how much they had done. He wasn't about to pay for another multi-head shower for a bathroom used for the occasional guest. He wanted to finish everything and finally relax in his home.

He didn't have anyone to start a family with. There was only one woman he wanted, and she'd made it clear they could never be anything but friends.

After the night of Hulk's wedding, she never mentioned anything about what happened, and Crash didn't bring it up. Of course, he'd only seen her once after that. He still got pissed about the idiot who almost ran over him and never found out who it was. Some teenagers were probably trying to find a place to do God knows what, but he still felt uneasy about it. He didn't know why.

He kept his distance from Allyson over the last few weeks. Being close to her was so hard, knowing he could never have her as more than a friend. He'd fallen in love with her a long time ago. His heart knew it, but when Bethany told him about her patio door, he didn't hesitate to make certain Allyson was safe. He'd dropped off the bar for her door that morning, and thankfully, her dad was there instead of Allyson.

"It shouldn't take long to refinish the floors. They aren't as bad as the rest of the house was. They'll make nice rooms for a few kids," his father hinted.

Crash felt that familiar punch in the gut at his comment because the truth was it wasn't in his future. When he was a teenager, he ended up with mumps, and a rare side effect caused him to become infertile. He'd accepted that he'd never have children but hoped to marry and adopt one day. After all, there were far too many children in the world who needed loving parents.

"Shit, son. I'm sorry." His dad's eyes widened.

"Dad, it's okay," Crash assured him.

"I forget about it, you know," his father squeezed Crash's shoulder.

"It doesn't mean I'll never be a dad." Crash slapped his dad on the back.

"That's true," his dad smiled.

Crash's phone vibrated in his pocket, and he cursed under his breath when he saw his friend's number on the screen. Wyatt tried to call him earlier, but Crash was in a meeting with Keith and couldn't answer.

"Hang on, Dad. I got to take this." Crash held up his finger as he put the phone to his ear.

Wyatt returned to Newfoundland a year earlier and was doing well. He'd gotten help for his addiction as well as his mental health. It was still difficult for both of them, but the man worked hard to keep his life on track for his family.

His parents helped Wyatt the same way they helped Crash. Thanks to them, Keith offered him a job even after Crash drove his car into the back of Keith's jeep.

That day, Crash was leaving a meeting with his therapist, whom his dad had found for him, and he hit a patch of ice. He lost control of his vehicle and drove into the back of Keith's Jeep. He also caused a chain reaction, and when Crash finally exited his car, four cars were damaged. He was sure the huge red-headed man was about to knock him out, but instead, he bought Crash a coffee while they waited for the police to arrive.

Crash was surprised by how easily he opened up to Keith, who was genuinely interested in Crash's story. By the time he arrived home, Crash had a new friend and a new boss. After his parents, the first person he called was Wyatt.

Now that Wyatt was clean and sober and had his life on track, Crash got him an interview with Keith. It was probably the reason for the call. Crash knew Wyatt would be a excellent asset to NES.

"Hey, buddy," Crash answered.

Nobody said anything, but Crash could hear sobbing. It sounded like a woman, but he couldn't be sure. He heard the rev of an engine, and for a second, he thought Wyatt butt-dialed him. He heard a muffled voice but couldn't make out anything they were saying. He waited for a moment and then spoke again.

"Hello? Wyatt?" Crash tensed when he heard a motor rev.

"Please, let her go. She doesn't know anything." Wyatt's voice was barely audible.

"Wyatt? Let who go?" Crash glanced at his father.

They both knew how easy it was for someone to fall off the wagon. Crash had a beer occasionally but knew the possibility of sliding down that slippery slope again. His father wouldn't because he always said if he had one, he wouldn't stop at that.

Crash hit the speaker on his phone so they both could hear the call. The sound of a revving engine had them both looking at each other with the same anxious expression.

"Wyatt? Where are you?" Crash's father shouted.

"Mack? We can't escape…" there was a sob. "I fucked up. I fucked up big time, and I trusted the wrong people. Protect them, Brent. Don't let them get her."

"Wyatt, where are you? Let us come get you, and we can talk," Crash begged.

"It's too late. You need to be careful, Brent. You and Ax can't… You got to… Fuck."

A loud scraping sounded like metal, and then there was a rustle, as if Wyatt was driving through trees. It didn't make sense, but the last thing he heard was a shriek before the call ended.

Crash immediately tried to get Wyatt back on the phone. It rang several times before going to voicemail. He tried again as he and his father ran out of the house to his dad's truck.

"Damn it, Wyatt. Answer the fucking phone," Crash shouted as they pulled onto the highway leading to St. John's.

"What is he talking about, Brent?" his father asked.

"I have no idea. Jesus, Dad. I thought he was doing great." Crash choked on the words.

"That didn't sound like it," his father snapped.

"I should've answered his call earlier," Crash said mainly to himself.

"Don't you dare go down that road. You're not responsible, and he knows when he gets low to call his sponsor," his father said as he grabbed Crash's arm. "Do you hear me, son?"

"Yeah, Dad." Crash closed his eyes.

"Was that Ellie screaming?" His father asked the question Crash was afraid to think about.

"I don't know. Jesus, the kids." Crash choked out the words.

With his phone gripped in his hand, Brent watched the scenery as his father sped through the streets to get to Wyatt's house. Hopefully, Ellie was at home, and the scream he heard wasn't her.

Chapter 6

"Thank you, Dr. Sullivan," a young nurse said as she took the chart from Allyson.

Allyson finished the last of her charts with only an hour left on her shift. She enjoyed the Emergency Department, but the long hours weren't as easy as they used to be. Although she would miss the fast pace of the hospital, having a set schedule where she would be home most evenings was appealing. Maybe she could finally find a hobby she enjoyed and get that dog.

She'd discussed turning one of her extra bedrooms into an office with Crash, so maybe she could turn another into a hobby room, not that she had time for hobbies. She could keep the fourth bedroom as a guest room when a family member came to stay. She wasn't looking forward to all the work but needed to do something with the extra space. However, she wasn't sure if Crash would be willing to help after how she'd avoided him.

Crash always gave her something to look forward to. Now she felt lost without her friend, probably her best friend next to her sister. It was selfish to call him when she needed help, but he was the first person to come to mind when she needed someone to talk to.

Her life was one massive punch in the gut after another. First, she struggled to carry her son to term and almost lost him during delivery. Then she lost her little girl and her chance of ever having another child. The last straw was to be on the verge of divorce, only to have her husband die defending his country.

Cameron was only eleven when Trent died, and it shattered her to tell him. Even though they were ending their marriage, it didn't mean she'd wanted anything to happen to the father of her child. Trent was a decent man and an incredible dad.

Now, she was a widow living alone. Cameron was nineteen and moved into the city to go to university. She missed him even though he visited regularly, but it wasn't the same as having him stay in the room down the hall.

The house was deafeningly silent at night; she had even considered selling it and moving into an apartment in St. John's as her father did. When they returned to Newfoundland, Lewis Donnelly gave up living the small-town life and moved into an apartment for seniors. He was happy and started seeing a lovely woman who lived in the same building. Vera Greeley was precisely what her dad needed, and Allyson was delighted for him but admittedly a little jealous that her dad had a better love life.

"Dr. Sullivan, we have two ambulances coming in. A car went over a cliff," Leah called out to her.

"Okay, prepare for intake." Allyson ran behind Leah.

The first ambulance arrived, with the paramedics giving chest compressions while they rushed into the trauma room. The other doctor, Dr. Adam Cramer, ran behind them.

Before Allyson had a chance to help, the other ambulance arrived. The vehicle's doors flew open, and Allyson knew it was critical. The woman was bleeding heavily with a severe head injury. Her eyes were swollen shut, and her nose looked broken. Allyson went to work on the patient while the paramedic gave the report. She listened intently without stopping until she heard the name.

"Her identification says her name is Ellie Christopher," the paramedic held out the card.

Allyson grabbed the card, causing Leah to stare in confusion. As she studied the picture, Allyson's heart raced. The woman was Crash's friend, and her condition was critical.

"She's crashing," Leah shouted.

They worked to bring Ellie back for twenty minutes, but nothing worked. Allyson stepped back from the gurney and closed her eyes before calling the time of death. For several minutes, she scanned Ellie's body from head to toe. Something about all the injuries didn't scream a car accident. Ellie looked as if someone had beaten her. Badly.

She glanced toward the other trauma room to see Adam walk out, ripping off his gloves. He lifted his eyes to meet Allyson's and shook his head, telling her the man was also deceased.

"What's his name?" Allyson asked, knowing what Adam was about to say.

"Wyatt Christopher." Adam shook his head. "He didn't have a chance. Between you and me, those injuries didn't come from the accident. Someone beat the shit out of that man."

Allyson glanced into the room and saw the white sheet covering Wyatt. She went to the nearest computer and looked up Ellie and Wyatt on the system. Of course, they were each other's next of kin, but Wyatt also had Crash down as a second.

"Are you okay, Ally?" Leah walked next to her.

She shook her head as she looked through the report from the paramedics. It said Ellie was in the backseat of the car, and she wasn't wearing a seatbelt. Something told her most of Ellie's injuries were not due to the accident. She looked down at herself; Ellie's blood covered her, but she needed to call Crash to let him know about his friends.

Leah followed Allyson out of the room and stood beside her in the corridor. She didn't say a word for a moment, but then she touched Allyson's shoulder.

"Did you know them?" Leah asked.

"No, but they're Brent's friends. They have two small kids." Allyson found it hard to contain her emotions.

"Oh no." Leah glanced back into the room where Ellie's body lay. "Life isn't fair, is it."

Ellie and Wyatt had no family other than the Adams. Brent told her all about them one night after Wyatt and his wife moved back to Newfoundland. The couple grew up in foster care, and as far as she knew, they had no family.

"The police are here," Leah pointed to a couple of officers at the reception desk.

Allyson hurried over to the two uniformed men to let them know both victims were deceased. She wished she knew one of the police, but they were all rookies.

"Thank you for letting us know, Dr. Sullivan." One of the officers nodded.

"Neither has any family, but they have a very close friend who is an emergency contact. If you don't mind, I'll contact him. He's a friend," Allyson told the young man.

"Of course, I'll let my supervisor know." The other officer stepped away with a phone to his ear.

Allyson walked into an empty room and took several deep breaths before pulling out her phone. It was almost dead, but hopefully, she had enough battery to make the call. Leah walked in behind her.

"Everything okay?" Leah asked.

"No, it isn't. I need to call Brent."

Leah left the room, leaving her alone to do something she was not looking forward to doing. Allyson let her finger hover over his name for several seconds before she finally tapped it.

"Hey." He sounded strange.

"Hi, Brent," Allyson said with a hitch in her tone.

"I can't talk right now. I'm in the middle of something. Can I get back to you?" Crash sounded as if he had been running.

"I have something to tell you. I'm at the hospital, and a bad accident came into emergency," Allyson began.

"Who is it?" Crash practically shouted.

"It's Ellie and Wyatt," Allyson continued. "You were Wyatt's emergency contact."

"Are they okay?" Crash asked.

She hated to be the one to tell him he'd lost two friends in the blink of an eye, and she certainly didn't want to do it over the phone, but what choice did she have?

"No, they're not," Allyson said gently.

"How bad?" Crash asked.

"The worst."

There was silence for several seconds, and for a moment, she thought he'd hung up. Then he started cursing, and she could hear him banging against something.

"I'm sorry, Brent. We tried everything, but their injuries were too extensive." Allyson felt the need to tell him the hospital did everything they could.

"I don't understand," he choked out the words.

Allyson heard the sound of a car door and then boots clicking against the pavement.

"Have the police shown up?" Crash snapped.

"They're here, although I'm unfamiliar with them. They look like they should still be in high school." Allyson glanced toward the two officers standing in the reception area.

"I'm on the way." Crash didn't give her a chance to say anything.

"Dr. Sullivan?" A male voice came from behind her.

Allyson almost dropped her phone and spun around. She had to bite back the groan when she saw who was addressing her. The last thing she wanted to deal with was Witt and his stuck-up attitude.

"Dr. Davenport," Allyson said, trying to keep her tone from sounding annoyed.

"I've left a few messages, but I haven't heard back from you," Witt said as he glanced at himself in the window behind him.

Allyson rolled her eyes and turned back to the chart in her hand. She needed to make notes before Crash arrived, or the police needed a statement. When she lifted her head, Leah looked at her and mimicked the act of sticking her finger down her throat as she sneered at Witt.

Allyson shook her head and tried to keep her composure. Leah told her once that Witt seemed to want to date his way through all the female staff at the hospital. Allyson agreed, but he wanted a second date with her for some reason. That wasn't going to happen.

"I'm sorry. I'm swamped. On my time off, I'm doing some things with my house and trying to join Dr. O'Connor's practice." Allyson forced a smile.

It wasn't a lie. She was doing all those things, but it wasn't taking up all of Allyson's time. She wasn't interested in spending time with Witt ever again outside of the hospital.

"You should hire a personal assistant. I'd be lost without mine. Anyway, now that I have you here, I have tickets to the Arts and Culture Center opera this Friday. When should I pick you up?" Witt said as he checked his manicured nails.

Allyson stared at him for a moment. He didn't seem to notice the blood or the tears in her eyes because she'd had to tell Brent his friends were dead. No, Witt was too selfish to see anything but his own reflection.

"Sorry, I'm not a fan of the Opera, and I've already got plans this weekend." Allyson almost laughed at his shocked expression.

Before he could answer, Crash ran up to her and stepped between Allyson and Witt. Crash glanced over his shoulder at the police officers before he spoke.

"Have you talked to them yet?" Crash asked her.

"Excuse me, I was speaking with Dr. Sullivan." Witt stepped between Crash and Allyson.

Allyson would've laughed at Witt if it weren't such a serious situation. At barely five feet nine inches and maybe one hundred fifty pounds, he looked like a little boy to a man over six feet tall and over two hundred pounds of solid muscle. She had to give Witt credit when he pushed Crash; he had guts.

"I suggest you step aside, Chad." Crash sneered.

"My name is Witt Davenport, Doctor Witt Davenport." Witt snapped.

"Well, *Witt*," Crash said, emphasizing the name. "I just lost two friends, and your overinflated ego is the last thing that concerns me. Now get the fuck out of my way so I can talk to Ally."

The veins in Crash's neck bulged as he clenched his jaw. His face was red with rage, and Allyson shivered because she'd never seen him lose his cool. She stepped around Witt and placed her hands on Crash's chest.

"Let's talk in there." Allyson nodded toward a small office off the nurse's station.

"Allyson, I need an answer," Witt called after her.

"I told you, no," Allyson said before entering the office.

"But this is…" Witt began.

"Are you fucking deaf? She said no. Now back off," Crash roared.

Before Crash could lunge at Witt, Allyson pushed him into the office and closed the door. The room was tiny but seemed even smaller, with him pacing like a caged animal.

"Who the fuck is that asshole, Ally?" Crash snapped when he finally stopped pacing.

"An asshole," Allyson returned.

"Are you dating him?" Crash glared through the small window of the door.

"No." Allyson sighed. "Now, please sit down."

She pointed to one of the chairs, but Crash linked his fingers and placed his joined hands on his head. He swallowed several times before he spoke.

"I can't." He swallowed several times before he spoke again. "They're really gone?"

When she nodded, tears filled his eyes. Allyson grabbed a couple of tissues from a box on the desk and handed them to him. With a shaky hand, he accepted them as he blew out a puff of air.

"Do you know what happened?" Crash whispered as he eased down on one of the chairs.

"I don't. I haven't talked to the police, and I called you as soon as they both passed." Allyson sat next to him.

"Whose blood is that?" Crash nodded toward her soiled scrubs.

She glanced down and cringed. It was hard enough for Crash to know his friend was dead, but to see Ellie's blood all over Allyson was the same as a slap in the face.

"I worked on Ellie. I'm sorry, I should go change." Allyson stood up.

"What am I going to do?" He grabbed her hand as he shot to his feet.

"You'll get through it." She reached up and cupped his cheek.

"They were family to me. Jesus, the kids." Crash's eyes grew huge, and his face paled.

"They'll be okay," Allyson assured him.

"You don't understand. Wyatt and Ellie made me the kids' guardian in the event of their deaths. They filled out wills after Mila was born." Crash plowed his fingers through his hair.

"I'm sure you'll have all the help you need." She dropped her hand.

"Ally, I don't know anything about raising kids. Christ, they're still babies." Crash started to pace again.

"Your parents will help, I'm sure, and I'm only a phone call away," she promised.

Crash stopped pacing and stood staring out the office window for a few minutes. He needed time to process everything, but she had an overwhelming urge to pull him into her arms. She wished she could tell him neither Ellie nor Wyatt's injuries seemed consistent with a car accident, but until the medical examiner confirmed it, Allyson couldn't say a word.

"Can I see them?" Crash asked.

"I'll take you in, but I have to warn you—they have a lot of injuries," Allyson said.

"I've probably seen worse," he muttered.

Allyson didn't doubt that, but there had to be a vast difference between seeing horrific sights during wartime and seeing close friends who died so violently. She motioned for him to follow her and brought him to the trauma rooms. Thankfully, Witt didn't wait because she was sure Crash probably would've put the guy in one of the ED beds if he'd accosted Allyson again.

She closed the door as they entered the room, and Crash's step faltered as he moved next to the first gurney. The police put Wyatt and Ellie in the same room, probably to keep a better eye on the bodies. Allyson fought back tears as Crash spoke softly to Ellie and Wyatt.

Chapter 7

Crash couldn't believe his eyes. A beautiful couple died because of a stupid car accident. He didn't think the amount of damage done to them was possible from a car accident.

The phone call from Wyatt played repeatedly in his head as Crash stared down at his friend. They'd been through so much together, but Wyatt sounded terrified on that call.

"What happened to you, buddy?" Crash whispered.

Crash wished he could shake Wyatt and get the answers he wanted. None of this made sense. Why had Wyatt warned him to be careful? What did he mean when he said he'd fucked up and trusted the wrong people?

"Jesus, Ellie. Why the fuck are you both here? You shouldn't be gone. You should be home with your babies." Crash took a shaky breath. "I promise they'll never forget either of you. Damn... Keep watch over me, you two. I need all the help I can get."

He bent down, kissed Ellie's temple, and said goodbye one last time. Then he turned to Wyatt and grabbed his hand.

"Who the fuck did this to you?" Crash hissed.

"We'll find out," someone said behind him.

Crash turned and noticed a police officer inside the room. The guy looked familiar, but it was hard for Crash to think with his brain in a spin.

"Who's looking after the investigation?" Crash asked.

Crash was sure the young officer was qualified, but he didn't want a rookie investigating his friends' case. He needed experienced police to handle this, and several officers, including all four of his boss' brothers, fit that bill.

"Inspector O'Connor is on the way," the young officer said.

"Which one?" It didn't matter which one.

"A.J.," the officer told him.

"What's your name, kid?" Crash asked.

"Constable Ray, Dillon Ray. I'm from Hopedale as well." Dillon told him.

"I thought you looked familiar. I want the best to look after this case," Crash explained.

"I understand." Dillon met Crash's eyes.

"Good. No offense." Crash turned back to Wyatt and Ellie.

"None taken. This is my first year with the department, and I know I don't have enough experience to deal with this, but for what it's worth. I don't believe they got all these injuries from the accident. Neither does A.J."

Crash hated to leave his friends, but he was now responsible for two lives that didn't deserve to experience this loss at such a young age. He'd ensure they knew everything about their parents and how much Ellie and Wyatt loved them.

"I'll never let them forget you," Crash murmured.

Crash pulled the sheets up over both his friends and then slowly walked out of the room, swallowing down the colossal lump threatening to strangle him.

He stepped outside the room with Dillon behind him. The young officer stood guard outside the room as Crash walked away. Obviously, the police didn't believe this was a typical car accident. Crash tried to get the picture of his friends' battered bodies out of his head, which was why he was frantically looking around the ED for the one woman who could help him get through this, whether she knew it or not.

He spotted her talking to Aaron next to the main desk. He stomped toward them, trying to control all the anger raging inside. He was not upset with them; the itch at the back of his head told him he needed a drink to deal with this. It was the first time he had felt that urge in a very long time.

"I want to know who the hell put them here and find out why. They shouldn't be here. I want to know every fucking step in this investigation." Crash shook as he looked Aaron in the face.

"I know, Crash, but you need to let me do my job," Aaron replied.

"Well, do it." Crash snapped.

"It'll be okay, Brent. A.J. will get answers," Allyson said, using Aaron's nickname.

Allyson placed her hand on his shoulder, which shouldn't have affected him, but he couldn't control how he felt, so he stepped away and pulled out his phone. He was sure she winced but tucked her hands into her pockets and turned away.

"I need to call my family. I don't know where the kids are," Crash sighed.

"I called your dad, and he said Megan doesn't have them," Allyson told him.

"Megan is going to be devastated. Ellie is her best friend…" Crash stopped when he heard a familiar voice.

"Brent."

Megan sprinted down the corridor, followed by his father, mother, brother, and sister-in-law. All of them had the same shattered expression on their faces.

Ryan and Nancy stopped beside him, but Megan practically threw herself into Crash's arms. She sobbed into his chest as he held her, but while she cried.

"Is it true? Is Ellie and Wyatt…" Megan gazed up at him with tear-filled eyes.

"I'm afraid so." Brent hugged her.

"What the fuck happened?" Ryan asked as he wrapped his arm around his wife.

"Their car went over a cliff." Crash tucked his sister under his arm.

"I can't believe this," Nancy whispered.

"Where are the kids?" Crash asked.

"I don't know. Lacey called Ellie's regular babysitter, but she doesn't have them either," Ryan told him.

Lacey was Crash's nineteen-year-old niece. She recently started university to study Marine Biology, and his brother couldn't be prouder.

Allyson stood next to him and helped keep him from completely losing it. Although, the asshole doctor talking to her when he arrived was back in the reception area pretending to scroll through his phone. Crash didn't miss how he glared and was about to ask what the problem was when he spotted Ellie's nanny running toward them.

Very few people knew who Sidney was, and with her rainbow-colored hair and tattoos, nobody would guess. She was a sweet girl and knew what she'd escaped as a child. The people who adopted her made sure she was never in any danger.

"This can't be true," Sidney whispered as she stepped beside Nancy.

"I'm afraid so, sweetheart," Crash's mom murmured.

"Where are the kids, and what will happen to them?" Sidney broke into tears.

"I'll be their legal guardian. Wyatt and Ellie made wills when Mila was born, and the police are checking the house," Crash assured the weeping girl.

"I'm glad they're going to be safe." Sidney took a deep breath. "If you need anything for the kids, please let me know. I love those babies."

She pulled a piece of paper from her purse and wrote on it. She handed it to Crash and then shoved the pen into her bag. For a moment, she stood there staring at the floor. When she finally lifted her head, tears were streaming down her cheeks.

"I can't believe this. Wyatt and Ellie were family to me," Sidney whispered.

"They loved you, Sid. We all do." Crash hugged the young nanny.

Sidney was brought to Newfoundland when she was little, and Ellie's former foster parents took her in. They had special skills for caring for high-risk kids. It didn't matter what kind of situation the child came from; they did everything to keep all the children safe.

"I'll keep in touch," Crash told Sidney.

Before she could respond, Aaron joined them. His jaw clenched, and his eyes narrowed. He had his phone to his ear, and whatever he heard wasn't good news.

"Thanks. Please make sure I have the full report as soon as you've got it." Aaron ended the call and put the phone back in his pocket.

"A.J., was that about Wyatt and Ellie? Did you find the kids?" Crash asked.

"They weren't at the house, and the neighbors weren't home," Aaron said as he glanced at the group around Crash.

"They may be out of town for the weekend. I can try to call them," Sidney offered.

"I'd appreciate it," Crash said before making introductions.

"I'm so sorry about your friends, Crash." Aaron gently squeezed Crash's shoulder.

"Thanks." Crash hugged his sister tighter.

Sidney walked away with her phone to her ear as Aaron stepped next to Crash. It wasn't difficult to see the man didn't like what he'd heard.

"That call was from the team recovering the vehicle. It's all preliminary, but they believe someone pushed the car off the cliff." Aaron explained. "If the car hadn't gotten tangled up with the trees, we probably wouldn't have found them for a long time. They would've dropped down into the ocean."

"Whoever pushed them off the road didn't want them found," Crash mainly said to himself.

"Probably, but we'll have answers after the autopsies and the forensics team take a better look at the car," Aaron explained.

"Both their phones are going to voicemail. Service is not great at the cottage." Sidney sighed. "I'm sorry I couldn't help."

"It's okay, Sid." Crash squeezed her shoulder gently.

"I've got to get back to my dorm. I've got a paper due. Please let me know when you find them." Sidney wiped the tears from her cheeks.

"We will," Megan hugged the young girl.

When she walked away, Megan tucked herself into her father's side. Crash's mind was racing. He needed to find the kids and pray they were okay.

"Thanks, A.J., but where the hell are the kids?" Crash was worried.

"I'll let you know the minute I know something." Aaron turned to leave but then stopped. "Again, I'm sorry about your friends, and we've already put out an amber alert for the kids. I'll make sure whoever did this ends up behind bars."

Crash looked around and found Allyson talking to a man in the reception area. He couldn't see his face but clenched his fists when the guy touched her shoulder. He had no right to be jealous, but he couldn't help how he felt.

"What happens now?" Crash asked Aaron as he turned away from Allyson.

"You take care of yourself, and I promise we'll find out what happened," Aaron promised.

"I can't sit around and do nothing, A.J.," Crash whispered.

"I know it's hard, but you need to trust us," Aaron told him and looked behind Crash.

He followed Aaron's line of sight and saw Allyson leaning against the wall with her head resting against it. The man from a few seconds ago was nowhere to be seen. Her eyes were closed, and she looked exhausted.

"She should've gone home a while ago," Crash muttered.

"She's staying for you," Aaron informed him.

"I don't think so. She probably has paperwork to do." Crash sighed.

"She cares about you, Crash," Aaron told him.

"We're friends, A.J.," Crash replied.

"Bethany thinks Allyson is afraid to admit her feelings for you, but she doesn't know why."

"She says I'm too young for her." Crash rolled his eyes.

"For the love of God, what is it? four or five-years difference?" Aaron snorted.

"I'm four years younger," Crash explained.

"Bull is six years older than Kristy, and you never met a happier couple," Aaron said.

Kristy was Aaron's cousin, and she married Keith's best friend and business partner, Dean 'Bull' Nash. Bull. Crash remembered that in the beginning, Bull had issues with the age difference, but mostly, he didn't think he was good enough for Kristy.

"Age doesn't matter to me, but right now, I need to give all my energy to finding the kids," Crash said.

"You're not alone. You know that, right?" Aaron stepped in front of Crash.

"Thanks. That means a lot." Crash shook hands with Aaron.

He was now responsible for two lives and didn't even finish his house. It was liveable enough for him but not for small children. He'd probably have to stay with his parents and ask for help to finish the other bedrooms and the other bathroom. He ran his hand through his hair and blew out a breath.

"Where the hell are the kids? The only people they trusted were my family, the babysitter, and their neighbor," Crash said.

"We'll try to get in touch with the neighbors," Aaron told him.

Crash nodded as Aaron shook his hand again and then walked over to where the other police officers waited. What was he supposed to do now? His mind was going a mile a minute with images of what could've happened to three-year-old Caleb and one-year-old Mila. He needed to remain hopeful before putting himself into a pit of despair he couldn't escape.

Crash turned to his father and mother.

"I need to find Caleb and Mila," Crash told his family.

"I hate to say it, but do you think the people who did this could have them?" his dad asked.

"I can't go there, Dad." Crash plowed his fingers through his hair.

"We'll find them," his father assured him.

"I'm going to drive by their house and see if the neighbors are there," Crash said. "When I find them, I'll need a place to stay until I finish my house. It's not ready for small kids."

"We'll worry about that when we have those babies in our arms," his mom hugged him.

"I know, but it's going to be a priority when I find them," Crash said.

"You can stay with me until you finish the house," Allyson said from behind him.

When he spun around, her lips pressed together as if she hadn't meant to say it. She shifted from one leg to the other before pulling out her phone as if she were about to make a call.

"I've got to go." She practically ran down the corridor.

Did he hear her correctly?

Chapter 8

What possessed her to blurt out an invitation for Crash to stay with her? At her house, where they would be in close quarters. She knew what it was—the pain in his voice and her feelings for him. When she heard him mutter his concerns about the house, her words came out like verbal vomit. She couldn't stop it.

"Ally," Crash called as she tried to make her escape.

"Damn it," she muttered under her breath.

It wouldn't be easy to contain her attraction or feelings if he said yes to her offer. As much as she wanted it, they didn't have a future. He needed someone who could give him the family he said he wanted. She needed to keep reminding herself.

"Ally?" Crash grasped her hand as he caught up with her.

She turned and forced a smile, but as her gaze lifted to meet his, her breath caught. He stared into her eyes for a moment without releasing her hand. She pulled from his hold and shoved her hands into her lab coat.

"Yeah." She tried to sound casual.

"Did I hear you correctly?" Crash asked.

"If you heard me offer my house for you and the kids, then yes. I have plenty of room, and you need a place close by to finish the renovations without traveling back and forth to the city. I can help with the little ones until your place is ready to move in."

Allyson impressed herself with her confidence but was glad he couldn't hear her heart pound. She'd spent plenty of time with Crash over the years, and only once did she almost allow herself to give in to what she so desperately wanted. How long would it take to complete a couple of rooms? A week? Two weeks? She could manage to have him in her house for that long without stepping over that line.

"Ally, thank you, but I can't accept." He shook his head.

She should probably shut up and be relieved she dodged a bullet, but she couldn't help herself. Her mouth seemed to have a mind of its own.

"Why not?"

"I can't take over your house with two small kids. Do you know how much of an inconvenience that would be?" Crash pulled her aside as a man walked by.

"Brent, those babies need a comfortable place to stay, and you need to be able to finish your house. This is my last two-week shift, and I can watch them while you and your dad finish everything."

Allyson didn't know if she was trying to convince him or herself. The mess of mixed feelings swirling around in her head gave her a headache, but when she looked into his eyes again, she made her own decision. She felt an overwhelming need to be there to help Crash.

He wasn't alone; he had his parents, sister, brother, and sister-in-law. The way they rushed to the hospital as soon as they heard about Ellie and Wyatt showed that they cared, but if she was honest, she wanted to be the one to help.

"I can stay with my parents," Crash reminded her.

"They live in St. John's, and traveling back and forth will get tiring. Plus, when you take a break from renovating, you can come to check on the kids anytime you want." Allyson smiled as he glanced back into the room.

"Those sweet angels have a rough road ahead of them. Both their parents are gone now, and they have no other family." Crash turned away with tears in his eyes.

Allyson placed her hand against his cheek and pulled his attention to her. She hated the pain in his eyes. Those kids were orphans now, but Crash lost two friends. How could she do anything but help him care for the babies?

"They have you. They have your parents, Megan, Ryan, Nancy, and Lacey. Now, they have me, and I can almost guarantee that when everyone in Hopedale finds out what happened, you'll have all the help you need. Now, go find them and bring them home." Allyson wiped a tear from his cheek.

When he covered her hand with his, she tensed. To anyone watching them, they probably looked like two people in love. It was perhaps why she felt the urgent need to be there for him.

"Ally, are you sure?" Crash locked his gaze with hers.

"One thousand percent," she lied.

"Thank you," he choked and turned his head to kiss her palm.

"You don't have to thank me, but we should probably leave and get things set up for them. It's getting late." Allyson pulled her hand away.

Crash glanced at his watch and cursed. It was after nine in the evening, and the kids were probably asleep. She could head home and move some things around to make room for them.

"Look, let me know when you find them. Tomorrow, come to my house, and we'll go from there. Okay?" Allyson shoved her hands in her pockets to keep from touching him again.

"I don't know how to thank you," Crash whispered as he tucked a piece of her hair behind her ear.

"You don't have to. It's what friends do for each other," she said, trying not to lean into his touch.

"Yeah. Friends." Crash sighed and walked away.

She was so glad her shift was over. As she made her way through the hospital parking lot, a wave of exhaustion hit, making her feet feel weighed down with rocks. It was close to midnight, and she'd been at the hospital since six that morning. She couldn't wait to get home.

Someone grabbed her shoulder as she pulled open her car door. Allyson gasped and turned around, ready to defend herself against an attack.

"Hey, sorry." a familiar man held up his hands.

"Jesus, Julian. You don't approach people in a dark parking lot without warning them you're there." Allyson tossed her purse on the seat.

Julian Burgess was in pharmaceutical sales, and they'd spoken earlier because he had misplaced his briefcase. He was checking with the doctors he'd met over the last couple of days to see if they'd seen it. Allyson promised to call if she found it, but she hadn't looked.

"Sorry, I wanted to let you know I found it. I left it in the men's room, and someone brought it to the main reception." Julian shook his head. "I should be more careful."

"Probably," Allyson chuckled.

Julian always seemed to make her nervous, but not because he'd said or done anything. It was something she couldn't put her finger on. He talked fast and couldn't sit still for long. It was as if he was always looking over his shoulder. She wasn't sure if it was some hyperactive disorder or if he was overly energetic.

"Well, I should head home. I'm glad you found it," Allyson said as she sat in her car.

"Me too. I was going to see if you wanted to go for a drink, but you look tired." Julian leaned on her open car door.

"I am, but thanks for the offer." Allyson smiled.

"Maybe another time." Julian stepped back as she closed her door.

"Goodnight," Allyson said without committing to the drink offer.

She'd had one date with the man about six months earlier, but it was awkward. His questions weren't the type someone asks on a date. Julian seemed more interested in who she spent time with and if she had any friends in the military.

By the time she arrived home, she had taken a shower and crawled into bed; it was after two in the morning. The problem was that she was exhausted, but her mind wouldn't shut off. It was always hard when she lost a patient, but the fact that Ellie and Wyatt were Crash's friends made it hit home a little harder.

Then, there was blurting out an offer for Crash and the kids to stay with her until he finished his renovations. She honestly didn't mind helping out, but she wasn't sure her mental health could handle living with Crash. It certainly wouldn't be easy to keep him at arm's length if they were under the same roof.

"Well, you can't take it back now," she muttered as she flipped over on her stomach.

Allyson had to keep reminding herself she wasn't the right woman for Crash. He needed someone who could give him children, not an older woman who had her childbearing years behind her. At least she had one amazing kid who got her through each day.

She closed her eyes and prayed Crash had found the sweet babies and sleep. What she wouldn't give to have Crash hold her at night so she could drift off in his arms. She'd have no issues with snuggling into the warmth of his embrace. Then again, being that close to him would probably have her libido in overdrive.

A loud crash downstairs had her bolting upright. She reached for her phone on the nightstand only to come up empty. She didn't want to turn on her bedroom light in case whoever was in her house would realize she was home. Then again, they had to be pretty stupid not to see her car in the driveway.

"Where the fuck is my phone?" Allyson whispered as she gently slapped her hand around her nightstand.

She smoothed her hands around her bed, thinking she may have left it next to her as she often did, but there was nothing. She threw back the blankets and tiptoed to the corner of the room where she kept Trent's old baseball bat. He bought it to show Cameron how to hit a ball when their son was in little league.

After he died, Cameron kept it in his room, but when he moved to town, he gave it to her to keep in her bedroom for safety. Allyson had laughed because she never expected to need it.

"Thanks, Cam." she sighed and gripped the bat handle, holding it as if ready to play ball.

Allyson slowly opened her bedroom door and tiptoed to the top of the stairs. The only light downstairs was the light over the stove, and she could see a shadow move around the kitchen. She needed to call the police, but she couldn't find her damn phone.

One step at a time, she crept down the stairs, bat ready to swing if anyone came close. She was on the bottom when she heard a male curse. Her heart pounded when she spotted her phone charging next to the stove.

She plastered herself against the wall outside the kitchen entrance and reached around the doorjamb to switch on the light. Surprising the intruder with a room full of light, she jumped into the doorway with the bat held over her head.

"What are you…" Allyson gasped. "Elijah?"

"Holy fucking Jesus. You scared the living shit out of me, Ally." her cousin blew out a breath of air.

"Why are you creeping around my house at one in the morning?" Allyson snapped.

"I texted you to tell you I was coming back to Newfoundland tonight. I sent you all the information," Elijah explained. "If you don't mind, can you put down the bat? You look nuts."

Allyson looked at her shoulder, realizing she still had the bat ready to attack. She placed it next to the door as she walked into the kitchen. It was when she noticed the broom in Elijah's hand and a dustpan full of glass.

"I dropped a glass," he said.

"No shit." Allyson grabbed her phone.

She tapped the screen and saw several texts from her cousin, one from her sister, one from Cameron, and several from Witt. She looked at all the crucial ones before checking to see what her annoying co-worker wanted.

She rolled her eyes when she scrolled through numerous memes that he seemed to think were funny, but she thought they were stupid. They all involved plastic surgery.

"I'm sorry. I haven't checked my phone since supper time, and then it died. When I got home, I plugged it in and went to bed." Allyson placed it back on the counter.

"I'm glad I didn't get a bat to the head." He chuckled and tossed the broken glass into the garbage.

"You would've deserved it. Most people call a few days in advance, not a few hours," Allyson chastised as she hugged her cousin.

Elijah Grant was the only child of her mother's brother. Her uncle Oliver was a retired teacher. Allyson didn't see him very often, but they talked at least once a week.

"I didn't know I'd be coming here a few days ago. I only found out eighteen hours ago." Elijah kissed her forehead.

Elijah used to work with a company that helped veterans who struggled with civilian life. He was sent all over the country, but three years ago, he joined NES. Keith usually sent him out of the province because he enjoyed traveling, and none of the other staff wanted to do those jobs.

"Keith doesn't give you much notice, does he?" Allyson laughed.

"The joys of private security," Elijah sighed.

"Anyway, how long are you here for?" Allyson asked as she grabbed a glass of water.

"Not sure. Keith was kind of secretive about the whole thing. Said it would be a long contract, and I'd be based mostly here." Elijah sat at the table.

Allyson overlooked the pizza on the table until her cousin took a bite out of a piece. She grabbed a slice for herself and joined him for the snack.

"So, I'm guessing you'll be staying here?" Allyson asked with a hint of reluctance.

If Elijah remained with her, it would possibly be an issue having Crash and the kids stay at her house. She couldn't take back her offer and didn't want to. She also couldn't turn away her cousin.

"I'm going to crash at one of the bunkhouses on the compound. Not that I don't love staying here, but I'd rather have my own space if I'm here for an extended period." Elijah grabbed a second piece of the pizza.

The compound was what everyone called Keith's extensive property. He lived there with his family and kept the offices for NES and his construction company in a separate building, a stone's throw from his house. Keith also erected several bunkhouses at the back of the area for staff or anyone who needed a short-term stay. It was completely secure, and a fence surrounded the entire property. Nobody got through the gate without being let inside.

"Okay, good," she said without thinking.

"Good? Thanks a lot, cuz." Elijah chuckled.

Allyson stopped chewing and placed her pizza on top of the napkin. She put her hands on the table and lifted her eyes to meet Elijah's amused gaze.

"I have some people staying here for a couple of weeks," she told him.

"What? Are you going to run a bed and breakfast from this place?" Elijah questioned.

"No, a friend needs a place to stay for a bit." Allyson was being evasive.

"A friend?" Elijah smirked. "Are you seeing someone, Allyson?"

"No," Allyson almost yelled. "Brent is staying here until he finishes his house."

Elijah's eyes grew wide, and his mouth hung open. He'd been one of the people who constantly hounded her to take a chance on Crash. Before she could tell him the situation, he threw his head back and laughed.

"I fucking knew you'd give in sooner or later," Elijah said.

"It's not like that, Elijah. It's a long story." She took another bite of the pizza.

"I slept on the plane. Let's hear the long story." Elijah smirked.

She could tell by the expression on his face he didn't believe anything was going on between her and Crash. She was exhausted, but the only thing that would shut him up was if she told him the whole situation. After she grabbed another piece of pizza, she explained.

"That's terrible," Elijah said.

"Yeah, we both know losing a mom is not easy, but to lose both parents before you're old enough to retain memories of them, that's cruel." Allyson sighed. "They're just babies, and I'm praying he found them."

"Between Crash's family and the guys at NES, he won't be short of help looking." Elijah stood up. "I'm going to catch a few hours shut-eye before heading to the compound."

"I should get some sleep too." She placed the leftover pizza in the fridge. "I'll see you in the morning."

Elijah hugged her and then headed to Cameron's old room. He was lucky she hadn't cleared anything out yet, or her cousin would be sleeping on a bare floor—although it wouldn't be his first time.

She wanted to call Brent to see if there was any news, but it was late. If he had managed to get some sleep, she didn't want to wake him. Allyson didn't want to think about what could happen to kids if the wrong people got their hands on them.

By the time she crawled back into bed, she barely had the strength to tug the covers over herself. She closed her eyes and drifted to sleep; her last thoughts were of Cameron, Caleb, Mila, and Crash.

Chapter 9

His truck was quiet as he and Megan drove the five minutes from his parent's home to Wyatt's place. It was as if both were afraid to say anything because it would upset the other. Driving by the house where their friends lived would be difficult, but they had to do it.

He'd drove by the previous night, but the neighbors still weren't home, and Aaron hadn't gotten hold of them. With little to no sleep, Crash wanted to check again, hoping by some stroke of luck, the older couple would be home.

It took him and Megan several minutes to get out of his truck. When they finally did, Crash noticed the front door of the house ajar, and he grabbed Megan's arm to stop her from going any further.

"Get back in the truck and call the police," Crash ordered.

Megan didn't resist. She quickly yanked open the door and jumped back into Crash's truck. Crash slowly made his way up the front steps and listened for any noise inside. He gradually pushed open the door, keeping himself ready to deal with anyone who decided to escape. When nobody came out, he stepped inside and carefully looked around. He didn't see anyone, but someone left chaos behind them.

Crash stepped over the debris scattered around the floor of the small foyer as he moved further into the house, anger built in his gut. He backed out the door and briefly walked around the house to see how the intruder got in without a key since the front door didn't look damaged.

When he hopped over the fence in the backyard, he spotted the rear door wide open and a large footprint in the middle of it. His anger grew as he fisted his hands and turned away from the damage.

"Fucking heartless bastards," Crash hissed through his teeth.

When he jogged around the house, he found Megan outside the truck with the phone held against her chest and tears in her eyes. Crash tugged her into his arms until she could pull herself together.

"Hey," a woman shouted as she walked toward them from the house next door.

Crash turned to see the neighbor they'd been hoping to speak with. For his life, he couldn't remember the woman's name. He'd been introduced to them a few times because they were Ellie's former foster parents, and they'd been the ones who adopted Sidney.

"I called the police when Roger and I returned from our cottage. We left yesterday morning, and as soon as I pulled into the driveway, Roger noticed the door open. He went over to see if Ellie and Wyatt were home, but he stopped when he saw the mess. Let them know we're sorry." The woman glanced at the house and shook her head.

"I'm afraid I have bad news." Crash swallowed the lump in his throat. "Ellie and Wyatt were killed in a car accident yesterday." Crash didn't know how else to tell the woman.

She grabbed her chest and staggered back. Both he and Megan reached for the lady to keep her from falling. He probably should've been careful telling her about the deaths. After all, the woman was the only parent Ellie ever knew.

She clung to Crash's arm as he walked her back to her house while Megan waited by the truck for the police to arrive. She was trembling, and tears filled her eyes.

"Those poor, sweet babies." The woman sobbed as her husband bolted through the door.

"What's wrong, Ethel love? Are you okay? Are you having chest pain?" Roger took his wife's hands and scanned her from head to toe.

Ethel. Crash mentally slapped himself for forgetting her name. Then it all came back to him. Ethel and Roger Collins lived in the house for over thirty years. They helped Wyatt and Ellie find their home.

"I'm fine, dear. I got some horrible news." She squeezed her husband's hands.

"What is it?" Roger glanced at Crash.

"Wyatt and Ellie, they died in a car accident." Ethel started to sob.

"Are you serious?" Roger stared at his wife and then glanced at Crash.

He always hated it when someone asked whether you were serious when given bad news. Did people joke about things so terrible? He didn't say anything to the man; he simply nodded.

"I can't believe this. Ellie." Roger hugged his wife to his side.

"It was a shock, but right now, we're trying to find the kids," Crash explained.

"The kids…" Roger stopped when Ethel grabbed his arm.

"They weren't in the car with Ellie and Wyatt, nor with the babysitter," Crash interrupted.

"You talked to Sidney?" Roger asked.

"Yes, she came to the hospital." Crash couldn't read Roger's expression, but Ethel looked scared.

The three of them stood in silence for several seconds. Crash was about to tell them he needed to talk to the police when the car pulled up behind his truck. He said his goodbyes and sprinted over to greet the officer.

"We need to talk to them as well," Ethel shouted as he left.

"I appreciate you giving them any information. Thanks." He nodded and headed back to his truck.

Crash stepped next to his sister as two police officers exited the cruiser. One was the young man he'd met at the hospital, and the other he knew well. Relief washed over Crash as Nick O'Connor walked toward him.

"I was in the area," Nick explained as he walked closer.

He'd become close friends with Nick and knew the man was the recruit trainer, which was probably why Dillon Ray was with him.

"The neighbor said she called as well." Crash pointed to the couple, who were in a deep discussion.

"Dillon, can you take a statement from them?" Nick asked the young officer.

"Yes, sir."

As Dillon hurried over to the neighbors, Crash told Nick what he'd seen inside and found at the back of the house.

"We need to get in there," Megan reminded Crash.

"We can't go in right now." Crash hugged her.

"The kids need their things." Megan rested her head against his chest.

Crash didn't bother to remind her that they needed to find the kids first, but when she looked up at him, he saw tears. He kissed the top of her head and swallowed hard.

"Look, I'll go in with you. We'll head to the kid's room, get what you need, and when it's cleared, you can come get the rest." Nick offered.

"I'll go in." Crash grabbed a couple of duffle bags out of the truck.

"Okay," Megan whispered.

When he got inside, Crash got a better look around. Whoever broke in was looking for something specific because they didn't appear to touch any of the electronics. There was a large television in the living room, Wyatt's gaming system, a laptop on the coffee table, and an iPad beside it.

"What the hell were they looking for?" Nick used a tissue to open the laptop.

"Clearly not electronics," Crash muttered as he scanned the living room.

"Come on, let's get what you need out of the bedrooms." Nick motioned toward the stairs.

Crash carefully walked up the steps, avoiding the debris tossed down from the second floor. Nick was ahead of him, and they stopped at the top of the landing.

"The two rooms on the right are the kids. The two on the left are a guest room and the master bedroom." Crash told Nick.

He headed down the hall to Caleb's room with Nick behind him. When he pushed open the door, he cursed under his breath.

"What the fuck? Why would they destroy a kid's room?" Nick shook his head.

"They didn't take anything belonging to Caleb." Crash dropped one of the duffle bags on Caleb's bed.

"Take what you need." Nick grabbed the other bag. "I'll get whatever is in the other room."

"You sure you know what to take?" Crash asked.

"I'm a dad, remember," Nick reminded him and left the room.

Crash picked up all the clothes scattered around the floor. He checked the dresser drawers, but all the clothes were emptied on the floor or bed. He knew the kids had a lot of clothes because Wyatt complained about Ellie always buying new ones, but the amount around the room was ridiculous.

When he shoved as much as he could into the bags, he tossed it on his shoulder and grabbed the toy box next to the bedroom door. He prayed he wasn't taking the kid's things only to find out they were… Nope, he wasn't going to let that thought enter his head. Exiting the room, he heard Nick shuffling around Mila's bedroom.

He walked into the room and froze. Mila's crib lay tipped over, and the floor covered with baby clothes. He locked eyes with Nick as he picked up handfuls of clothing and shoved them into the duffle bag.

"I thought my kids had too much shit, but this is nuts." Nick shook his head. "Sorry, I didn't mean to say that out loud."

"It's okay. I agree this is a lot for a kid that will grow out of it in a month or two."

"Sometimes they grow out of it in a week," Nick sighed.

"Why would one baby need all this?" Crash shook his head.

"Why did they beat the shit out of the crib, and why tear open the mattress." Nick threw the bag on his shoulder and grabbed the basket filled with baby toys.

Crash wanted to look around the rest of the house, but Nick bent the rules by allowing him to enter the place before forensics went through the home.

"Let's get out of here. I got a text saying the guys are ready to get in here, and Dillon has some news." Nick led the way down the steps.

Dillon was standing by the front door when they stepped outside.

"Sir, I have some information." Dillon glanced at Crash.

"You can speak freely in front of Crash, Dillon," Nick assured the young officer.

"The couple next door said they'll only speak with Brent Adams. They have something to tell him." Dillon probably didn't know Crash's real name.

"Dillon, my name is Brent Adams," Crash told him.

"Crash is a nickname," Nick explained when Dillon looked confused.

"Oh, sorry, I've only ever heard the guys with NES referred to by their nicknames." Dillon shrugged.

"I should go talk to them." Crash ran down the steps.

After tossing the bags and toys into the truck, he told Megan he'd be right back and jogged back to where Ethel and Roger stood. They looked concerned as he climbed the steps to join them.

"You know I'm Brent Adams, right?" Crash asked them.

The couple glanced at each other as if they were silently communicating. Roger took a step forward with his hand out.

"Can I see something to prove that?" The man asked.

"Sure." Crash reached into his pocket and pulled out his wallet.

He handed his license to Roger and waited while the man seemed to study the card. He gave it to his wife, and when she finished, she returned it to Brent.

"Wyatt said you and your family were the only people he could trust besides Roger and I." Ethel's voice cracked. "I know we met before, but we still need to be sure you are Brent."

"We might have been Ellie's foster parents once, but she was like our daughter. We love her and those kids." Roger swallowed.

"Both of them thought a lot of you both. They talked about you all the time," Crash assured them. "The officer said you would only talk to me."

"Yes, because Wyatt made us promise that no matter who came here, we were only permitted to tell you." Ethel sniffed.

"Tell me what?" Crash asked.

The couple motioned for him to come inside, and he followed, trying not to lose his patience with the couple. He wanted to know what the hell Wyatt told them that was so damn secretive. He was about to ask when Roger opened a door to a room off of the living room.

"They're sleeping right now," Ethel whispered.

All the air whooshed out of Crash when he saw Caleb curled up on the sofa, cuddling a teddy bear, and Mila softly snoring in a portable crib. He grabbed the door frame to steady himself. The relief of seeing the kids safe and sound was overwhelming.

"Wyatt was scared when he came here in the middle of the night. He begged us to take the kids to our cottage and not return until today. He was worried about Sidney too, but she was in class, and she's safe where she is," Roger began.

"He said if they didn't return for the kids by the end of the week, we were to contact you. They gave us all your information and an envelope to give you." Ethel grabbed a large yellow folder on the bookcase next to the door.

"Since we know they won't be..." Roger shook his head.

Crash took the envelope and ripped it open. He found the kids' IDs, medical cards, birth certificates, and Wyatt and Ellie's banking information and wills inside. All this meant the couple knew they were in danger and may not return to their kids.

"Did they say anything else?" Crash asked.

"Only to keep ourselves and Sidney safe. They said everything you needed is in there." Roger wrapped his arm around a sobbing Ethel.

Crash took a deep breath and blew it out slowly. He didn't want to wake the kids, so he asked the couple if he could leave them there until he went to talk to the police.

"But Ellie said they couldn't go to the police." Roger looked frantic.

"Trust me, the man outside I trust with my life," Crash assured them as he hurried back to Nick.

Nick leaned against Crash's truck, talking to Megan. Her shoulders relaxed when he ran toward them, and Nick stood up.

"What did they want?" Megan practically shouted.

Crash didn't answer until he was next to them, and he didn't speak until he was sure nobody else was nearby. Ellie and Wyatt were paranoid about something, so he didn't want to chance that someone would overhear him.

"The kids are in there." Crash whispered.

"What?" Megan gasped.

He explained everything and held up the envelope that Roger had handed him. With Crash's permission, Nick went through all the contents. It took several minutes before he finally handed everything back to Crash.

"It's as if they knew something was going to happen to them." Megan wiped a tear from her cheek.

"I'm not sure what's going on, but I just want to get the kids and worry about everything else later." Crash hopped in his truck.

"I thought you were going to get Caleb and Mila," Megan said as she got beside him.

"I am," Crash told her as he drove into the Collins' driveway.

He had no idea what the fuck was going on. All he knew was that he had two lives depending on him and would do everything in his power to ensure the kids were safe.

Chapter 10

Allyson breathed when Crash texted to tell her he'd found the kids. He didn't go into details, but what mattered was that they were found and safe. She wasn't sure Crash would survive if anything happened to the kids.

To kill time while she waited for Crash and the kids to arrive, she cleaned and freshened the guest room after Elijah left. She didn't know if Crash wanted to stay in the room with the kids or a separate room, so she got both rooms ready.

She took one last look around the living room to confirm nothing was there to hurt curious little hands. She always did the same thing when her sister visited with the kids. It was difficult not to be envious of Bethany because she was married to the love of her life and had an amazing little family.

Allyson didn't have that because she wanted someone she couldn't have. She cared too much about him to deny him the family he deserved.

She glanced at the patio door and froze. She'd cleaned the glass two hours ago, but now it had a large smear across the center. As she walked closer, it was clear it was outside. If she didn't know better, she'd say someone had their cheek pressed against it.

After she'd removed the bar from the door to open it and clean the streak, she checked around the deck. Nothing looked out of place, but something felt off. Allyson quickly hurried back inside and put the bar back on the door when she heard him.

"Knock, knock." Crash's voice echoed from the foyer.

"I'm in the living room," Allyson replied, setting aside the cloth and cleaner.

Footsteps shuffled down the hallway, and Crash stepped into view. He held the hand of a little boy and carried the most adorable baby she'd ever seen.

"Well, hello." Allyson walked toward the trio.

"Caleb, this is Dr. Sullivan." Crash crouched to be at eye level with the child.

Allyson did the same and smiled at the little boy, who shyly lifted his head. His huge blue eyes glanced back and forth between Crash and Allyson. The poor kid was probably so confused. It was hard for adults to understand the death of a loved one, but for a child, it had to be impossible to comprehend.

"It's nice to meet you, Caleb, but you don't have to call me Dr. Sullivan. All my friends call me Ally," Allyson told him.

"Hi," Caleb said.

"You know what? My nephew left some toys here. They're next to the table and bookcase with all those cool books." Allyson pointed to the corner of the living room.

Caleb looked at Crash, and when he nodded, the little boy made his way to the box of toys. Allyson saw the hint of a smile when Caleb pulled out a small truck and began to roll it around the floor. At least he found something to make him happy. She and Crash stood silently, watching for several seconds before Crash spoke.

"Thank you," he whispered.

"You don't have to thank me. I'm happy to help," Allyson met his gaze.

Crash was the first to look away when the baby started to squirm in his arms. Allyson was surprised when the little girl leaned forward and stretched her arms.

"Mila likes you." Crash chuckled.

Allyson took the little girl into her arms and held back the tears as the baby rested her head on Allyson's shoulder. Crash gently ran his hand over the top of the baby's soft curls.

"She doesn't go to just anyone," Crash informed her.

"She's probably tired," Allyson whispered.

"After I found them, we stayed at my parent's place. Neither of the kids slept well last night. It's been a long day." Crash sighed.

"I'm glad you found them so quickly," Allyson said as she began to sway with the baby.

"I'll tell you about it, but I have stuff in the truck. Nick gave me a portable thing for her to sleep in. Are you okay with them while I bring it in?" Crash asked.

"I'm fine." She smiled as Mila snuggled into her neck.

He glanced between the kids and Allyson before rushing outside to get everything. After several trips to the car, he closed the front door, and she escorted him to her son's old room.

"I hope this is okay," Allyson said as she bounced the baby in her arms.

"It's perfect," Crash assured her.

She left Crash to set up the crib while she kept an eye on Caleb. She didn't know if the little boy would be afraid or get into something he shouldn't. She found him in the same place, pushing the same little car around the floor.

She was playing with Mila on the floor next to Caleb when the front door opened again. Allyson glanced up as her son appeared in the doorway. Cameron's blue eyes grew large, but only for a few seconds. When he leaned against the door jamb, he raised an eyebrow.

"I know it's been a week since I've been here, but is there something you haven't told me?" Cameron narrowed his eyes. "Do I have new siblings, Mom?"

"You don't have siblings. This is Mila, and that's Caleb. It's a long story, but…" Allyson stood with Mila in her arms.

"I like stories," Cameron laughed.

She walked closer to her son so Caleb didn't overhear her. She didn't know if he knew about his parents yet or even if he understood what was going on. How could he? The child was barely out of diapers.

"They lost their parents, and Brent became their legal guardian. They were friends of his," she whispered.

"Damn, that's tragic." Cameron looked over at the little boy.

"Yeah." Allyson cupped Mila's tiny cheek.

"Wait, if Crash is caring for them, that doesn't explain why they're here with you." Cameron smirked. "Have you finally decided to…"

"Brent and I are friends, and he's staying here until he can finish the renovations to his house. It's easier than having to drive back and forth to the city. I'm off for a few weeks, so I offered to watch the …"

She stopped when Crash came down the stairs, looking like he'd just crawled out of bed with mussed hair. His face was a little red, but she wasn't sure if he was mad or embarrassed.

"Hey, Cam," Crash said with a smile.

"Hey, Crash." Cameron raised an eyebrow at seeing Brent coming downstairs.

"He was setting up the portable crib for Mila. She's ready for a nap," Allyson explained.

"Yeah, about that." Crash plowed his fingers through his thick hair and blew out an aggravated breath. "I think it's broken. I can't get it to stay up."

Allyson chuckled as she handed Mila to Crash and began to head toward the stairs. Anyone who set up a portable crib knew how frustrating it could be.

"Come on, I'll bet you it's not broke." Allyson headed toward the stairs. "Cam, can you stay with Caleb while I help Brent with the crib?"

"On it." Cameron sat on the floor next to the little boy.

Caleb looked at her son as if he was a movie star, especially when Cameron lay on the floor and started playing with the small matchbox cars. The little boy was in the best hands.

Allyson entered the guest room and pressed her lips together to prevent the giggle from escaping. The crib lay upside down on the floor. She shook her head at Crash, who shrugged as he shifted Mila to his other arm.

"I'm telling you, it's broken," Crash grumbled.

Allyson set it up in less than a minute with blankets at the bottom. When she turned around, Crash stared, his mouth hung open. Mila giggled as if she understood how funny the situation was.

"What kind of witchcraft is that? I swear it wouldn't open." Crash grumbled.

"They can be pretty tricky if you've never set one up before," Allyson reassured him.

"Is that your nice way of saying even an idiot can do it?" Crash asked.

"No. The first time I had to set one up, I sat on the floor and cried," Allyson admitted.

She wasn't lying, but Crash narrowed his eyes, wondering whether to believe her. Before he could say a word, Mila drew his attention when she yawned and placed her head on his shoulder.

"Do you want to put her down?" Allyson stepped aside.

"I'll try. I hope she'll go to sleep in another strange place." Crash gently lowered the baby into the crib.

"When babies are tired, they don't care where they sleep." She hoped.

Allyson walked to the doorway and turned. Crash leaned over the crib, whispering to Mila as he pulled a blanket over her. The baby babbled as she fisted the material and pulled it against her face.

"Go to sleep, sweet girl," Crash whispered and backed out of the room.

They stepped into the hallway, and Crash froze as Mila whined. He then chattered as she wiggled around for a few seconds. He peeped into the room, and after Mila exhaled, there was no other noise.

"I think she's going to sleep." Crash sighed.

"Leave the door open so you can hear when she wakes up. You should probably pick up a monitor," Allyson suggested.

Crash nodded, and they headed back downstairs. They found Cameron still playing cars with Caleb. Allyson smiled, remembering how much her son loved the tiny diecast vehicles when he was little. She still had a box of them in the attic because she couldn't bring herself to throw them out when he stopped using them.

"Vroom, vroom, eeek." Cameron pushed a little car across the floor to a smiling Caleb.

"That's the first time I've seen him smile since I found him." Crash leaned close, and his warm breath tickled her ear.

It took everything in her not to moan and lean closer to him. The fact that his scent was already playing havoc with her libido didn't make things any better. She quickly stepped into the kitchen to put some space between them.

"You never said where you found them," Allyson reminded him.

"With Ellie's former foster parents. They told us Wyatt and Ellie dropped them off the night before the accident, and if they didn't come back, they weren't to tell anyone where the kids were except me." Crash kept his voice lowered.

"It sounds as if they knew they weren't coming back," Allyson whispered.

"I know, and Caleb hasn't asked for either of them. I wonder if they told him something before they dropped the kids off, or he's waiting for them to show up." Crash's eyes moved to the little boy.

"I'm sure he's wondering where his mom and dad are. You haven't told him yet, have you?" Allyson asked.

"No. I don't know how I'm going to tell him." Crash sighed.

"Cam was eleven when Trent died, and it was hard for him to understand. I'd suggest talking to a therapist. I can recommend someone from the hospital," Allyson told him.

"I'd appreciate it." Crash turned his gaze to her, and her breath hitched. "Thanks, Ally."

"That's what friends are for," she whispered.

"Yeah." Crash sighed.

"I think us men need a snack. What do you think, little man?" Cameron shouted from the living room.

When Cameron stood up, the little boy nodded and jumped to his feet. It seemed her son had made a friend in young Caleb. Then again, Cameron was fantastic with small children. She wondered if he would follow in her uncle's footsteps and become a teacher. He hadn't picked a major at university because he was still thinking about what he wanted to do.

"I'll get you something," Allyson offered.

"Nope, me and Caleb are going to get a big boy snack. Don't need help." Cameron winked at his mother as he scooped Caleb up into his arms.

"He's good with Caleb," Crash said.

"Cam's always had a way with small kids," Allyson said proudly.

They stepped into the living room, and Crash sat on the edge of the couch. He rested his elbows on his knees, clasping his hands under his chin. It wasn't hard to see he was exhausted and wound tighter than a drum.

"You look tired." Allyson sat next to him and gently touched his shoulder.

"I don't remember the last time I slept. I've been running around like a chicken with its head cut off. Mom and Dad took one thing off my plate and went to make the funeral arrangements," Crash told her.

"Why don't you take a nap while Mila is sleeping? Cam and I will keep Caleb entertained," Allyson suggested.

"Thanks, but it's no use in trying. My mind won't shut off." Crash leaned back and dropped his head against the sofa.

"You won't be able to help anyone if you're exhausted. At least sit here and close your eyes. Even if you don't sleep, you can rest briefly." Allyson stood up. "I'll keep Caleb and Cam in the kitchen."

Crash didn't argue and closed his eyes. For a moment, she watched him. Tension marred his handsome face, and she wished she could do something to relieve all that stress.

"I can't relax with you staring," Crash muttered.

"Sorry," Allyson muttered and then hurried out of the room.

Cameron and Caleb were eating cookies and drinking milk when she found them. They both looked up at her as she walked in, and her son gave her a huge grin.

"Greatest cookies in the world, Mom," Cameron told her.

"You say that because you want to take some back to the apartment with you." Allyson narrowed her eyes and pointed her finger at him.

"Well, yeah, but I'm going to stay here tonight. Me and Caleb are going to watch a movie." Cameron held out his hand, and Caleb slapped his little hand on top of it.

"Oh, I see. Don't you think you should okay that with Brent first?" Allyson asked.

"He can watch it too." Cameron chuckled.

"I'm sure he'll be overjoyed," Allyson said sarcastically.

"Do you know Caleb has not seen Toy Story?" Cameron looked utterly shocked.

"That's tragic." Allyson gasped.

"I gotta Buzz Lightyear. Daddy got it for me," Caleb said in a low voice.

"And you never saw the movie?" Cameron feigned a gasp.

"No. Daddy and Mommy went to heaven before we could watch it." Caleb lowered his head.

Allyson locked eyes with Cameron. Crash said he hadn't told Caleb about his parents, but somehow the kid knew. She wasn't sure who told him, but Crash was probably going to be pissed.

"Who told you that, Caleb?" Allyson asked.

"Nanny Adams talked to her friend on the phone and said Mommy and Daddy died. When my fish died, Daddy told me it went to heaven." Caleb explained.

Iris was going to be upset that Caleb overheard her. Crash told her Wyatt and Ellie called his parents, Mom and Dad, which was probably why Caleb called Iris Nanny.

"My daddy is in heaven, too," Cameron said, placing a comforting hand on Caleb's back. "But that means he's up there watching over me, so I'm safe."

"I miss them." Caleb lifted his head and looked up at Cameron.

"I miss my dad too, but I have lots of people who love me, which makes things a little easier. Hey, that's the same as you. You have lots of people who love you, too." Cameron nudged the little boy with his shoulder.

Caleb's face lit up with a huge grin as he stared at Cameron like he was the best person in the world. Allyson knew how the little boy felt because, watching her son with Caleb, she felt the same way.

Chapter 11

Crash pushed his way through the trees, running as fast as he could. He needed to save them. His friends had left him the most precious things in their world to care for, and now he was running to save them.

He broke through the thick forest to see little Mila and Caleb strapped to the back of a car. The car slowly rolled toward a cliff, and they were screaming. Crash tried to run, but his feet felt weighted down.

Crash looked down to see large rocks tumbling around his ankles. He tried to throw them out of the way, but more continued to fall. He glanced up at the car, but it was gone. Instead, Wyatt stood next to him, holding a sniper rifle and dressed in a ghillie suit.

Crash was confused by Wyatt's attire and why the man wasn't running to save his children. He was about to ask what his friend was doing when Wyatt spoke.

"I got your back, bro. They won't get away with it again," Wyatt whispered as he dropped to the ground.

"Wyatt, we got to save your kids," Crash shouted.

"I got the target in my sight." Wyatt held up his rifle. *"I won't be fooled again."*

Crash followed the line of sight, and his heart almost stopped. In front of him, Caleb held hands with Ellie, and Mila was in her arms. Allyson smiled at the little girl who touched her face.

"Target in focus," Wyatt whispered.

"Wyatt, what the hell are you doing?" Crash reached for the rifle, but he couldn't grab it.

Crash watched as Wyatt gently squeezed the trigger, and then there was the sound of a crying baby. He looked over where Ellie stood, but she lay on the ground covered in blood with Mila crying on her chest, except it wasn't Ellie. It was Allyson.

"No," Crash shouted.

"Brent, wake up."

Crash jolted upright, but for a moment, he didn't know where he was. He frantically looked around the room before finally realizing he'd been dreaming.

"You were shouting," Allyson crouched in front of him. "Are you okay?"

Crash wanted to pull her into his arms because the nightmare had been so vivid, and he couldn't get the image of Allyson's bloody body out of his head. He wanted to hold her to prove she was still here.

"It was just a dream." Allyson took his hand.

"Where are the kids?" Crash shook his head.

"Mila is still napping, and Cameron took Caleb out in the yard to play," Allyson told him.

"How long was I out?" Crash pulled his hands down over his face.

"About an hour." Allyson stood up and stepped back.

Crash didn't realize he'd fallen asleep. The last thing he remembered was resting his head against the back of the couch. He needed rest, but if his nap indicated the type of dreams he faced, he didn't know if he wanted to go back to sleep.

"You need to get some sleep, Brent," Allyson told him.

"I know, I know." Crash sighed.

"You said the nightmares from your time overseas had gotten less." Allyson sat next to him.

"I'm fine." Crash turned his head to look at her.

He hated to see the worry on her beautiful face, but what was he supposed to say that he dreamed about his dead friend killing her? That type of dream would have Sigmund Freud shaking his head.

"I'm okay, Ally. I think it's all hitting me at once," Crash told her.

"Maybe you should talk to someone, too. A professional, I mean," Allyson said with a slight hitch in her voice.

"I'll make an appointment with the woman Keith suggested." Crash promised.

A couple of months earlier, Keith decided to have a psychologist on retainer for his staff since there had been some traumatic things happening over the last several years. Keith's dad recommended Dr. Nicole Westcott. Crash had seen her several times over the last couple of years. Especially when Keith found out Crash was having night terrors about Afghanistan.

"I met her at the hospital. She's great." Allyson smiled.

Crash met her gaze, and as always, his heart pounded. Her dark blue eyes were like sapphires. When the light hit them a certain way, they almost looked purple. It was the most beautiful thing he'd ever seen. Then again, he was intoxicated by her beauty the first day he met her.

He knew she was attracted to him; that kiss at Hulk's wedding was proof, and it pained him not to be able to feel her lips against his again.

When her eyes dropped to his mouth, he held his breath and slowly leaned into her. When she didn't pull back, he lifted his hand to cup her face, but before he could touch her, Mila's soft cry broke the spell, and Allyson jumped to her feet.

"I'm going to start supper."

After those words, she practically ran out of the living room. Crash slowly stood up and headed upstairs to get the baby. It was time he gave up the dream of being with Allyson and moved on. If he pushed it, he'd lose her friendship, and the last thing he wanted to do was not have her in his life.

Supper was a mix of giggles and messes. Thankfully, the kids ate a lot, and Crash was glad Cameron kept Caleb busy while he dealt with Mila. After she managed to cover her body with food, he bathed her.

Allyson walked in as he was getting the baby dressed and helped him figure out the sleepers with too many snaps. He sighed as he sat on the bed next to the giggling baby. Was he ready for this? He couldn't set up the crib or figure out a stupid pair of baby pajamas.

"I thought you should know that Caleb knows about his parents." Allyson sat next to him.

"What?" Crash shot to his feet.

"Yeah, apparently, he overheard your mom talking to a friend. I don't think he fully understands, but you may want to talk to him about it," Allyson explained.

"He must have heard Mom on the phone when we stayed there last night. Damn it." Crash sat back down.

"It will be okay. He's young, and he'll probably have spurts where he misses them and gets upset, but Caleb has you and everyone else." Allyson touched his arm.

Crash nodded because he couldn't talk with the lump in his throat. It was killing him that his friends were gone. Axel and himself were the only ones left from that extraction mission when he thought about it. It was unbelievable. He hoped Aaron figured out who killed Wyatt and Ellie.

A week flew by a lot faster than he expected, and the coroner finally released Ellie's and Wyatt's remains. He'd had a long talk with Caleb, and although he wasn't sure the kid understood any better, at least the communication lines were open. Caleb knew he could go to Crash or anyone in the family with questions.

Crash was getting ready to bury his friends and contacted Axel to let him know about the funeral arrangements. Unfortunately, his buddy couldn't make it that quickly. He was devastated and broke down when they talked on Facetime. Thankfully, Axel had someone he could speak to where he lived, so Crash didn't worry about his friend falling off the wagon.

Crash decided not to bring Caleb or Mila to the service because they wouldn't understand what was happening, and the last thing the kids needed was to be around such a sad event. Cameron offered to watch Caleb while Keith's niece watched Mila. Lily was Ian's and Sandy's daughter, and he felt comfortable leaving her with the baby.

He was fixing his tie in the kitchen when Sandy walked in with Lily and Keith. Keith's clenched jaw and narrowed eyes told Crash his boss was about to hit him with bad news. He wasn't sure he wanted to hear anything else.

"Where's the baby? I want to squish her cheeks," Lily cooed.

"She's down for a nap, but she should be up soon," Crash told the excited girl.

"Ah, shoot. I guess I'll have to annoy Cam until she gets up," Lily motioned toward the living room.

"Why do I get the feeling those two will never stop harassing each other and go out on a date?" Sandy shook her head.

"Leave them alone. Lily doesn't need to be dating at her age." Keith grumbled.

"She's nineteen years old, and she's been dating since she was sixteen." Sandy rolled her eyes.

"Well, my daughter is not dating until she's thirty or I'm dead," Keith returned.

"I need to remind Emily to call me the first time little Scarlett gets picked up for a date." Sandy laughed.

"Not going to happen," Keith grumbled.

"Whatever gets you through the day, Keithy." Sandy patted the large man's shoulder.

Keith's daughter was only five, so he had a few years before he would completely freak out about little Scarlett dating. Crash thought about Mila and how someday he would be the man screening the guys she wanted to date. Suddenly, he agreed with Keith's views on dating.

"There *is* a reason you're still here," Keith snapped.

"Yes, asshole." Sandy pulled out her phone. "You asked me to come here because you don't know how to use video conferencing."

"Why do I torture myself by keeping you on staff?" Keith sighed.

"'Cause you *love* me," Sandy returned.

"As much as I'm enjoying this banter, I need to get to the church," Crash told them. "So, whatever you need to tell, spill it."

Sandy tapped the screen on her phone as her and Keith's expressions turned serious again. Crash didn't want to hear any more bad news, but he needed to get it over with.

"A.J. asked us to be here when you talked to him. The crash, Ellie's, and Wyatt's injuries weren't because of the accident—at least most weren't." Sandy held out her phone.

"What do you mean?" Crash wasn't all that surprised.

"Here, A.J. will explain. He's at the coroner's office." Sandy handed him her phone.

Aaron was on the screen with a man Crash didn't know. He assumed the guy was a doctor because he wore scrubs and a lab coat.

"Hey, Crash. This is Dr. Aubry Lucas. He's the medical examiner," Aaron explained.

"Mr. umm… Crash," Aubry seemed confused by the nickname.

"My name is Brent Adams, but everyone calls me Crash," he told the doctor.

"Okay, well, Mr. Adams, A.J. wanted me to explain my findings when I completed the autopsies on Mr. and Mrs. Christopher." Aubry pushed his glasses up on his face. "I understand you're their next of kin."

"Yes, they had no family other than their children." Crash felt a tightness in his gut.

"I understand that the preliminary report said they died due to injuries sustained in a car accident, but the intake doctor who worked on Mrs. Christopher asked for a more in-depth examination," Aubry explained.

"Allyson?" Crash asked.

Allyson had gone to the church to help his mother with some things. He needed to wait for Cameron and Lily to arrive, but she never said she talked to the medical examiner.

"Yes, Dr. Sullivan," Perry confirmed.

"She…" Crash began, but Aaron stopped him.

"Before you get bent out of shape because she didn't tell you, she couldn't, at least not until it was confirmed," Aaron explained.

Allyson was doing her job, and she confirmed her suspicions before saying anything. While Aubry went on about what he'd found, Crash missed most of it. The one thing he knew was Ellie and Wyatt were beaten badly, and now he was pissed.

"Thanks, Dr. Lucas. I appreciate you telling me all this." Crash sighed. "A.J., I'm assuming there will be an investigation."

"Yes, there were some things with the vehicle, too, but I'll explain that to you later," Aaron said. "I'll keep you informed, and Crash,"

"Yes," Crash said.

"I'm so sorry for your loss. We'll figure this out. I promise." Aaron told him. "I'll see you at the church."

"I appreciate it, and thanks." Crash handed the phone to Sandy and left the house.

"Hey," Keith shouted behind him.

"What? I got to go," Crash barked.

"Let A.J. handle this," Keith warned.

"I'll do exactly what you would do, Rusty. Don't worry," Crash returned and left before his boss could respond.

Chapter 12

Walking out of the church behind hundreds of people who were there to celebrate the life of a military veteran and his wife hit way too close to home. Allyson swallowed the lump in her throat as she watched Crash prepare to bury his friends. How does this happen to people?

She'd spoken to Aubry before the funeral, and he'd confirmed what she suspected. He said Wyatt wouldn't have been able to move his legs, and Ellie probably wasn't conscious when the accident happened. Aaron had assured her he would keep Crash updated on everything.

Over the last week, having him and the kids under her roof hadn't been bad. She enjoyed spending time with Caleb and Mila while Crash, Mack, Ryan, and some of the guys from NES helped finish the house. Keith had even got his brothers together to help move things along faster.

When she'd offered to watch the kids for the funeral, Crash asked if she would come. At first, she wasn't sure because, as a military vet, Wyatt would get the whole veteran send-off, and she knew it would bring back memories of burying Trent.

Crash expressed that he needed her for moral support and that she wanted to be there for him. She may have put a stop to a romantic relationship between them, but next to Bethany, he was her best friend.

She watched Crash hug and shake hands with people, but she was worried about him. When he arrived at the church, he looked furious and barely spoke to anyone before the service. He didn't seem to be dealing well with the grief of losing his two friends, but who would?

"He knows about what the coroner found," Keith said as he stepped beside her.

"You mean about their injuries?" Allyson asked.

"Yeah, A.J. called before we left for the funeral." Keith towered over her.

Allyson turned her gaze back to Crash. His eyes met hers, and a shiver ran through her body. Was he angry with her? He'd never looked at her like that before, and when she mouthed the words, 'Are you okay?' His lips formed into a tight line.

The rest of the afternoon, he seemed to avoid her. At his parents for the reception, he spent most of his time with his brother or the people he worked with. Her only solace was Megan sitting with her for a while, and she thanked her for helping Crash while he was finishing his house.

When she was ready to go home, Crash disappeared, and nobody seemed to know where he'd gone. When Mack approached her, she grabbed her coat and pulled it on in the foyer.

"Thanks for coming, Allyson," Mack held her coat while she shoved her arms into the sleeves.

"I'm glad I could be here for all of you," She zipped up her jacket and smiled at Crash's father.

"Well, at least they won't be under your feet too much longer. We'll have everything done by the end of next week," Mack told her.

Her heart dropped. She enjoyed having Caleb and Mila around, and if she was being honest, she was getting used to seeing Crash every day. She knew the whole arrangement wasn't permanent, but a small part wished it was.

"That's wonderful, not that I mind having them here. They're the sweetest, and considering what they've been through, I see they're adjusting well." Allyson forced a smile.

"Brent said Caleb knows about his parents." Mack sighed.

"Yes, but he seems to be dealing with it okay," Allyson said.

"Iris feels horrible that he overheard her." Mack shook his head.

"She didn't realize he was there." Allyson knew Crash's mother would never hurt anyone, especially those kids.

The little boy would talk about how his mom and dad were in heaven, and now he would always have angels watching over him. She was glad Cameron had told the little boy because Caleb seemed to open up.

"I guess I'm going to head home. Let Cameron and Lily leave. They have school in the morning." Allyson opened the door.

"Brent already left to pick up the kids." Mack stared at her with confusion.

"Oh, yes, I forgot." Allyson stepped through the door.

She left the house feeling embarrassed that Crash hadn't told her he would get the kids. Allyson had no idea where he would take them since the house still needed some work done. Maybe he was spending the night with his family; after all, they had all lost Wyatt and Ellie.

When she pulled into her driveway, his truck was still there, but Cameron's vehicle was gone. She assumed her son had brought Lily home or Sandy had come to get the girl. Lily didn't drive.

Allyson entered the house, and the only light came from the living room. She pulled off her coat, hung it next to the door, and noticed how quiet it was. She found Crash next to the window with his back to her.

"They were murdered." His voice was barely above a whisper.

"I know," she replied.

"They think Ellie wasn't awake when the crash happened, and Wyatt was… paralyzed… but… I heard her scream." Crash sniffed.

He'd told her about the call from Wyatt the day they died. She wasn't sure she'd be able to deal with knowing she'd heard her friends scream as they plunged to their deaths.

"Did you tell A.J. that?" Allyson wasn't sure how much he'd told Aaron.

"No," Crash returned.

Allyson walked toward him, but he turned around and held up his hands. His jaw clenched, his eyes had turned a dark hazel, and all signs of the green flecks were gone.

"Talk to me," Allyson whispered.

"Why? You didn't tell me the injuries weren't because of the accident." Crash's voice cracked.

"I couldn't tell you because I didn't know for sure," Allyson stepped closer.

"I know that in here," Crash pointed to his head. "But in here." He pointed to his chest. "I'm pissed that a stranger told me."

Allyson closed her eyes briefly to blink back the tears that had formed. She never wanted to upset him, but she also couldn't break the rules at the hospital, no matter how much she cared about him.

"I'm…" She began, but he stopped her.

"You don't need to apologize. You were doing your job." Crash walked around her and sat on the couch.

He rested his elbows on his knees and dropped his head into his hands. Allyson's heart broke for him, and she wished she could do something to fix it all. She'd give anything to take away his pain.

"Megan took the kids for the night. She's staying at my parents' place. I think Mom asked her to do it because she saw how pissed I was. I may have broken a bottle when I threw it at the shed." Crash sighed.

Allyson sat on the coffee table in front of him. She itched to pull him into her arms and tell him everything would be okay. Holding him would let him know she cared about what he was going through. She'd do anything to take away the pained look on his face.

"What if I can't do this? I don't know anything about raising kids." Crash's voice trembled.

"Brent, no parent knows everything." She certainly made her share of mistakes.

"But I'm not their fucking parent. I'm their consolation prize because some bastard decided to take two of the best people in the world." Crash fisted the hair at the top of his head.

"You're not a consolation prize, and I'm damn well sure Ellie and Wyatt made you their guardian because they knew you would take care of their babies." Allyson gripped both his hands and held them between hers.

"I couldn't even tell Caleb his parents were gone. He had to overhear it from a conversation my mom was having." Crash shook his head as tears streamed down his cheeks.

"You would've told him, and you would've made sure he knows everyone loves him. He knows, and that's what matters. He's dealing with it okay right now, but you'll be there for him when it gets hard," Allyson encouraged.

Crash lifted his gaze to meet hers. Allyson physically hurt seeing the agony in his eyes. She moved closer and cupped his face as she wiped the tears away. She kissed his cheek and then pulled back.

"You're the only person for those babies. Don't you know how wonderful you are? How loving and sweet you are to everyone?" Allyson whispered as her eyes blurred with tears.

How could he not know what an incredibly amazing man he was? He was kind, intelligent, strong, and would give the shirt off his back to someone who needed it.

"Ally," Crash whispered.

"No, those kids are so lucky to have you. Do you know how I know?" Allyson moved closer.

"No."

"Because I thank God every day that you came into my life. I'm lucky to have such an amazing friend. I care about you so much, and if things were different..." Allyson stopped herself before she told him exactly how she felt.

"Ally," Crash lifted his hand to cup her cheek.

His thumb glided featherlike across her jaw, and her mouth parted. She was playing with fire, but having him touch her was something she couldn't resist anymore. When he leaned forward, she held her breath as his lips touched her cheek.

"Brent." She sighed.

His lips moved to the corner of her mouth as his fingers slipped around her neck. He pressed soft kisses along her jaw to her chin, then he tilted his head and put his mouth a breath away from hers.

"I need you, Ally," Crash murmured against her lips.

"I..." She closed her eyes when he lightly touched her lower lip.

"Ally, please don't push me away," Crash whispered as he pressed his mouth against hers.

Allyson whimpered as his other hand slipped into her hair, and she tilted her head. His mouth moved against hers in a slow, seductive dance, and when he licked the corner of her lips, she opened for him. Crash plunged his tongue into her mouth, and she sucked it into her mouth, driving him crazy with desire.

Allyson moaned as he stood up and pulled her with him. She snaked her arms around his waist and fisted the back of his shirt, pulling his hard body tight against hers. One of his hands moved down to the small of her back, and the other stayed tangled in her hair.

Crash didn't hold back; this kiss was more heated than the last one. Allyson could feel his hardening length against her belly, and she squeezed her thighs together to ease the arousal.

"Brent," she breathed into his mouth.

"Ally," he returned with a groan.

The sound snapped her small amount of restraint, and she tugged at his shirt until it was out of his pants. Crash pulled away from her lips long enough to tear the garment over his head in that sexy, one-handed, over-the-head move. Her hands glided up his warm, hard body, feeling every muscle flex under her touch.

"Fuck, I've wanted your hands on me for so long." he sighed against her cheek.

She held her breath as his fingers worked the zipper at the back of her dress. Ever so slowly, he lowered it as his kisses traveled down her neck. His lips moved across her shoulder as her dress slipped down her body.

"Brent," she gasped when his fingers glided across the top of her breast.

"I need you, Ally. I need you like I need air," Crash whispered when her dress slid to the floor.

"Brent, we…" Allyson began.

"We can, Ally. We belong together, and if the last week taught me anything, life's too short for regrets." He ran his hand down her body.

"But…" Allyson tried again.

"Let's be together, even if it's only for tonight." Crash kissed the side of her neck.

Allyson knew he wouldn't listen unless she stepped away from him. It took all her strength, but she managed to step back far enough that his lips and body couldn't distract her.

"Ally," Crash moved toward her.

"Let me speak." She pressed her hand against his chest.

"Okay," he whispered.

"I need to lock the door so nobody walks in. Nobody in this town knocks anymore." She smirked as she picked up her dress.

"Huh?" Crash stared as if she was speaking another language.

"I'm locking the door and going to my room." Allyson backed out of the living room. "You can meet me there. If you still want to."

With those words, she quickly checked the front door and sprinted up the steps to her bedroom. She hung her dress over the chair next to the window and sat on her bed, her heart racing and her hands trembling.

Allyson wasn't sure how she should feel when he walked into the room—if he did. She shouldn't be doing this, but she was tired of fighting her feelings for him. He deserved to know the truth, but she first needed this one night with him. It was selfish, but at least she would know how it felt to be with the man who owned her soul.

Chapter 13

Crash could practically hear his heart pound as he went to Allyson's bedroom and prayed it wasn't all a dream. With everything that happened over the last week, he wasn't sure he could take her rejection again. The door was open, and she stood at the foot of the bed wearing only a lace bra with matching panties.

The sight took his breath away, and he was sure he'd have the imprint of his zipper on his dick. Her long brown hair lay over her shoulders, and he could see shimmers of auburn when the light hit it a certain way. Her flawless skin, lightly covered with freckles, looked soft as silk. Her blue eyes locked with his as he closed the door.

He stepped before her and lifted his hands to cradle her face. His cock was painfully hard, but he wanted to savor every second with her. This could be the only time they would be together.

"You're so damn beautiful, Ally," Crash said with a catch in his voice.

Her hands leisurely slipped around his waist as his lips found hers. She sighed when he fisted her hair and tilted her head to give him access to her sweet mouth again. She pulled his body tight to hers, and he groaned when her skin touched his naked chest.

"Ally." Crash kissed across her jaw and the soft skin between her shoulder and neck.

"Brent," she murmured as her hands slid down to cup his ass.

He lowered her to the bed and continued to kiss, nip, and suck her silky skin while he slipped her bra strap off her shoulder. He almost swallowed his tongue when she pushed her hands down the back of his pants and dug her nails into his ass.

"Fuck." He gasped.

"Did I hurt you?" Allyson asked.

"It hurt in a good way, trust me." Crash smiled.

"Take off your pants." She bit down on her lower lip.

He didn't have to be told twice and jumped up to unbuckle his belt. He lowered his zipper, and his dick practically sprung from his boxers. He slipped them down over his hips and stood completely naked in front of the one woman who could bring him to his knees.

He wasn't shy because he worked hard to stay in shape. His few tattoos meant something to him, and his dick was thicker than some men, but the way Allyson took in his entire form made him self-conscious.

"You're a gorgeous man," she whispered.

Allyson reached behind to undo the bra but held the cups to her breasts as the straps slipped down over her shoulders. He met her eyes as he gently dragged her hands away and pulled the garment away.

"Don't hide from me, Ally," Crash whispered.

She slipped her thumbs into the waistband of her panties, slowly sliding them down her shapely legs. Crash almost blew his load when he looked down to see her bare pussy as she tossed her underwear to the floor.

Crash moved slowly down her body and skimmed the tip of his nose around each nipple, giving them a flick of his tongue with each pass. Allyson gasped and gripped onto his shoulders when he sucked one nipple into his mouth. He could smell her arousal, and his dick ached to be buried inside her.

She whimpered his name over and over as he kissed down over her stomach and licked across from one hip to the other.

"I want to taste you, Ally," Brent growled against her belly.

Her legs fell open, and she raised her hands above her head to grip the headboard. He hummed at the sight of her wet pussy, and the scent was intoxicating. He quickly flicked his tongue out to taste it, and she jumped at the sudden touch. She moaned when he gripped her hips and slipped his tongue between her folds.

"Yes," Allyson hissed with an arch of her back.

Crash circled her swollen bundle of nerves with his tongue as he slipped a finger into her opening. He sucked as he moved the digit in and out of her soaking opening. Her hips flexed up, and she cried out his name.

"You're so wet." Crash pressed a second finger inside her.

"It's been a long time," she admitted.

Crash groaned at those words because knowing she hadn't been with another man in what she called a long time made him want to beat his chest and roar 'mine' at the top of his lungs.

He curled his fingers and pressed against the front wall of her sex as he sucked harder on her clit. She started to close around his fingers and cried out with a shiver.

Crash didn't stop until he'd pulled the second wave of pleasure from her. Only then did he kiss his way up her warm body. She let out a small sigh as he lay beside her and kissed her face.

"That was the most beautiful thing I've ever witnessed," he whispered into her ear.

"It was pretty great to experience too."

She smirked and ran her hand down his abdomen. When she wrapped it around his shaft, he grabbed it and pulled it away. If she jerked him, he was done and wouldn't get the chance to drive inside her.

"I want to touch you," she rolled onto her side to face him.

"Ally, I want nothing more than to feel your hand wrapped around my dick, but if you touch it now, I'm going to embarrass myself," he admitted.

Allyson rolled over on top of him and straddled his hips. If she thought this was helping stop the need to blow all over her, she was sadly mistaken. Seeing her sweet curves on top of him was making him want to drive into her desperately.

"Ally, this isn't helping me get control." He reached up and cupped her full breasts.

She eased up to her knees and moved her opening directly over his swollen head. His heart almost stopped when she began to lower herself onto his bare cock.

"Condom," he grunted as he tried to hold off from ramming right into her.

"I haven't been with anyone since Trent." She gazed into his eyes.

"I'm clean. I'm tested regularly. Not that I need it. It's been a while for me, too," Crash told her.

"We don't have to worry about pregnancy either. I'm… protected." She closed her eyes as she dropped slowly onto his rock-hard dick.

"Sweet fuck," Crash grunted.

He should've told her he couldn't get her pregnant anyway, and he'd always used a condom to prevent anything else, but at that moment, his brain couldn't form the words. When he was fully seated inside her, he squeezed his eyes shut to keep from exploding in less than two seconds.

"I'm so full." She lay on top of him and kissed his chest.

Neither of them moved for a few seconds, but when he felt he had better control, he grabbed her hips and lifted her a little, then slammed his hips up.

"Oh, God," she panted.

"Fuck," Crash groaned when she dropped down again.

Crash wrapped his arms around her and flipped them over until she was on her back, and he knelt between her legs. She grabbed the edge of the mattress while he drove into her wet heat. He could feel her inner walls start to squeeze around the sensitive skin of his bare shaft. While he continued to slam his cock into her knowing he wasn't going to last much longer, he pinched her swollen nub and drove her over the edge.

"Brent," she cried out.

"Fuck, Ally,"

That was all he needed, and he exploded inside her. His body convulsed with the most intense orgasm he'd ever experienced. Every muscle in his body contracted; at one point, he wasn't sure if it would stop. He barely kept himself from falling on top of her.

With shaky arms, he rolled them on their sides, trying hard not to slip from her body. Crash wasn't sure if he'd ever be with her again, so he wanted to keep them connected as long as possible.

She snuggled into his body, and they were quiet even after their breathing returned to normal. Even when he slipped from her body, she didn't move, and at one point, he thought she'd fallen asleep, but then she spoke.

"I didn't lie," Ally whispered.

"About what?" Crash rolled on his back and tucked her into his side.

"I haven't been with anyone since Trent." She lifted her head and rested her chin on his chest.

"I didn't think you were lying." He pushed the hair back from her face.

"I just wanted you to know that." She placed her head against his chest again.

"It's been over two years for me," Crash confessed.

The last woman he was with was a one-night stand he'd gone home with after he'd found out Allyson had gone out on a date with some guy from work. He was smart enough not to get drunk but ended up going home with a woman from his meeting.

"Okay," she whispered.

She was silent for several minutes, then pulled out of his arms. The loss felt like a knife in his chest, but as she headed into the bathroom, he prayed she'd come back. Several minutes passed, and she didn't return; Crash grabbed his boxers off the floor and pulled them on.

He sat on the bed for a few minutes, and that's when he heard it—a soft sniffle from the bathroom. Was she crying? Crash padded to the bathroom door and knocked.

"Ally?"

"I'll be out in a minute," she called, but there was something strange in her voice.

"I'm coming in," he told her.

Before she could respond, he opened the door and found her wrapped in a bathrobe with tears streaming down her cheeks. He wanted to punch himself. Did she regret what happened?

"Ally, what's wrong?" Crash pulled her into his arms.

"It's nothing," she tried to pull away.

"Ally, don't tell me it's nothing. Did I do something wrong?" Crash stepped back and looked down into her weepy eyes.

"It's not you. You're amazing." She wiped her fingers under her eyes. "I need to tell you something, and I know it'll change things forever."

"You can tell me anything; nothing will change how I feel about you." Crash cupped her cheeks. "I lo…"

She pressed her fingers to his lips and shook her head. She wouldn't let him tell her that he loved her. He had for so long that it was difficult to remember when it started, and now that they'd been together, he didn't have doubts about the world.

"Don't say it, please." She pulled away and escaped back into the bedroom.

"Why? Because you think we can't have a relationship? Age doesn't mean shit, Ally. I love you, and I'm not going to take it back. With everything this week, I don't want another day to go by without telling you that. Life is too damn short." He stepped in front of her, and she closed her eyes.

Allyson took a deep breath before she finally opened her eyes again. She lifted her hands and placed them against his cheeks as she stared into his eyes. She pulled him closer and pressed her lips to his.

"That may change when I tell you," she said as she pulled away from him. "You deserve so much more."

Allyson sat on the bed and folded her hands on her lap. She didn't look up as he sat beside her, but she tensed when he wrapped his arm around her.

"Talk to me," he whispered.

He wanted answers here and now because, after having her once, he was sure that he couldn't let her go. Crash had lost too many people, and he wasn't about to let her leave his life. He didn't care what she had to tell him.

Chapter 14

Allyson's heart was about to jump out of her chest. She was sure of it. The minute she told him, he'd see her differently. She was selfish in letting things go as far as they did. Still, she needed at least one night before she lost him forever.

His words echoed in her head, and she wanted to scream that she loved him, too. She couldn't remember having feelings so intense, even with Trent. Telling Crash could destroy everything.

"I can hear you overthinking," Crash whispered against her ear.

It was precisely what she was doing because now that she'd been intimate with him, she felt him touch her and had him tell her he loved her; hiding her feelings would be impossible. When he moved on and found someone else, it would rip her heart out.

"We didn't do anything wrong, Ally." He kissed her temple.

She needed to let the chips fall where they may and rip the Band-Aid off. Crash wanted his kids, and she couldn't give him that. She couldn't give him the family he desired and deserved.

"You asked me once why Trent and I didn't have more kids," she began in a whispered voice.

"I remember," Crash replied.

"The truth is we did. The pregnancy had a lot of complications, and she didn't make it." Allyson blew out a shaky breath.

"I'm sorry." Crash gently caressed her back.

"I almost died. Trent had to make a decision that changed both our lives." Allyson dropped her head. "I couldn't because I was unconscious, and my life was in jeopardy. It was up to him, and he did what he thought was right."

"What did he do?" Crash asked.

"He saved my life." She lifted her head.

"Ally, that's a good thing." Crash cupped her face.

"Yes, but it also took away something I can never have back," she sobbed.

"What?"

"My ability to have children," she choked out the words so quietly she wasn't sure if he heard her.

Crash's silence alarmed her. How could he love half a woman? She'd kept this secret for so long it was hard to believe she'd told someone. Her sister and father knew about her losing the baby, but they didn't know she'd had an emergency hysterectomy. When his silence continued, she was about to get up and walk away when he spoke.

"He saved your life," he spoke softly.

"Yes, but it took away my ability to…"

Crash pressed his finger to her lips and shook his head. He pulled her until she was straddling his lap, and she could look into his handsome face.

"But you're alive, and if Trent hadn't made that choice, Cameron would've lost both his parents before he was twelve." Crash had tears in his eyes.

"I don't blame him, but you don't need to suffer for that decision." She touched his cheek.

"Wait? Is this why you believe we can't be together?" Crash brow furrowed.

"You said you'd love to have kids someday and deserve to be a dad. I can't give that to you," she said.

"Ally," Crash began.

"No, don't say it doesn't matter because it does. You love kids, and you said you wanted a bunch," Allyson continued.

"Ally," Crash said again.

"This world needs little Brents running around, and you deserve to find someone who can give you that." She shook her head.

"Ally." Brent raised his voice.

"What?"

Crash held her head in his hands and gazed into her eyes. The slight smile confused her; maybe she was seeing things, and he was frowning.

"Even if I listened to you and decided to find another woman, there still wouldn't be any little Brents running around," Crash informed her.

Allyson didn't want to picture him with anyone, but she needed to let him go. She pulled away from his touch as if his words finally made sense.

"Why not?" Allyson asked.

"When I was a teenager, I had the mumps. I got sick and ended up with orchitis, which, as a doctor, you know what that is." Crash raised an eyebrow.

"Yes, it's caused by an infection and can affect a man's…"

He stopped her from continuing. He probably didn't need to hear the explanation of how a childhood disease caused both his testicles to become inflamed. It was rare, but it happened. It meant there were no chances of little Brents running around.

"You can't have kids," Allyson said.

"No," he admitted.

She let that bit of information sink into her addled brain because if this was true, she'd wasted years holding back from the one thing she wanted. She stared into his eyes and felt a sense of relief for the first time in forever.

"Ally?" Crash reached for her when she jumped off his lap.

"I've been fighting my feelings for you because I didn't want you to be stuck with an old barren woman." She sighed.

"You're not old." Crash rolled his eyes.

"I'm older…than you." Allyson tried to stop the laughter from bubbling up.

"Okay, I'll give you that, but still." Crash chuckled.

"I'm sorry," Allyson cleared her throat. "It's not funny."

"It kinda is," Crash laughed.

Suddenly, Allyson stopped laughing and stared at him. If he'd told her about this, they could've been together. She slapped his arm and put her hands on her hips.

"What the hell?" Crash laughed.

"Why didn't you tell me?" Allyson threw her arms up in the air.

"It's not exactly dinner conversation, Ally, and you never told me either." Crash moved toward her.

"I wouldn't have pushed you away if I'd known," Ally whispered as he wrapped his arms around her.

"How was I supposed to know that?" Crash chuckled.

"I've been so foolish." Allyson allowed her eyes to take in his handsome face.

"Does this mean you're going to stop pushing me away?" Crash asked.

Allyson's eyes moved to his mouth and then back. She didn't move or pull away from his embrace as he dragged her closer. He lowered his lips to meet hers and stopped before they touched.

"Are you done pushing me away?" Crash whispered against her lips.

"Yes."

"Thank fuck." Crash slammed his mouth against hers.

She couldn't believe they'd wasted so much time and that it took a tragedy to finally reveal the truth. It was as if everything that weighed her down suddenly lifted, and she could finally be in love with him. She didn't have to deny herself happiness anymore.

They made love again before falling asleep wrapped around each other. She fell into a deep, content sleep to the sound of Crash's beating heart as she lay on his chest.

Allyson groaned when she tried to throw off the heavy blanket, which made her so hot she could barely breathe. She couldn't move, and for a second, panic started to build until she opened her eyes and saw the muscular arm thrown over her body.

She glanced at the clock on the nightstand. It was only a little after three in the morning, and she snuggled closer to Crash, but his body heat was bringing on a significant case of hot flashes.

"Brent." Allyson turned her head.

No response.

"Brent, honey." Allyson tried to push him back.

The man groaned but didn't move an inch. As much as she enjoyed being in his arms, she needed to breathe, and his body weight was not helping.

"Crash," Allyson shouted.

"Huh, What? What's wrong?" Crash jolted up in the bed.

"You were making it very difficult for me to breathe," Allyson sat up.

"Did I hurt you?" Crash's panicked expression made Allyson feel terrible.

"No, you're very heavy and have a lot of body heat," Allyson smirked.

"Wait? Did you call me Crash?" He looked at her with confusion.

"Brent wasn't working."

Allyson tried to get up to go to the bathroom, but before she could get out of bed, he yanked her back and hovered over her. His eyes scanned her face before he lowered his lips to hers. The kiss was tender and sweet. When he lifted his head, he was smiling.

"I think that's the first time you've ever called me Crash." He chuckled.

"Don't get used to it. Brent is much better." Allyson cupped his face between her hands.

"I love you, Ally," Brent whispered.

Allyson swallowed the lump that formed in her throat. She'd said the words for years but could never tell him. This was the first time she could tell him how she felt.

"I love you too, Brent." Her voice cracked as her eyes filled with tears.

"You don't know how wonderful it is to hear those words come out of your mouth," Crash murmured against her lips.

Chapter 15

Crash couldn't move. It was as if something pinned him down, but it was warm and soft. He opened his eyes and smiled at Allyson practically on top of him, making the cutest little snore. He wrapped his arms around her and closed his eyes again. It hadn't been a dream.

An annoying buzzing sound kept him from falling back to sleep. Crash snatched the phone off the nightstand and sighed at his sister's number on the screen. It meant she was probably on the way with the kids.

"Who is it?" Allyson grumbled against his chest.

"Megan." He kissed the top of her head and tapped the phone. "Hey."

"Did I wake you?" Megan asked.

"It's okay. I need to get up anyway." Crash yawned.

"Dad is meeting you at your house. Is Allyson still able to watch the kids?" Megan asked.

"Can you still watch the kids?" Crash asked.

"Uh-huh." Allyson sighed.

"Wait? If I woke you, then…" Megan got cut off when Crash ended the call.

He didn't have the phone out of his hand when it rang again. Allyson lifted her head and furrowed her brow at the buzzing sound.

"I think Megan may have figured out we're in bed together," Crash warned before he answered his sister.

"Rude," Megan snapped.

"Sorry, I hit the end button by mistake." Crash chuckled.

"Liar," Megan exclaimed. "Seriously, are you two… together?"

"What time will you be here?" Crash ignored the question.

"In an hour, and I want details." Megan hung up before he could respond.

"Good thing I'll be gone when she gets here." Crash grinned as he wrapped his arms around Allyson.

"Why?" She kissed his chest.

"I mistakenly asked you about babysitting after telling her she woke me. My sister was quick to put two and two together," Crash whispered against her neck.

"I'm not ashamed," Ally sighed when he nipped her earlobe.

"I'm glad because I want to shout it from the rooftops," Crash rolled over on top of her. "But first, I've got a little problem."

He pushed his erection against her belly and groaned when she enclosed the length of him in her hand.

"I wouldn't exactly call this little, but I'm happy to help you with the problem. How long do we have?" Allyson stroked his cock slowly.

"Megan said an hour, but you keep that up, and I won't last five minutes. We can save time by finishing in the shower." He jumped out of the bed and tossed her over his shoulder.

"Brent," she squealed.

She slid down his body, and before he tugged her into the shower, he kissed her as if he needed it to take his next breath. She melted into his embrace and followed him until they were both under the warm spray of the water.

He'd wrapped a towel around his waist when his sister's voice echoed from the first floor. Ally smirked at him through the mirror, where she brushed her hair next to the sink.

"That was not a fucking hour," Crash grumbled.

"It kinda was." Allyson grinned.

"I'm coming up if you don't answer me," Megan bellowed.

"We're coming. Keep your shirt on," Crash shouted.

Allyson was still getting dressed when he left the room, but not before kissing her. He found Megan in the living room with Mila on her lap and Caleb playing with the toys in the corner.

"It's about time." Megan snorted.

"You said an hour." Crash picked up Mila and kissed her on the cheek.

"I'm not talking about that. I'm talking about you and Allyson." Megan poked him in the chest.

"Please keep this quiet for a bit. We've got a lot on our plates right now, and as much as I want to make it known, I need to get my shit together for these two." Crash motioned to Caleb and Mila.

"Have some faith, big brother. Things happen for a reason, but I can't understand why the hell…" Megan stopped.

"I know. It doesn't make sense why two terrific people would be ripped away so violently," Crash whispered.

Megan turned to watch Caleb as the little boy pushed a tiny firetruck around in circles. Crash swallowed the lump as he tried to contain the sadness. He needed to be strong for the kids and make sure he was there for them whenever they were ready to know the truth about their parents.

It was way past time to talk with Caleb about his parents and the whole situation, but Crash wasn't sure if the little boy would understand. He'd be turning four soon, and it was up to Crash to make sure the little boy still got to celebrate his day. He handed Mila to Megan and crouched next to Caleb, where he played on the floor.

He was supposed to meet his father and work on the house, but this conversation was overdue. He sent a quick text to his dad to let him know he needed to take care of something and wasn't surprised when his dad messaged back with a thumbs-up emoji.

"Hey buddy, do you want to take a walk on the beach with me?" Crash asked.

"Yeah." Caleb leaped up from the floor.

"Isn't it a little cold for the beach?" Allyson had her shoulder braced against the doorjamb.

Crash met her beautiful blue eyes and smiled. She looked stunning with all the tension off her face. She'd told him before they fell asleep that she felt anxious whenever he was around because it was difficult to keep her feelings covered. He knew how she felt.

"We'll dress warm. Caleb and I need to talk," Crash explained, hoping both women understood.

Allyson gave a slight nod, and Megan snuggled Mila into her chest. Crash took Caleb's hand, and after bundling the little boy up in his warm coat, he pulled on his jacket and headed out of the house.

The walk wasn't far from Allyson's house, but instead of letting Caleb walk there, Crash popped the little boy on his shoulders, and they talked about what they would find at the beach. Caleb was excited.

They strolled the length of Hopedale Beach, finding several rocks, seashells, and driftwood that Caleb swore were special and wanted to take home. When Crash reached the large sitting rock, his pockets were weighed down.

"Caleb, let's sit here for a bit before we head back. There's something I need to talk to you about." Crash leaned against the rock.

Caleb struggled to climb on the huge boulder, but in the end, Crash had to give him a boost. They watched the waves crash against the shore for a few minutes. It was calming, and he always found himself in the same spot when he needed peace. Crash hoped it would help him find the words to explain everything to Caleb.

"Uncle Brent, you look sad." Caleb leaned forward and stared into his face.

Crash scanned the sweet face of the little boy he adored. It was hard to comprehend that this child would grow up without knowing what incredible people his parents were, how his dad worked his ass off to kick drinking. How his mother worked with Ethel to help foster kids find safe homes so they wouldn't bounce around from one to the other.

"I am, bud." Crash put his arm around the little boy and kissed the top of his head.

"You miss Mommy and Daddy too, doncha?" Caleb stared up at him.

"I do, Caleb. Very much." Crash admitted.

"Nanny said they're in heaven." Caleb's innocent little face was breaking his heart.

Crash swallowed down the bile rising in his throat because telling this kid that he was right was tearing his heart out. He took a shaky breath and squeezed the little boy closer.

"Yes, buddy. They are." Crash kissed the top of Caleb's head.

"Why?" Caleb's voice cracked.

Crash was asking himself the same question, but he had to answer in a way that wouldn't traumatize Caleb. Telling a kid his parents were murdered was not an option.

"Sometimes God needs special angels to watch over people, and he looks for the best ones he can find. Nobody was better than your mommy and daddy." Crash blinked back tears.

"Who's gonna take care of me and Mila?" Caleb asked.

Crash took the little boy up in his arms and held him close to his chest. Caleb wrapped his little arms around Crash's neck and tucked his head into his neck.

"You and Mila will live with me in my new house." Crash told him as he started to make his way back to Allyson's house.

"What about my toys?" Caleb lifted his head.

"You'll have all your things at my place. I'm going to have it all brought to my house. It'll be another day or two at Allyson's, and we'll be moving." Crash promised.

"Ally, too?" Caleb lifted his head and stared into Crash's face.

Crash smiled because he'd love to have Allyson live with him, but since they had barely been together a day, asking her to move in with him might be extreme.

"She'll visit a lot." Crash hoped.

"I love you, Uncle Brent," Caleb said as he hugged Crash's neck.

"I love you too, buddy." Crash choked out the words. "You know you have a birthday coming in a couple of weeks. Do you want to have a party?"

Crash wasn't sure if it was appropriate, but he would move heaven and earth to ensure Caleb and Mila never missed out on anything their parents would give them. He knew from previous years that Ellie had always thrown a big celebration for Caleb's birthday.

"I'm gonna be four." Caleb held up his tiny hand with four fingers.

"I know. You're such a big boy." Crash smiled.

"I love chocolate cake," Caleb told Crash.

Caleb's chatter filled the time on the walk back to Allyson's place. He went on about what he wanted to do for his birthday, not to mention what he wanted in his new room. One thing being a picture of his mom and dad. He wished he had the resiliency of a child. At least

Caleb wouldn't feel the grief Crash felt every time he thought about Wyatt and Ellie.

Caleb bolted inside as soon as Crash opened the door. He was about to follow when a black car across the street caught his eye. Living in Hopedale, he recognized what vehicles belonged to whom, and this one wasn't familiar. It appeared as if someone was watching him, and he questioned if it was the person following him. The person could've switched cars.

"I'll be back in a minute," Crash shouted before closing the house door.

He texted Crunch and Hulk before shoving his phone back into his pocket. They lived closest to each other and knew about the strange vehicle Crash saw. It made the hair on the back of his neck stand up.

He slowly made his way down the steps, and by the time he reached the end of the driveway, Hulk and Crunch had joined him.

"Someone's in that car," Crunch informed him.

"Let's go see who our guest is," Hulk stalked toward the car with Crash and Crunch behind him.

The driver's door opened as they approached the car, and someone stepped out. Hulk immediately reached into the back of his jeans, where he had a Sig 9MM. The man came prepared, and as he wrapped his hand around the grip, Crash looked up at the man standing next to the car.

"Hulk, wait." Crash grabbed his friend's arm.

"Last time I was in Newfoundland, I got a better reception than this." Axel rested his arms on the roof of the car.

"Maybe you shouldn't be lurking outside people's houses," Crunch returned.

"Axel fucking Wright," Crash made his way around the car.

"Brent fucking Adams," Axel turned and slammed his arms around him.

"What the fuck are you doing here?" Crash asked when Axel released him.

"I finally decided to move back home," Axel replied.

"Where's…" Crash glanced into the car.

"Don't ask. Let's say when I stopped handing over cash, her ass was gone." Axel glanced toward Hulk and Crunch. "Are these guys here to kill me?"

"Sorry, we're having some security issues. These are my buddies, Hulk and Crunch. They work for NES as well," Crash explained.

"Good to know you got friends close when you need them." Axel closed the door to the car.

"Axel and I served together," Crash explained to his friends.

"Nice to finally meet you. Crash told us a lot about you." Crunch shook Axel's hand.

"That nickname still makes me shake my head." Axel laughed.

"It's a rite of passage when you work for Keith." Hulk shook Axel's hand.

"Since things are okay here, I'm going to head home," Crunch waved as he headed back toward his house.

"Me too. Carolyn is pregnant, and I'm afraid she's going to move me outside to make room for the baby." Hulk chuckled, then jogged off toward his home.

"Great friends." Axel leaned against the car's hood.

"The best," Crash admitted.

"I need to say it. I can't believe they're gone." Axel shook his head.

"It's surreal, that's for sure." Crash moved next to Axel.

They didn't say anything for a while, then Axel turned and slapped a hand on his back.

"If I weren't a recovering alcoholic, I'd say let's go have a drink for them, but how about a coffee?" Axel squeezed his shoulder.

"Coffee we can do," Crash said.

"We need to talk, B. There's stuff I found out that you should know… about…" Axel stopped.

"We'll talk." Crash nodded.

"It's bad." Axel sighed.

"Come inside. Megan and the kids are there, and I want you to meet someone." Crash motioned toward the house.

"Oh, someone, huh." Axel pushed away from the car.

"It's Allyson, yes." Crash admitted.

Axel chuckled because Crash told him about her and how much he cared about her. Even when he'd given up on ever being together, Axel would remind him that things would happen if it were meant to be.

"Did she finally get her head out of her ass and realize age is nothing but a number?" Axel slapped him on the shoulder.

"It had nothing to do with age. It was something else, but we talked and hopefully headed in the right direction." Crash opened the door.

Megan practically leaped into Axel's arms when she saw him. He was like another big brother to Crash's sister. He introduced his friend to Allyson. Caleb knew about Uncle Axel, but he hadn't seen him since he was a baby.

Axel had tears in his eyes as he watched the kids on the floor. Crash felt it, too, the grief for Caleb and Mila because they weren't old enough to understand. It was obvious to anyone who knew Axel that there was something on his mind. Crash needed to find out what, but it would have to wait for now.

"Are you staying for good?" Crash asked his friend after supper.

"Yep." Axel didn't look at Crash.

"Where are you staying?" Crash would make room if he needed somewhere to go.

"With my dad." Axel stood up and brought his plate to the sink.

"What about a job?" Crash wanted to know if his friend was serious about staying in Newfoundland.

"What is this? An interrogation?" Axel turned around to face him.

"What did you expect when you show up out of the blue?" Crash punched his friend in the arm.

"I was wondering if your boss is hiring," Axel admitted.

"I can give him your name. Keith is always looking. He was going to hire Wy…" Crash leaned against the counter.

"I'm here to stay, Brent. There's nothing for me on the mainland anymore." Axel plowed his fingers through his messy blonde hair.

"I'm glad you're here, but…" Crash stopped to make sure nobody could hear them. "What's going on?"

"Let's not ruin the evening. We'll talk soon." Axel nodded toward Allyson.

"I feel guilty for feeling happy." Crash and Axel headed out to the front porch.

"Don't do that, brother." Axel shook his head.

"I should've answered the phone that morning," Crash whispered.

"Brent, you can't blame yourself for this." Axel placed the cup he was holding on the rail.

"Can't I? He called me that morning, but I was in a meeting and didn't answer." Crash sighed. "Their kids are never going to know them. Those babies have to grow up without knowing how hard Wyatt worked to give them everything they needed or that their mom was one of the sweetest women in the world." Crash pulled his hands down over his face and blew a shaky breath.

"We'll make sure they know," Axel promised.

"Ax, why would someone do this to…" Crash stopped speaking.

His eyes narrowed as he spotted that damn car at the end of the driveway. He skirted around Axel and darted toward a vehicle, but before he got there, the car raced away, squealing tires and leaving a puff of dust behind it.

"What the fuck do you want?" Crash bellowed as the car disappeared around the corner.

Axel joined him in the middle of the road as Crash pulled out his phone and called Sandy. Crash was pissed. He would find out who owned that car and why they were watching him.

"I got a plate number. Can you find out who owns the car and let me know?" Crash demanded.

"Well, hello to you too," Sandy said.

"I'm not in the mood for sarcasm, Sandy. Can you get me the information or not?" Crash shouldn't be yelling at her.

Sandy was considered one of the best data analysts in the country. She was the only female employed with NES, but the woman didn't take shit from him or any of the men who worked with her. She wasn't going to put up with Crash's attitude.

"Maybe I would be willing to help if you weren't being a dick."

Crash blew a frustrated breath. Yelling at Sandy wouldn't get her to do anything, and she didn't deserve his anger. She would do anything for all the guys who worked for NES, because they were like a family.

"I'm sorry, Sandy. I want to know who the fuck is following me. It's the same car that almost plowed me down the night of Hulk's wedding, but this is the third time I've seen it in the last two days. This time, I got the plate number."

"I'll see what I can find out." Sandy wouldn't let him down.

"Thanks, Sandy, and I'm sorry for yelling," Crash apologized before he ended the call.

"Are you okay?" Axel asked.

"I want to know who the hell is in that car." Crash pointed to where the vehicle had disappeared.

Allyson stepped outside as Crash and Axel walked up to the porch. She glanced between them before she spoke.

"Can I get you something? Coffee?" Allyson asked.

"No," Crash snapped.

"Okay." Allyson's brows furrowed.

"Fuck. Ally, I'm sorry. I'm... That car was out there again, and I feel bad about it. I'm convinced it's connected to what happened to Wyatt and Ellie." Crash closed his eyes and then blew out a breath. "I didn't mean to snap at you."

Allyson closed the door behind her as she moved onto the porch. She looked up into his eyes, noticeably disturbed by his outburst, and he felt like an enormous ass.

"I understand. Really, I do, but you have to keep your feelings in check. The kids will sense your anger." Allyson moved closer and wrapped her arms around his waist.

"She's not wrong, B. You've got to keep that shit under control." Axel dropped a hand on Crash's shoulder.

"I know, and I'll do better. The last thing I want is to upset Caleb and Mila." Crash embraced Allyson and pressed his lips to the top of her head.

She rested her cheek against his chest as Axel stepped inside, leaving them alone. Crash held her in his arms as they stood in silence. When she pulled back and looked up at him, he kissed her forehead before walking back into the house.

Axel and Megan were in the living room with the kids, and Crash placed his phone on the coffee table to make sure he heard it when

Sandy called. He soothed himself by watching the kids play. It wasn't very long before his phone vibrated.

"Hey, Sandy," Crash answered on the second ring.

"Okay, are you still yelling?" Sandy asked.

"No, I'm not." Crash rolled his eyes.

"I wouldn't want to come over there and kick your sorry ass," Sandy retorted.

"I'd like to see that." Keith's rough voice echoed in Crash's ear.

"Keith, I'd kick all your asses and not even break a sweat," Sandy promised.

"Why do I put up with you?" Keith grumbled, and Crash could picture the large man glaring at his sister-in-law.

"Many reasons, actually. First, I'm the greatest. Second, I'm married to your brother, and lastly, you love me," Sandy teased, but she wasn't wrong.

"Tell him, for fuck's sake, and stop pestering me," Keith grumbled with pure exasperation in his voice.

"Hey, you come in my office, you get what I give you," Sandy goaded.

The woman didn't care that Keith was not only twice her size but also her boss. She was confident enough that she knew he would never fire her because she'd be snapped up by someone else in a heartbeat.

"Did you find anything?" Crash interrupted the banter.

"What's going on?" Megan whispered to Allyson.

"He's concerned about some car outside. Not sure if it's anything, but you know, safety first." Allyson explained.

"I'm sure he's being over-cautious. Especially with what happened." Megan's voice cracked.

Crash wasn't the only one grieving over the loss of Ellie and Wyatt. Megan was also, but she couldn't hide her grief very well.

"The plate didn't match the car. Pretty sure it's stolen." Sandy told him.

"That's fucking great," Crash sighed.

"I'm not surprised because if someone is trying to be invisible, they aren't going to use something that will tell us who they are." Sandy cleared her throat. "I'll check the footage on the cameras outside the compound. All cars have to pass Keith's property when they drive into Hopedale."

"Are you hacking my security cameras again?" Keith complained.

"Would you expect anything less of me?" Sandy snorted.

"Thanks, Sandy. I do appreciate it. You're the best," Crash hoped his compliment would make Sandy forget he'd snapped at her earlier.

"I know, and I'll let you know if I find anything." Sandy ended the call.

For the next hour, he talked about anything but the car. Megan asked about his house, and he admitted it wouldn't be long before he and the kids could move in. He didn't miss the surprise on Axel's face when Crash said only he and the kids would be moving, but his friend didn't say anything.

He'd almost forgotten about his dad working on things at his house. He sent him a quick text and received a message that Keith had sent some guys to help. Crash had to remember to thank the man for everything he did, not as a boss but as a friend.

"Is Cameron coming today?" Caleb asked from the living room.

"I don't think so, buddy. He has school." Crash informed the little boy.

The look of sadness on his little face broke Crash's heart. The little boy seemed to connect with Allyson's son, probably because Caleb knew Cameron had lost his father, and maybe, on some level, he believed Cameron was the only one who understood.

"How about I text him and ask if he can stay for the weekend?" Allyson suggested.

"When is the weekend?" Caleb asked.

"In two sleeps," Megan interjected.

"That's a long time," Caleb groaned.

To a three-year-old, waiting for two days seemed an eternity. Crash was sure as soon as Allyson told Cameron that Caleb was asking for him, her son would probably drop by that evening.

Allyson texted on her phone for a few minutes and then smiled. She handed Crash her phone, and he read the texts she'd sent to her son.

Allyson: Hey, Caleb has been asking when you are coming by again.

Cameron: He knows a great guy when he meets him.

Allyson: Of course he does. I told him I'd ask if you could come spend the weekend.

Cameron: Actually, I can come by tonight and stay until

Monday. I've got no classes for the next two days. We have an extra long weekend because of the Thanksgiving holiday.

Allyson: I won't tell him. You come by and surprise him.

Cameron: Hold on. Is this your way of having me around kids so I'll want to make you a grandmother.

Allyson: Absolutely not. I'm too young to be a grandmother and you need to finish school.

Cameron: Ha Ha, just pulling your leg, Mom. Love you, and I'll see you this evening.

Allyson: Love you too.

"I forgot about Thanksgiving on Monday." Crash gave her back the phone.

"Why does Canada have a different Thanksgiving than the United States?" Megan asked Axel.

"How would I know?" Axel shrugged.

"It's because October is the end of the Canadian Autumn harvest," Allyson interjected.

"Beautiful and smart. You're a lucky man, B. I guess this means we'll have a big turkey dinner on Monday." Axel rubbed his hands together.

"We?" Crash raised an eyebrow.

"Hey, I've been out of Newfoundland a long time, and a good ole Jiggs dinner would be heaven." Axel grinned. "Dad doesn't cook. He has all his meals delivered at the senior's apartment building."

Jiggs dinner was something all Newfoundlanders missed when they lived off the island. The traditional meal included salt beef, potatoes, carrots, turnip, cabbage, and split peas boiled in a bag called peas pudding. Most households in the province had it every Sunday with a turkey or a beef roast, and it was mouthwatering.

"I guess I better get a turkey and all the fixings." Allyson sighed. "Especially if Cam is going to be here."

Allyson's face suddenly looked as if she was going into a state of panic. Something about the thought of Cameron being home for the weekend was concerning her.

"What thought just went through your head?" Megan noticed.

His sister picked up on the sudden change as well. It hit him when Allyson glanced at him and looked away quickly. He gave her knee a gentle squeeze and winked.

"I can sleep in the room with the baby. Cam can have his room. Caleb will want to sleep in the same room with him anyway." Crash hoped she understood he wouldn't put her in any awkward situation with her son.

"Yeah. Most likely," Allyson replied.

By the time Allyson had written a grocery list and Crash got Mila bathed, Megan informed them she was headed home, but not before she told them how happy she was for them.

Axel stayed until Cameron arrived, promising Crash he would talk to him soon. Considering Axel's talk seemed important, Crash was surprised he left without mentioning it.

The minute Cameron showed up, Caleb followed him around. They watched a movie and set up a fort in the living room that got knocked down when Mila decided to crawl over to it and yank the blanket off the coffee table. By bedtime, Mila was ready to sleep, and Caleb was so tired he didn't even complain when Cameron told him he had to shower before bed. By the time Cameron finished, Caleb was sound asleep.

"Little man is out like a light." Cameron joined Crash and Allyson in the living room.

"Thanks for entertaining him, Cam. I'm sure you probably had better things to do being a university student," Crash stated.

"I can't think of anything. I'm not a big party person. Lily and Evie also mentioned some fair at the community center. We're going to take Caleb, Mila, and a few of their cousins tomorrow. Lily told us her grandmother has it running the entire weekend." Cameron shrugged. "I think Daniel and Mason are coming with us too."

Evie was Lily's sister, and Daniel and Mason were two of the numerous O'Connor cousins. Mason just finished high school and was taking a year off before he started university, and Daniel would graduate at the end of the school year. Both boys were going to follow in their father's footsteps and join the police force, which was no surprise to anyone.

Crash lost count of the number of O'Connor children and hoped Cameron knew what he was getting himself into if they planned to take all the kids to the center.

"I'm going to call it a night. I'm sure I'll fall asleep before Caleb tomorrow night." Cameron chuckled.

"Thanks again, Cam. I appreciate it." Crash smiled.

"Not a problem, Crash." Cameron waved as he headed to bed.

For a few minutes, they sat in comfortable silence. Allyson seemed surprised when he wrapped his arm around her shoulder and pulled her close to his side.

"I wish you could sleep next to me tonight," he admitted against the top of her head.

"Me too," she whispered.

"We aren't going to keep this from everyone, are we?" He kissed her temple.

"No, I'll talk to Cam tomorrow, but I'm sure he won't be surprised." Allyson turned to look at him.

"I don't know. You've been pretty adamant about keeping us in the friend zone," he teased.

"Be glad you got promoted to the more-than-friend zone." She poked his chest.

"I'm thrilled. Trust me." He poked her back. "Want to sit on the front porch for a while? We need to enjoy the weather while we can. It won't be long before winter hits."

The evening was crisp, but they snuggled on the wicker loveseat with a blanket over their legs. Allyson made some hot chocolate to help them stay warm as they breathed the fresh sea air surrounding them.

By the time he went to bed, the evening air and the lack of sleep from the previous night had helped him drift off quickly.

Chapter 16

What a difference a week made. With Thanksgiving over and everyone in Hopedale finding out she and Crash were finally together, she felt happier than she had in a long time. Nobody seemed surprised by the news, not even her son.

Cameron was happy for her but warned Crash to treat Allyson right. She wasn't worried about that. He'd always treated her with respect and never lost his temper, at least with her. She was lucky to have him in her life.

Allyson wasn't surprised when her father dropped by to give his opinion on her new relationship. He liked Crash, but Lewis Donnolly wasn't about to admit that to anyone. Her dad looked Crash in the eyes and told him if he didn't take care of Allyson, he knew people who could take him out.

Allyson laughed because her dad, at sixty-four, spent his time with senior citizens and his woman friend, as he called her. Her dad didn't have a violent bone in his body, but to Crash's credit, he hadn't laughed; he told her father that he would treat her with all the respect and love she deserved. That seemed to appease her dad, and he shook Crash's hand.

Allyson folded the last of the second load of laundry and smiled as she piled the clothing into the basket. Most of it belonged to the kids. It wasn't surprising the little ones accumulated so many dirty clothes in the two weeks they'd been there.

Crash joked that Mila seemed to hate being dressed in clean clothes because she would end up with something staining her shirt or pants as soon as he changed her. Caleb tended to be less likely to spill something, but the knees of all his pants would always somehow have dirt on them by the end of the day. As a little boy, she remembered Cameron had been the same way.

Crash told her he and the kids would move into his house in two days. He'd spent the last three days cleaning out Wyatt and Ellie's house to put it up for sale. He wanted to put the money into a trust fund for the kids. Keith's brother Mike was helping with that since he was a family lawyer.

Allyson lifted the clothes basket off the counter and left the laundry room. She wasn't looking forward to being alone again but knew the arrangement was temporary from the beginning. It was depressing to think about sleeping alone again. She sighed and tried to push the thoughts from her mind, but she'd gotten used to the noise, so with the kids and Crash gone for the afternoon, it was way too quiet.

"Maybe I should sell this place," she muttered.

Cold air swirled around her legs as she walked by the living room to head upstairs. She glanced into the room, but the patio door was closed. She hadn't opened it since Crash put the security bar on it. She placed the basket on the bottom of the steps and checked the front door. It was closed, but before she could turn around, a hand covered her mouth, stifling her screams.

"Allyson, it's me," a male whispered into her ear.

She couldn't place the voice and struggled to pull away, but he held her tightly against him. Why would someone try to keep her quiet if they were friendly?

"I'm going to let you go, but you have to promise to be quiet," the man said.

Allyson nodded but fisted her hands, prepared to fight him when he released her. He slowly lowered his hand, and she spun around, ready to shove her fist into his nose.

"Axel?" Allyson froze with her hand in the air.

He pressed a finger to his lips and motioned to get behind him. Axel leaned forward and peeked out through the small window in the door as if he was hiding.

"What's going on?" Allyson asked, keeping her voice quiet.

He didn't say anything, but he locked the door and continued to peek out through the window. Allyson knew this guy was Crash's friend, but his behavior made her uncomfortable.

"Allyson, I need you to get your phone and find somewhere safe in the house. Call Brent and tell him someone is creeping around your house. I didn't grab mine out of the car when I ran in here." Axel stated without looking away from the window.

Allyson moved as fast as she could upstairs and locked the door to the master bathroom. She fumbled with her phone and dropped it twice before unlocking it and hitting Crash's number.

It rang several times, then went to voicemail. She tried again but got the same result. She cursed under her breath as she tried to think. Crash was probably running power tools at his house, and he couldn't hear his phone. She knew she could call any of the guys from NES, and they would be there in a heartbeat, but she tried Crash again before contacting any of the others. After the third ring, she almost cried when she heard his voice.

"Hey, Ally," Crash sounded out of breath.

"Brent… Brent… Oh my God. Axel is here, and he said to tell you someone is creeping around my house." Allyson whispered.

"Where are you?" Crash asked.

"He sent me upstairs. I'm in the bathroom, but Axel is by the front door watching whoever it is." Allyson sat on the floor by the locked door.

"Ok. I'm coming for you. Ally, don't leave that bathroom until you hear one of us." Crash told her.

"Okay," she choked.

She hugged the phone to her chest and waited. Allyson heard no noise, but that didn't mean someone hadn't entered the house. She dropped her head on her knees and prayed.

"I'm coming for you."

Crash's words played in her head. He was going to come and probably run into someone who was there to hurt her or maybe him, and she was hiding in the bathroom. She wouldn't let someone harm him, but what could she do? Then she remembered the bat.

Allyson jumped up and hurried into her bedroom. She put the bat back in her room after the day Elijah showed up in her house. She picked it up and took a deep breath. She wasn't going to let anyone hurt Crash.

She opened her door and tiptoed down the hallway to the top of the stairs. As she crept down each step, she held the bat up so she could swing if someone came at her. She hit the bottom step as Axel and Crash dragged the last person she expected to see into the kitchen.

"Witt?" Allyson glared at him.

"I knew I saw you before," Crash snapped as he pushed Witt into one of the kitchen chairs.

"Who are these Neanderthals, Allyson?" Witt tried to stand up, but Axel shoved him down again.

"We're the men going to beat your ass if you don't tell us why the hell you're creeping around outside of Ally's house." Crash grabbed Witt by the front of the shirt.

"Get your hands off me," Witt shouted.

"Buddy, I'd tell him why you're here because he's about five seconds from rearranging that preppy face." Axel stood next to Crash and crossed his arms over his large chest.

"Allyson, are you going to let them disrespect me?" Witt didn't sound as confident as he usually did.

"Don't talk to her. Why the fuck are you here?" Crash shook him.

"I wanted to ask Allyson to dinner," Witt finally said.

"Not happening." Crash shoved Witt back in the chair.

Witt looked toward Allyson as if she would stand up for him, but she wasn't about to do that. She'd told him one too many times that she wasn't interested.

"Allyson?" Witt stared at her with wide eyes.

"Don't talk to her. I told you it wasn't happening." Crash grabbed Witt by the neck and pulled him to his feet.

"Brent, wait." Allyson walked toward him.

Witt smirked, but it disappeared when she glared up at him. With Axel on one side of her and Crash holding the cocky doctor by the back of the neck, the guy must have known better than to open his mouth and say something stupid.

"Why were you on my property?" Allyson demanded.

"I... I was..." Witt winced when Crash's grip tightened.

"No bullshit," Crash practically growled.

"Well, if you'd stop trying to strangle me..." Witt didn't finish because Crash spun the man around and slammed him against the wall.

"You're lucky I don't fucking beat you senseless for creeping around like some sort of stalker," Crash said through gritted teeth.

"I wasn't creeping, and I'm not a stalker," Witt explained, his voice slightly quivering.

Allyson needed to stop Crash before he hurt Witt. The last thing he needed was an assault charge because she knew the doctor well enough to know he would do it.

"Brent, let him go so he can explain." Allyson touched Crash's shoulder.

She didn't think he would for a moment, but with one more shove, he backed away. Witt slowly turned around and glared as he tried to muster some of his dignity.

"Talk," Crash snapped.

"I was in Hopedale to consult with a patient. I was driving by and saw someone sneaking behind the house." Witt straightened his tie.

"I was outside, but I didn't see anyone going around the house," Axel interjected.

"You wouldn't have seen him from the front of the house. If you let me move, I'll show you." Witt pointed to the living room.

"Show me." Allyson motioned for him to go ahead of her.

At first, he didn't move because Crash and Axel blocked his movement. Both men moved when she cleared her throat, and Witt quickly shuffled around them.

He stepped next to the patio door and pointed toward the back corner of the house. It was the only part of her yard that didn't have a fence around it. It used to contain her father's old tool shed, but she tore it down several years ago because it was a hazard.

"A guy dressed in black was crouching next to that corner. I thought it was suspicious and came to see if you were okay. I'm not a bad person, Allyson." Witt turned to face her.

"No, you're a pushy bastard," Crash grumbled.

"I call it persistent," Witt replied.

"I call it annoying," Axel snorted.

"Can you describe the guy?" Crash asked.

"His back was to the road. I couldn't see his face." Witt shrugged. "Look, I wouldn't hurt anyone, and I certainly wouldn't stalk anyone. I wanted to ask Allyson out, but I get the feeling she's unavailable."

"You'd be right about that feeling, but why did you tell us you were here to ask her out instead of telling us about the guy in the first place?" Axel asked.

"Put yourselves in my shoes. Someone comes charging out of the house, and another grabs you from behind. You could've been with the guy at the back of the house. He looked as big as you two." Witt waved his arm up and down at Axel.

The man had a point, and Allyson couldn't blame him for panicking when he was shoved around like a rag doll. She glanced at Crash, who was starting to relax and, much to his credit, looked embarrassed.

"Look, I'm sorry we got rough. We've been having some security issues around here, and you were in the wrong place at the wrong time." Crash held out his hand. "Thank you for bringing this to our attention."

Witt slowly reached out and shook both Crash and Axel's hands. He glanced back out through the patio door and then back to Allyson before he buttoned his suit jacket.

"I doubt the guy is still there, but there is no way he didn't leave a trace of himself. Maybe you should check it out while I briefly talk to Allyson." Witt nodded toward the side of the house.

Crash's relaxed look turned tense in an instant at Witt's suggestion. When he stepped toward the doctor, Allyson quickly stepped between them and pressed her hands against Crash's chest.

"Witt is right. Please check outside," Allyson whispered.

"But…" Crash started, but she pressed her finger against his lips. "I'll be okay."

Crash and Axel finally left before Witt was given a not-so-subtle shove. When she heard the front door close, she turned back to Witt, who looked as if he was ready to bolt at any second.

"What do you want, Witt?" Allyson asked.

"Are you being held against your will?" Witt whispered.

Allyson stared at him for a few seconds before she burst out laughing. She held her stomach as he continued to suggest he could go to the police, and they could get her out.

"I don't see how this is funny, Allyson." Witt finally said with a huff.

"Witt…Witt, I'm more than safe, and I'm certainly not being held against my will. There's been some security issues, and he's worried," Allyson said as she tried to stop laughing.

"You're sure?" Witt pressed.

"Absolutely, but I appreciate the concern. Thank you for stopping by to let me know what you saw. I'm very grateful." Allyson gently touched his arm.

"Grateful enough to have a drink with me?" Witt grinned.

"No." Allyson rolled her eyes.

"I'm guessing the guy with the attitude is why you're off the market." Witt wasn't asking.

"Brent and I are together, yes," Allyson admitted.

When they entered the house again, Axel looked angry, and Crash was on his phone. Their expressions sent a chill up her spine when she realized what could've happened if Witt hadn't driven by her house. As much as he irritated her, she was grateful for his interference.

"I found some impressions, but I don't know if they'll be there when you arrive. It's starting to rain." Crash was frustrated.

"Someone was there, and from the footprints, they'd been there a while," Axel told Allyson.

"If you have a tarp or some plastic, you could put it over the prints until the police get here," Witt suggested.

Allyson had several tarps in her laundry room left over from when she'd had to repair her roof. She retrieved one and brought it to Axel. He quickly rushed outside, but when he returned, he was wet. The rain had gotten heavier.

"A.J. asked if you could leave your information so he can get your statement." Crash shoved his phone back in his pocket.

"I can wait around. I don't mind," Witt offered.

Crash didn't seem to like the idea, but what could he have said? Allyson wasn't going to kick the man out after he risked his safety. Not that he was in danger from the stranger, but Crash and Axel could've punched first and asked questions later.

"I'll make some coffee."

Allyson needed to do something before she let the panic bubble up. She wasn't sure what was happening, but knowing someone was sneaking around her home made her want to run and hide.

Chapter 17

Crash couldn't help himself, so he pulled Allyson into his side while they waited for the police. Witt wasn't all bad when he wasn't hitting on Allyson, but Crash wanted to clarify that the doctor didn't have a chance.

"Who were you in Hopedale to see?" Axel asked out of the blue.

"I'm sorry I can't divulge that information. The whole doctor/patient confidentiality thing." Witt sipped from the cup he held in his hand.

"You'd have to tell the police if they ask," Axel pushed.

"The only way I'd need to do that is if they had a warrant and I was in trouble." Witt stopped. "Which I'm not."

Crash wanted to grab the man and shake the information out of him, but that would upset Allyson, and he was pretty sure the guy would probably cry to the police. When he glanced at Axel, he could tell his friend was probably thinking the same thing.

"Besides, what would my patient have to do with your prowler?" Witt continued.

He wasn't wrong. What were the chances both situations were connected? Crash decided to let it go because he was concerned about a guy sneaking around Allyson's home when she was there alone. Thank God he'd asked Axel to keep an eye on the house while Crash was putting the finishing touches on his house.

"Do you want some advice?" Witt asked.

"Not from you," Crash grumbled.

"I'm going to give it to you anyway because if you care about Allyson, you'd probably be smart to put some lights and a camera on that part of the house. I've had the entire outside of my place examined and ensured there were no blind areas." Witt crossed his legs and picked a piece of lint from the fabric of his pants.

"Are you afraid of something?" Axel crossed his arms over his chest.

"Not afraid. I'm being prepared. I live in a wealthy neighborhood, and some homes have been burglarized. I won't let some hoodlums take what I work so hard to make." Witt sighed. "Could I have another cup of coffee?"

"Sure," Allyson said.

While she went about starting another pot, Crash motioned for Axel to join him outside. He wasn't worried about Witt doing anything to hurt Allyson; from what Crash could see, the guy was a snowflake.

He didn't understand why someone would lurk around Allyson's house. Then again, whoever was following him probably knew he'd been staying there, and he wanted to kick himself for putting her in danger.

The kids were currently with his mother for the evening because she and his sister-in-law wanted to pick up some things for the children's rooms. Crash had no idea what else they could pick up because between what he packed up at Wyatt's house and the things given to him, he wasn't sure there was room for anything else.

Axel seemed anxious, and Crash still had not found out what his friend wanted to talk to him about. He needed to know if his friend had any information that could help.

"What's got your back up, Ax?" Crash asked as soon as he closed the door.

"The fact that I missed someone lurking around your woman's house isn't reason enough?" Axel walked to the end of the deck and dropped down on the bench.

"No. You said you needed to talk to me about something, and I feel it's the reason you seem on edge." Crash sat next to him.

Axel was quiet for several minutes, then turned and pulled something out of his jacket. He handed it to Crash before he started to speak.

"Six days ago, I got that in the mail. I don't know who sent it, but it says if anything happens to any of the men from our team, I need to watch my back. I can't get any information on that son of a bitch that sent us over there, but I do know he's in hiding. With Otto dropping with a heart attack last year, we're the only two left." Axel leaned against the railing surrounding the deck.

"Why didn't you mention that when you got here?" Crash asked as he scanned the letter he pulled from the envelope.

"You had a lot of shit on your plate. It's why I've been sleeping in my car across the street in that opening in the trees. I'm pretty sure someone is trying to clean up after themselves. There is something about our team someone is afraid of." Axel shook his head.

"Why? Gibson was forced to retire because of all this. Do you think it's him?" Crash asked.

"I doubt it. According to his neighbor, the guy was scared of something." Axel tapped the envelope. "I don't understand why I'm the only one who got this."

"You said you got it six days ago?" Crash asked.

"Yeah."

"All my mail has been going to Crunch's place. I haven't been over to get it in a couple of weeks. His woman texted me to let me know there was some stuff there. I wasn't worried because I do all the important stuff online," Crash said, glancing down the road toward his friend's house.

"Maybe you should go grab it," Axel suggested.

"I'll get it after the police leave." Crash opened the door to step back inside. "Don't mention anything to Allyson. I don't want to worry her."

Axel nodded and followed him inside. Crash wasn't sure what the hell was going on, but knowing someone was possibly taking out his entire team made him think Wyatt's and Ellie's deaths were part of it.

Aaron showed up a few minutes later with several other officers who immediately checked around the house. It was probably useless;

after all, the guy was long gone, but he needed to have a report filed in case it happened again.

He was also less excited about moving to his home and leaving Allyson alone. God knows what would've happened if Axel hadn't been there or even Witt. Crash hated that he'd probably brought danger to her doorstep, but he had no idea what was happening.

"Looks to be typical work boots," one of the officers said when he walked inside.

"So, it could be anyone who bought a pair of boots." Allyson sighed.

"I'm afraid unless we have someone to match the prints too, we don't have much to go on," Aaron said. "Maybe you should put some extra cameras around that side of the house."

"See, I told you." Witt smirked.

"You can go now." Crash growled at the ass.

"I've got your information if I have any other questions," Aaron assured the cocky doctor.

"Call if you need anything," Witt said as he turned to Allyson.

"Thanks again, Witt." Allyson walked him to the door.

"I don't like that guy," Aaron muttered.

"You and me both," Axel agreed.

"I'm not a fan either, but if he hadn't warned us, something could've happened to Ally." Crash's voice quivered at the thought of her being in danger.

"I'm glad you're staying with her," Aaron told Crash.

He was, but only for another day or two. He hated to leave but needed to get Mila and Caleb settled into their new rooms. After all, he would be returning to work, and he couldn't do that if they were shuttled around to a different house every day. Maybe he could convince her to stay with him.

"I thought you were moving into your place this weekend?" Axel asked.

"I'm supposed to be, and I can't put it off because ..."

"The kids need to settle in, and I'll be fine here." Allyson interrupted Crash when she walked back into the kitchen.

"Maybe you could stay with..." Aaron began, but Allyson held up her hand.

"I'm staying here. I'll get Keith to put in some extra security cameras, and I'll make sure all the doors and windows are locked at all times," Allyson informed them.

There was no way any of them would convince her otherwise, and Crash knew that because if he'd learned anything about her over the years, it would be that she was stubborn. He would ask Keith about setting up a detail for her, but he needed to talk to Allyson about it first.

Aaron was headed out the door when Crunch walked up the front steps. He had a bundle of mail in his hand and seemed as if he was pissed about something.

"Why the hell didn't you call one of us?" Crunch didn't give anyone a chance to say anything.

"How did you find out?" Crash asked.

"Aaron was at the house when you called." Crunch handed Crash the mail he had. "That stuff has been at the house for weeks, but this one only came last week."

Crunch pointed to a large white envelope with his name on it. There was no return address, but the postmark showed that it was sent from inside the province.

"That's different from the one I got," Axel said.

"What do you mean?" Crunch asked.

Crash explained the letter Axel had received and that they figured someone was either warning or threatening him. Either way, Crash was anxious to check out the contents of the non-descript envelope. He tucked the rest of his mail under his arm while carefully opening the large envelope as if it would blow up in his hands.

He opened it and found a thick stack of papers inside. He pulled it out and began to read. Crash wasn't sure what he was reading, but it appeared to be medical records with the names blacked out.

"I have no idea what this is," Crash mainly said to himself.

He handed it to Aaron and waited as his friend scanned the papers. Crash, Axel, and Crunch waited while Aaron went into cop mode and flipped through the documents.

"These are autopsy reports. The names are redacted, but there are at least four different people." Aaron looked up at Crash. "Didn't one of your team die four years ago?"

"Yeah, Perry Brown. He died in a fire," Crash explained.

"In Ottawa?" Aaron asked.

"Yes," Axel and Crash said together.

"This report is on someone whose remains were found in a house fire, but their lungs had no damage." Aaron pointed to the paper.

"What does that mean?" Crunch asked.

"It means he was dead before the fire." Aaron moved his finger down the paper. "This means his body was covered in bruises, and this is several broken bones."

On one of the pages was a sketch of the front and back of a person. As he read all the notes on the drawing, he felt sick. Both Perry's legs were broken, as well as most of his ribs. All his fingers were shattered except for one, which had been cut off. Crash didn't know that this report was about his friend, but if it was, it meant Otto was tortured to death.

"What the fuck?" Axel gasped.

"This means someone set the fire to cover up a murder," Crash exclaimed angrily.

"Let me check into it and talk to the officer who investigated the case," Aaron held out his hand. "Can I borrow those to make copies?"

"Ally has a copier. It's not that I don't trust you, but I want to keep this and read them over. I'll copy them for you." Crash hurried into the house.

"Maybe I can also find out who the other reports are," Aaron offered.

Crash waited patiently while Allyson photocopied over a hundred pages of documents. She explained some of the information but said they could sit down and go through it.

"Thanks, sweetheart. I'd appreciate it." Crash kissed her cheek.

If one of the reports was about Perry, who were the others, and why was it sent to him?

Chapter 18

Allyson's eyes burned as she pulled off her glasses and rubbed her eyes. They'd been reading through the papers for hours, and the one thing they learned was these people died horrific deaths.

The one that Crash was convinced was his friend, Perry, stated that he probably died from blood loss. The man had to have been in terrible pain from the number of fractures and breaks he had.

Another of the reports had detailed notes on breaks and fractures, along with dozens of cuts and bruises. From what she could find, it was another man, but there was no way to tell who it was or where he was murdered. It did state that there was cardiac damage as well, so the person might have had a heart attack because of the beating.

"Didn't your friend Otto die of a heart issue?" Allyson asked as she rubbed her eyes.

"Fuck," Crash snatched the papers from in front of her. "Do you think this is his autopsy?"

"Brent, I have no way to tell who it is, but if it's plausible that the other is Perry, maybe this one could be Otto." Allyson sighed.

"Shit, sweetheart. I'm sorry for keeping you up. It's three in the morning, and you need to get some sleep. I'm glad my mom decided to keep the kids for the night." Brent pushed the papers into a pile and picked them up. "Let's go to bed. This can wait until we get some rest."

Allyson was relieved to go to bed, but she knew he wouldn't sleep. Brent had become obsessed with reading the reports, and they'd gone over them half a dozen times. She could probably recite the written part word for word at this point.

"If you're going to sleep, why are you taking the reports?" Allyson asked as she wrapped her arms around his waist.

"I want to make sure they don't disappear." Crash pulled her against his chest. "Thank you for helping with this. I wish Axel had stayed. I'm worried he could be in danger."

Allyson was worried that Crash was in jeopardy. If someone was trying to get rid of his team, he could be next. It terrified her because she'd lived through Trent's death, but she wouldn't survive if anything happened to Crash.

"Do you think he'd gone back to his dad's?" Allyson asked.

"Knowing him, he didn't. He'd stay as far away as possible if he thinks it could endanger his father." Crash kissed the top of her head. "Let's go to bed."

Neither of them slept much. Crash tossed and turned, which meant Allyson was getting woken up every time he moved. When he fell asleep, he shouted. He offered to sleep in the other room, but she didn't want him to leave her. She was scared; even if he kept her awake, she knew he was okay.

She was startled awake by a knocking on the front door. She sighed as she glanced over to see Crash had somehow gotten out of bed without waking her. She crawled out of bed and wrapped herself up in a heavy robe.

She heard the voices as she made her way down the steps, fully expecting to see Keith, Sandy, and Aaron. She was surprised to see Axel in the same clothes he had left in yesterday and looking as haggard as she felt.

"I hope there is one of those for me," Allyson muttered as she glanced over to her counter.

A large box with Tim Horton's logo sat on the counter with several paper cups. She smiled as Crash handed her a cup filled with coffee and cream. She moaned as she sipped the creamy concoction and eased into one of the kitchen chairs.

"I figured we could all use tons of that black gold today." Axel plowed his fingers through his messy hair.

"Well, thanks because it's exactly what I needed this morning." She glanced at Crash.

"I wasn't exactly the easiest to sleep next to last night," Crash admitted.

"So why is everyone here so early?" Allyson asked.

"We were right about it being Perry's autopsy report." Crash handed her another bundle of papers, but the name was on it.

"Do you think we were right about the other?" Allyson sighed.

"I'm about to find out." Sandy was clicking on the keys of her ever-present laptop.

"If this is what we think it is, you and the kids are moving to the compound." Keith pointed to Crash. "So are you."

"I'll be fine," Axel replied when Keith trained his eyes on him.

"I'm sure your buddy thought the same," Keith grumbled.

"Got it." Sandy interrupted.

She read something on the screen for several minutes, and the rest waited. The longer she took, the more Allyson felt they were right. When Sandy finally raised her eyes to meet Crash, she looked concerned.

"It's Otto Fudge," Sandy said.

"Fuck," Axel and Crash shouted at the same time.

"There's something else." Sandy turned her laptop around. "Did you know he was found with a woman?"

"No, his wife died years ago." Axel had kept in contact with Otto.

"The woman's name was Halima…"

"Hasan," Crash interrupted Sandy.

"No, her last name was…Gibson." Sandy showed them the screen.

"Are you sure?" Axel asked.

"She's sure," Keith answered.

Everyone knew Sandy wouldn't say it if she weren't positive. The woman was incredible at finding things, which is one reason she was in high demand by government agencies.

"It has to be the same Halima," Crash looked at Axel.

"Did she marry Gibson? That doesn't make sense." Axel dropped down next to Crash.

"This says she was single," Sandy interrupted.

Crash and Axel looked completely bewildered. She didn't know who Halima was or why they would be so shocked over her last name. She didn't get a chance to ask because Crash's phone rang.

"Hello." He put the phone to his ear.

She watched his expression change instantly and saw that whoever was on the other side of the call was telling him something he didn't want to hear.

"Don't go anywhere. I'll be right there." Crash ended the call and looked at Aaron.

"What's going on?" Keith asked.

"That was Roger Collins, you know, Ellie's foster dad. He said he received a call from someone claiming to be Sidney's father and wanted to make sure she was safe," Crash explained.

"So why is he calling you?" Keith asked.

"What you don't know is the Collins' take in children removed from dangerous situations. It's why Ellie was placed with them. Her dad was bad news and had tried to kill Ellie and her mom. Her mother didn't make it." Crash went on. "Sidney was placed with them for the same reason. She was in danger from a cruel man."

"I'll send a car over there now. Is Sidney with them?" Aaron asked.

"No, she's at the university." Crash grabbed his coat.

"Whoa, where do you think you're going?" Keith stepped in front of him.

"To get Sidney home to the Collins'," Crash said as he pulled on his coat.

"You're not going off on your own. You could still be in danger, or did you forget about your team," Keith reminded him, and Allyson breathed a breath of relief.

The last thing she wanted to see was Crash getting hurt or worse. Whoever hurt his team was brutal and heartless. She shuddered as she thought about the injuries she'd seen on those reports, not to mention what she'd seen on Wyatt and Ellie.

"I've got someone going to get her now." Aaron stood next to Keith.

"She's not going to go off with a stranger. She knows me." Crash didn't seem to be thinking about anything but making sure Sidney was safe.

"Is there something you're not telling us?" Keith asked.

Crash locked eyes with Axel, and for the first time since she'd known him, she had no idea what was going on. They talked about everything, but whatever this was, it was between Crash and his friend

Chapter 19

"Is there something you're not telling us?" Keith asked.

Crash looked over at Axel. They were the only two left besides Ethel and Roger, who knew Sidney was Aya Hasan. Halima had given her up to keep her out of the clutches of the man hunting her down.

It suddenly hit him; he knew who was responsible, and if it was Nasir, he wouldn't stop until he found Aya. She'd been told the whole story about how she was rescued when she was two and why she was placed in Ethel and Roger's care. For a kid, she adjusted well and never looked back.

Now, the girl was studying to be a doctor, and from what Wyatt told him, she was at the top of her class. He knew it was time to explain the situation because if that son of a bitch was hunting down Sidney, she was in more danger than anyone knew.

"Crash, if there's something we should know, you need to tell us," Aaron pushed.

"Sidney Collins is really Aya Hasan," Crash began.

"Our team rescued her and her mother, Halima. That was the mission where we lost two of our team. The one that caused Brent and me to leave the military." Axel blew out a breath.

"But Halima only died a year ago." Sandy reminded them.

"It was believed Nasir was hunting her, and she knew the only way to keep her daughter safe was to give her up. Roger and Ethel deal with kids who need to be protected. Aya was three when she went to live with them, and her mother already started calling her Sidney, so they kept the name." Crash explained.

"Does she know about her uncle?" Keith asked.

"Yes, she knows everything. It's why Wyatt trained her in self-defense and taught her to use a gun, but she's not aware how close he is." Crash didn't like this.

"Fine, you can go, but you're not going alone," Keith said with his phone in his ear.

Ten minutes later, Crash, Axel, Aaron, Keith, Hulk, and Trunk were on their way to the university. The dorm had been contacted and told not to let Sidney leave her room. She was to stay there until Crash came to get her.

"Are we sure this is Nasir?" Axel whispered.

"Who else would it be?" Crash asked.

"Gibson?" Axel suggested.

Crash hated the man, and he certainly didn't trust him, but would he kill his men and the woman he sent them to rescue? He was a bastard, but he did everything to get Halima and her daughter away from Nasir. Plus, he wasn't sure Gibson had the strength to overpower Wyatt, let alone Otto or Perry. He was barely five foot ten and wasn't in shape, at least the last time Crash saw him.

"I don't see it, but then again, who knows."

Crash breathed a sigh of relief when they pulled up to Sidney's dorm. Two vehicles pulled up on either side of Keith's car.

"Trunk, you and Hulk stay at this entrance while we go inside to get Sidney," Keith ordered.

"You do realize I'm the cop here." Aaron glared at his brother.

"Yep, that's why you have the gun." Keith motioned for Aaron to go ahead of him.

"Yes, and I'm sure you don't have one inside your coat," Aaron grumbled as they entered the dorm.

They hurried through the hallway to Sidney's room. Crash was relieved to see three officers standing outside her door, and they stepped back when Aaron knocked on the door.

"Who is it?" Sidney asked through the door.

"Smart girl," Axel whispered.

"It's me, Sid. Brent." Crash called out.

At first, he wasn't sure she would open the door, but there were several clicks, and the door opened slowly. She had a knapsack on her back and a suitcase in her hand.

"Mom called and told me to pack." Sidney didn't look scared.

"You'll be staying at the compound." Keith reached in and grabbed her case.

"The compound?" Sidney looked suddenly terrified.

"It's okay, Sidney. It's Keith's property and the safest place for you to be right now." Crash explained.

"He's really here?" She looked up at Crash.

"We're not sure, but we can't take chances." Crash pulled her into a hug.

"What about mom and dad?" She looked around at the men.

"I've sent someone to pick them up. They'll be with you." Keith answered.

Crash hadn't even seen Keith make the call, but he was thankful his boss was so thorough. Aaron closed Sidney's door, and they headed back down the hallway. On the way out, Axel stopped and glanced behind him toward a large window at the end of the corridor. When Crash followed his line of sight, he immediately observed what Axel was looking at.

"Is that a propane tank?" Axel asked.

"Why would that be…"

Before Crash could finish, the building shook as a loud explosion sounded overhead. A few seconds later, there was another.

"Run," Crash and Axel shouted as they grabbed Sidney and ran.

They were through the door when another explosion sounded behind them. They barely got out of the building when people started flooding out of the building and jumping from the windows of the three-story building.

"Oh my God, help them," Sidney screamed.

By the time the fire department arrived, Crash had lost count of the number of kids they'd helped climb out of the windows. He wasn't sure if everyone got out safely, but whoever set this whole thing up mainly wanted a distraction.

"Get Sidney back to the compound," Aaron ordered as he ran toward the fire trucks.

"Can't we help," Axel offered.

"No, you all need to get to safety." Aaron didn't turn back.

"Let's get out of here," Keith said as he opened the door for Sidney.

"I have friends who live there." Sidney sobbed.

"Hopefully, everyone got out safe," Crash whispered as he hugged her.

Keith sped out of the university parking lot with Trunk in front and Hulk behind, each driving one of the armored SUVs belonging to NES. If his boss brought out these vehicles, he was worried.

Crash and Axel sat in the back on either side of Sidney, but nobody seemed to want to talk as the line of NES vehicles made its way through St. John's streets and onto the highway. The only sounds inside the SUV were the soft music from the radio and Sidney's sniffing.

"I've had your family picked up, too, Crash. We're not taking any chances," Keith broke the quiet ride.

Crash nodded because it was too difficult for him to speak. His entire family was in danger because of something he did nineteen years ago. It was shitty, but when he glanced at Sidney, he knew her life was much better than if she had stayed in Syria.

"Your dad is picked up as well, Axel." Keith continued.

"He didn't give you any trouble?" Axel asked.

"Not that I was told. Rex said he explained the situation, and your dad was concerned about your safety." Keith turned off the highway into Hopedale.

Caden Rex Dixon was a former American soldier who started working for NES around the same time Crash did. He was formally from Georgia but never talked much about his family. He mainly kept to himself unless he was working or attending a mandatory get-together.

The gate to the compound opened, and the three SUVs pulled through. Keith had six bunkhouses at the back of his property, used for staff who didn't have a place. The only one staying there now was Allyson's cousin, but if Keith thought he needed the place for clients, Elijah would need to find other accommodations. There was also a three-bedroom safe house, so chances were they wouldn't need him to relocate.

"Where are we?" Sidney asked.

"This is Rusty's property," Crash told her, using Keith's nickname.

"Rusty?" Sidney looked confused.

"That would be the red-headed man in the front seat," Keith chuckled.

"I thought your name was Keith?" She leaned forward.

"It's a nickname that the staff uses. You can call me Keith," he told her.

Sidney nodded as the SUV stopped in front of the safe house. There were several vehicles, and men stood around. Crash opened the door and stepped out as his father walked toward him. He looked pissed.

"How long do we have to be here?" His dad didn't even wait until he was next to Crash.

"I'm not sure, Dad. It's a precaution." Crash helped Sidney out of the car.

As soon as the door of the car closed, Ethel and Roger ran toward her. They embraced, and Crash's father seemed to lose some of his anger. Crash wasn't sure where he was supposed to go, but when he saw Allyson sitting on the steps of one of the bunkhouses, he stalked toward her.

She stood as he stepped beside her and practically leaped into his arms. He kissed the side of her neck as they clung to each other for several seconds. Crash knew if his family was here, then the kids were as well, and he wanted to see them for himself to make sure Caleb and Mila were okay.

"They're inside playing with Cam," Allyson whispered as if she'd read his mind.

"Cameron is here too?" Crash asked.

"Keith is being cautious." She stepped back. "I heard about the explosion."

"It was close. Too close." Crash wrapped his arm around her shoulders, and they headed into the house.

Mila was sitting on Cameron's lap, playing with a musical toy, while Caleb watched something on his iPad next to them. Crash blew out a breath when he finally saw them.

"Caleb was a little upset that he wasn't returning to my place. He said he wanted to go home." Allyson whispered.

"He's got to be so confused with being dragged from one place to the next." Crash sighed.

"Cam told him they were on a kind of camping trip, but they didn't have to sleep in tents. He promised to roast marshmallows." Allyson laid her head on Crash's shoulder.

"If a marshmallow roast is what he wants, den dat's what he'll get."

Crash and Allyson turned around and smiled. They shouldn't be surprised to see Keith's sweet grandmother lugging bags, followed by her husband, Tom. The woman was always the first to lend a hand when there was a crisis.

"That's right, dear. I'll get one of the boys to head back to the store and pick up a few bags of them." Tom headed back out of the house.

"Nan, you didn't have to do all this." Crash took the bags from the woman.

"Now, don't you fret. It's what I do."

She headed to the small kitchen, and when Crash placed the bags on the counter, she began to pull food out of them. He wasn't surprised to see enough for an army, but chances were this was all for them. The rest probably got deliveries as well.

"Now, I did put a little extra in here for da little fella and da big fella," Betty pointed to Cam and Caleb. "Dere's also some pureed stuff fer da little one."

"Nan, what would we do without you?" Allyson hugged the older woman.

"Da whole lot of ya would fall apart." Betty didn't even laugh because she wasn't wrong.

An hour later, a massive fire pit was burning in front of the bunkhouses. They rarely used the fire pit, but considering the day's events, it was a good distraction. Keith's wife and kids joined them, as did several of the other O'Connor kids. It wasn't hard to see they were trying to make things as easy as possible for everyone.

"At least Caleb is enjoying himself," Crash's mother said as she sat beside him.

"I'm sorry about…" Crash stopped when his mother pressed her hand against his mouth.

"You don't have to be sorry. You didn't do anything." She kissed his cheek, and he knew that was the end of that conversation.

By the time everyone had left, Caleb and Mila were sound asleep, and Cameron went inside with them. He hadn't said anything about why they were there, but he assured Crash that he wouldn't miss any classes because he could go online.

While Caleb and Cameron slept in one of the bedrooms, Allyson, Crash, and Mila slept in the other. The bunkhouses never had huge bedrooms, but they had double beds, and there was just enough room to set up Mila's crib.

"You need to sleep," Allyson whispered as she snuggled into his body.

"I'm trying," Crash said.

"Do you think this guy is trying to get Sidney?" Allyson lifted her head and looked into his face.

"He killed a lot of people. It's why Titus sent us in, or at least that was the information we had." Crash didn't tell her the military didn't send them.

"Can't your former leader do something?" She asked.

"Nobody knows where he is, and all information about that mission is sealed." Crash pulled her closer.

They were told the information was sealed, but it was probably scrubbed from everything. It was such a fucked-up thing, and Crash thought the whole thing was behind him. They all did, but someone was trying to get a message across. What was it?

Chapter 20

Allyson was going stir-crazy. She felt caged, but she shouldn't have felt that way. Keith's property was enormous, and she could walk for an hour without seeing the same spot twice. Still, she wasn't home and needed to prepare to start at the clinic. Sean was counting on her to start the following week.

It had been over a week, and the first snowfall of the winter covered everything with a blanket of white. It looked beautiful, and she enjoyed the crisp air as she walked down the pathway around the property.

Crash struggled to keep his annoyance in check and spend time with the kids. Why he thought he wouldn't be able to handle it was beyond her because he was a natural.

Cameron had moved into the bunkhouse with Elijah because he said the couch wasn't comfortable. Allyson didn't believe that for a minute. It was probably because the kids were up at the crack of dawn, and Caleb liked to wake her son.

Everyone brought to the compound dealt with things better than expected, but Axel seemed to struggle. His dad let it slip that Axel had nightmares every night, and when Crash talked to him, his friend said things were under control.

"It's so pretty," Sidney smiled as she walked toward Allyson on the path.

"Yes, it is." Allyson stopped to chat with the young girl.

"I needed to stretch my legs, and Mom and Dad hovered. A lot." Sidney sighed.

"They're scared for you." Allyson understood completely.

"I know, and the truth is, so am I. All the stories I heard about my uncle make me wish I could scrub all his DNA from my system." Sidney leaned against a tree. "Too bad that's not possible."

"Your DNA doesn't define you. You're an amazing person, and that's because wonderful people helped you." Allyson smiled at the young woman.

"I know, and I'm eternally grateful for all those men who got my mother and me out of there." A tear ran down her cheek. "I miss her letters."

"You kept in touch?" Allyson asked.

"She sent letters every month. She wouldn't call because she was scared he'd find me. Her brother is a monster. I guess it was inevitable." Sidney wiped her face. "Do you think he'll give up?"

Allyson didn't know the answer, but she felt that if Nasir had searched for nineteen years, he wouldn't stop unless someone stopped him. The thought sent a shiver through her, and she wrapped her arms around herself.

"I wish I knew, honey, but you have some of the best people in the world doing everything to keep you safe," Allyson assured her.

"I don't remember anything about that time. I was only two, but I have this flash of a man running with me in his arms. Brent carried me to the helicopter, but this man isn't Brent." Sidney shook her head. "It's weird, right?"

"No. We all have flashes of memory from when we were little. It's hard to distinguish which is real and which is what we've been told," Allyson said.

"This is so clear, though. The guy is olive-skinned and has dark eyes. I wonder if he's the uncle who took us." Sidney sighed.

"It could be." Allyson shivered as a cold wind blew around them. "Let's go get some hot chocolate."

"That sounds like a plan." Sidney smiled finally.

They silently returned to the bunkhouse and found Crash outside with Caleb, building the worst snowman she'd ever seen. He glanced up when Allyson got closer and grinned.

"Mila is napping, so we decided to come play in the snow." Crash helped Caleb put snow on the pitiful snowman.

Allyson would never say anything because the little boy was working hard on it, and Crash seemed really proud of himself. Someone laughed behind her before she could tell Caleb how good it was.

"What the heck is that supposed to be?" Megan walked toward them.

"It's a snowman," Caleb grinned.

Megan looked at the little boy and crouched to talk to him. She took his little hand and pressed her lips together for a moment before she spoke.

"Did you make this yourself?" Megan asked.

"No. Brent made it, and I helped." Caleb hugged Megan.

"Brent made it." Megan looked up at her brother.

"Don't say a word, or I'll throw you in a snowbank," Crash warned his sister.

It was nice to see them forget about everything going on and enjoy the day. She wasn't sure how long they had to stay on the compound, but they couldn't do this forever. She wasn't sure if she needed to be there; after all, she and Brent had only recently gotten together. A lot of people still didn't know about them.

"You have seen a snowman before, right?" Megan continued to tease Crash.

"Keep it up, little girl, and you are going headfirst into that snowbank," Crash narrowed his eyes.

"Let me show you one on my phone," Megan went on as she pulled off her glove.

That was all Crash needed. He lunged toward his sister, and she shrieked as she turned to escape him. She didn't stand a chance. He caught her and tossed her over his shoulder. With her begging, screaming, and beating on his back, Crash walked toward the large bank of snow that had been plowed there when Keith cleared the roadway of the compound.

"Brent, don't you dare. My phone is in my…" Megan didn't finish as Crash tossed her into the pile.

He didn't stop there. He started taking handfuls of snow and throwing it on top of her. Allyson felt bad for her, but she wasn't about to get in the middle of that snow fight.

"Jerk," Megan shouted as Brent walked away, slapping the snow from his gloves.

"Next time, don't diss my snowman," Crash called over his shoulder.

"That wasn't very nice." Allyson chuckled.

"Bet she won't make fun of my snowman skills again." Crash grinned.

His smile disappeared as he looked past her toward the road from the main gate. Allyson saw two police cruisers and Keith's Jeep driving toward them.

"Megan, take Caleb inside," Crash said as his sister stepped beside them.

As the cars came to a stop, Aaron got out of one, Nick out of the other, and Keith out of the Jeep. When Nick opened the rear door of his cruiser, Crash seemed to hold his breath as someone stepped out of the vehicle.

"What the fuck?" Crash gasped.

"Who is that?" Allyson asked.

Crash didn't say a word but began to stalk toward Nick and the man who exited the car. Allyson also moved toward them but stopped when she saw Axel run down the bunkhouse steps and follow Crash.

She didn't know who this man was, but Crash and Axel seemed to recognize him. Neither of them looked particularly happy to see the guy either.

"Who is that?" Sidney asked.

"I don't know, but maybe we should go inside with Megan and the kids."

Allyson wrapped her arm around Sidney and guided the girl to the bunkhouse. As they stepped inside, Allyson looked over her shoulder in time to see Nick and Aaron stop Crash and Axel as they lunged for the unknown man. This could be trouble.

Chapter 21

"You fucking son of a bitch. You should be in fucking jail for what you did." Axel shouted.

"Can't go to jail when you run and hide like a coward," Crash tried to step around Aaron.

"You need to calm down," Aaron warned.

"Are you out of your fucking mind? This bastard is the reason we are all in this situation in the first place. Isn't it, Titus?" Crash yelled.

Titus didn't speak, but it seemed as if he was about to throw up or bolt. He stood behind the open car door as if it would protect him if Crash or Axel grabbed him.

"He's here for a reason," Keith stepped next to Nick.

Crash looked at his boss and shook his head. There was no way Keith was letting NES protect that prick. If anything, the guy should be thrown to the wolves and let him defend himself. He didn't deserve any pity for what he did.

"I swear, Rusty, if you tell me he's here under protection, I'll quit." Crash glared at Titus.

"You're not going to quit, but you're going to damn well listen." Keith rolled his eyes.

"To what? His bullshit?" Crash pointed toward the man he'd trusted.

Keith said nothing as he turned and walked back to his jeep. A few seconds later, he returned with a file about two inches thick. Before Crash could ask anything, Keith slapped it against his chest.

"This guy is the reason you're both still alive." Keith snapped.

"What the fuck are you talking about?" Axel yelled.

Crash didn't hear anything else as he started to flip through the folder. It was the papers he'd received in the mail, but the names were not redacted. They were the autopsy reports for Halima, Otto, and Perry, but the fourth one had him shaking his head.

"He's dead." Titus' voice was barely above a whisper.

"He can't be." Crash looked up at his old officer.

"He is, and there's a lot you need to know." Nick released Axel.

Crash's head was spinning because if Nasir Hasan was dead, then who the hell killed his friends, and who was after Sidney? None of it made any sense.

"How long has he been dead?" Axel asked.

Titus finally stepped around the car door's protection and closed it. He slowly moved toward Crash and Axel but stopped when Keith held up his hand.

"He showed up at my house five years ago. He wanted me to tell him where Aya was because his life was in danger." Titus blew out a breath.

"Who was going to kill him?" Crash asked.

"Aya's uncle," Titus said.

"Nasir is her uncle," Axel snapped.

"Yes, he is, but he isn't the only one. Nasir wasn't the bad guy. His brother was and still is." Titus pulled his hands down over his face. "Look, I was only trying to protect a woman and child from someone I thought was going to do them harm."

"Two of our team were killed. This guy couldn't be too good if he killed Canadian soldiers." Axel was pacing.

"Nasir wasn't the one who killed them," Titus informed them.

"What?" Crash closed his eyes to calm his rising anger.

When he opened them again, Titus had moved closer. Crash wasn't sure they should trust what the man was saying, but why would he make this shit up? Unless he was working with Nasir and was trying to get close to Sidney.

"Why should we believe any of this?" Crash asked.

"It's all in that file. I've been collecting evidence against this guy for years. I don't know what he looks like because he never shows his face to anyone outside his circle. Nasir said his brother was cautious about keeping his identity hidden from people." Titus held up a photo. "This is the only picture we could find of him, and he's only about ten years old."

Crash snatched the picture from Titus' hand. It was old, with three little boys holding rifles and grinning and a little girl in the background. They appeared to be happy kids having fun, but the boy in the middle looked more ominous than the other two.

"The boy on the left is Nasir, the one on the right is Akram Hasan, and the one in the middle is the oldest brother. His name is Emir, but he's been living between Syria and Canada for years. Nobody knows what name he goes by." Titus stopped.

Crash glanced toward Axel. His face was red, and he looked as if he was ready to explode. This whole thing only made things worse. Their team had been sent not to save a woman and child but to bring them back to danger.

"Okay, let me get this straight," Axel began. "You sent us to rescue a woman and child from another country, and you being a high fucking rank, didn't think to investigate."

"I went through the channels and was told absolutely not, but I was never given a reason why we wouldn't extract her. I was simply told no," Titus explained.

"So, you decided, fuck them. I'm gonna be the hero and send guys to get her, but not tell them that they're on our own over there. That backfired, didn't it?" Axel's agitation was written all over his face.

"The guy outside Ally's house, we think it's one of Emir's men," Aaron said.

Crash's gut clenched, and his heart pounded in his chest. If that man had gotten into the house, he could've hurt Allyson or worse. He wasn't a fan of Dr. Witt Davenport, but at that moment, Crash would give the guy a medal for being a nosey bastard. He did want to punch Titus square in the face for bringing all this shit to the doorsteps of people he loved.

"Do you know for sure?" Axel's voice was a deep growl.

"Not for sure, but who else would it be?" Nick glanced at Titus. "He's here to help."

"Cause he was so fucking helpful in the past," Crash said through gritted teeth.

"They were my friends, too," Titus whispered.

Before anyone could stop him, Axel flew between Nick and Aaron. None of the men were quick enough to stop Axel's fist from connecting with Titus' face. Crash's friend got two jabs in before Keith and Nick pulled him off the bleeding man.

"Your friends? You don't know the fucking meaning of being a friend. Those men gave their lives for something they should never have been thrown into. I shouldn't have to fight every God damn day to stay sober because every night, I see my friends blown to pieces in front of my face," Axel shouted. "What the fuck do you dream about, you prick? I'm sure it's nothing like me and Brent face in our dreams. You've never seen a day of active duty, yet you wore all those medals on your chest as if you're the fucking hero. You should be stripped of those, you fucking coward."

Keith and Nick were both large men, but it took all their strength to keep Axel from flying at Titus again. Crash understood the anger, but violence wouldn't solve the problem—there had already been too much of it. He needed to defuse the situation.

"This isn't helping, Ax," Crash stepped in front of his friend.

"It sure as hell felt great to feel his nose break," Axel yelled over Crash's shoulder toward Titus.

It was then he smelled it. Axel had been drinking. Usually, his friend didn't get out of control, but he had a short fuse when he drank. Crash grabbed his friend by the shirt, and Axel met his eyes.

"You need to go to a meeting?" Crash whispered.

Axel glared for a few seconds, but then the whole fight went off him. His legs buckled as he nodded. He would've dropped to the ground if Nick and Keith hadn't held Axel's arms.

"A.J., take my phone out of my pocket and call my dad." Crash kept his eyes focused on Axel.

"I'm sorry," Axel choked out the words.

"Nothing to be sorry for, man. We all trip," Keith said.

Crash knew his life could be in danger, but Axel was in a bad way, and he needed all the support he could get. That was why Crash, his father, Keith, and Elijah headed to the closest AA meeting an hour later. Keith was careful as they drove out of the compound, and unless someone had seen the people in the back seat get in the armored SUV, they would never have known Crash was inside.

Axel sat between Crash and his father while Keith and Elijah waited outside the building. They probably could've pretended they needed the meeting, but Keith said he didn't want to invade people's private struggles. Crash appreciated his boss for understanding.

"Do I need to go back there again?" Axel asked as they got ready to leave the meeting.

"It's for our safety," Crash reminded him.

"I can't go back there if that… If he's going to be there. I can't believe you aren't furious about him being there." Axel pulled on his coat.

"I hate this, and the truth is I think he should be held accountable for what happened, but you know it's not going to happen. Keith will keep him away from us." Crash hoped he was right.

Chapter 22

Allyson smiled as Caleb's little eyes closed. He'd wanted to wait for Crash to return but was exhausted after playing outside with a couple of the O'Connor kids. She checked on Mila in the crib and then closed the bedroom door. They'd moved her into the room with Caleb because Crash had woken her the previous night when he yelled out during a nightmare.

She had showered and tidied up the small bunkhouse, but there was only so much she could do. It was difficult not to worry when she knew Crash was in danger, but she also understood why he wanted to be there for Axel.

Allyson saw a change in Axel over the last few days and figured he was concerned. The last thing she expected was for him to start drinking, but Crash stood by his friend. There was a soft knock, and she made her way to the front door.

"How are you doing?" Bethany said as she opened the door.

"I'm okay. I'm worried about Brent and his friend," Allyson said, plopping down on the small sofa.

"Aaron told me what happened here earlier." Bethany was the only one who didn't call her husband A.J.

"I can't believe an officer would put his men in that situation," Allyson said.

"You can't? Even after what happened to Trent?" Bethany sat next to her.

"The men who serve know their lives could be in danger if they go into those places, but Brent and his friends were sent there when they shouldn't have been." Allyson sighed.

"I saw Sidney at the safe house. I dropped off some food from Nanny Betty and Kathleen. She's pacing the floor," Bethany told her.

"She's got to be scared."

The bunkhouse door opened, and Crash walked in. He stopped for a minute when he saw Bethany. The man looked exhausted, but he still made her heart race when he looked at her.

"Hi, Bethany," Crash said softly.

"You doing okay?" Bethany asked.

"Yeah," Crash dropped down onto the armchair.

"Axel?" Allyson wasn't sure she should ask.

"He's struggling, but Dad is staying with him tonight. Axel's dad is there, too. Mr. Wright is heartbroken he hadn't noticed Axel drinking again." Crash yawned.

"I should head home. You're exhausted." Bethany stood up.

"You don't need to go. I need a shower, and hopefully, I'll get some sleep tonight." Crash motioned for her to sit back down. "I wish I'd gotten back in time to put Caleb and Mila to bed."

"Caleb tried to stay up but couldn't stay awake." Allyson smiled as he leaned down and kissed her cheek.

"Thank you for taking care of them," he whispered against her lips.

She watched as Crash quietly checked on the kids and then disappeared into the other room. Allyson turned back to her sister. Bethany seemed to have something else on her mind, but she wasn't saying it.

"What's wrong?" Allyson asked.

"Why did you suddenly change your mind about being with Brent?" Bethany reached over and took her hand.

Allyson still hadn't said anything to her sister about what happened after she lost the baby all those years ago. She knew Bethany would be hurt that she'd kept it from her, but everything had been so screwed up back then. It was stupid to hide it, but it had caused problems for her and Trent that she didn't want to bring anyone else into the situation.

"I thought he wanted kids of his own." Allyson sighed.

"Doesn't he?" Bethany asked.

"He does, but…"

Allyson wasn't sure if she should say anything without Crash's permission, but this was her sister, and she knew Bethany wouldn't go out yelling it at the world. None of her friends would look at him any differently.

"But what?"

"Please don't say anything to anyone because I'm not sure if he wants anyone to know." Allyson glanced back at the bedroom door.

"You know I won't."

"He can't have kids." Allyson looked into her sister's shocked face.

"Seriously?" Bethany whispered.

"A childhood illness caused it." Her sister nodded.

"So, you don't want any more kids?" Bethany seemed surprised.

"I'd love to have lots of kids, but that's not possible," Allyson said as she swallowed the lump in her throat.

"Ally, you aren't that old," Bethany grumbled.

"It's not my age. Do you remember when I lost the baby?" Allyson asked her sister.

"Yes, I was pissed you wouldn't let me or dad come stay with you. I mean, it's not like we were in Newfoundland. We were only living an hour away from you in Ontario." Bethany squeezed Allyson's hand.

"The baby wasn't the only thing I lost." Allyson blinked back the tears that always threatened to fall when discussing that day.

As she told Bethany everything about almost losing her life and Trent making the decision to do the hysterectomy, her sister's eyes filled with tears. Bethany knew Allyson always wanted a bunch of children but never questioned it after losing her baby girl.

"I didn't want anyone to pity me," Allyson admitted.

"I can't believe you kept this to yourself, but it is ironic that the one man who can make you happy isn't able to have kids either." Bethany wiped the tears from her cheeks.

"I know. We wasted so much time because of it." Allyson smiled.

"I don't know if I'm ready to forgive you for not telling me yet, but I'm glad you and Brent are together. I wish you didn't have all this other stress going on with him." Bethany hugged Allyson.

"Me too," Allyson whispered.

When Bethany left, Allyson checked on the kids again before she headed into the bedroom. Crash sat with his back against the headboard with his eyes closed. His hair was still damp from the shower, and his full lips moved as if he were saying something to himself.

She watched him for several minutes before he finally opened his eyes and held out his hand. She quickly crawled onto the bed and snuggled next to him.

"I missed you," she whispered.

"I'm sorry. Lately, I'm always in the middle of a crisis, but I missed you too." He tucked his fist under her chin and pulled her lips to his.

He kissed her slowly, taking his time tasting her. She lifted her hand and pressed it against his cheek, running her nails through the two-day-old stubble. She opened her mouth as his tongue begged for entrance and swirled against hers.

When he finally pulled his lips away from hers, she whimpered with need. He hadn't touched her anywhere else, and still, her body was on fire with a kiss. His eyes gave him away because his pupils dilated as he rolled her onto her back and hovered over her.

"I love you, Ally."

He slid his hand under her shirt, and the heat against her skin caused goosebumps to erupt all over her body. She could feel the full length of his erection against her thigh as he lifted the thin material of her top to expose her bare breasts.

When his mouth clamped over the stiff peak of her nipple, she gasped and squirmed against him. She needed to feel his skin against hers, and she wiggled around until her shirt got tossed to the side. The whole time Crash sucked, licked, and kissed from one breast to the other. Then he ran his rough hand down her stomach and slipped into the waistband of her yoga pants.

The tips of his fingers barely grazed the top of her sex, and she lifted her hips to try and get his hand where she wanted it. He chuckled as he moved over her and knelt between her legs.

"Do you need something, baby?" He whispered while slowly pulling her pants down her legs.

"I need... I need you to..."

When she looked up, he was completely naked, and his thick cock stood up hard and waiting for her touch. When he tossed the rest of her clothes to the side. She wrapped her hand around his dick, pulling a deep groan from him.

"Ally, baby." Crash's head fell back as she slowly stroked his length.

"I need to taste you," she whispered as she sat up.

"Fuck, yes," Crash bit his lower lip as he sat back.

She lowered her mouth to the tip of his cock and rubbed her lips around the swollen head. He lifted his hips a little as if begging her to take it deeper into her mouth. With her hand wrapped around the base of his shaft, she flicked out her tongue and traced the head of his sex. He was the first circumcised man she'd been with, and she loved how it looked. He gently tugged her hair when she took the tip into her mouth.

Crash groaned as she hollowed her cheeks and began to move up and down his length. She squeezed the base of his cock as her lips and tongue slowly worked his shaft.

"Fuck, that feels so good," Crash murmured.

The way he fisted her hair and tried to take control of how she moved her mouth set her on fire. Did she want to be dominated and never knew it, or did she simply enjoy Brent doing it?

"Ally," Crash moaned as he tried to tug her from his dick.

"Yeah?" Allyson stopped for a moment and then took his slicked tip back into her mouth.

"I want to be inside you," he groaned.

Allyson wanted that too, and after a couple of long sucks, she popped her mouth off his cock. He was breathing like he'd run a marathon, but he picked her up and flipped her onto her back when she sat up.

"You drive me crazy," he growled against her mouth.

Allyson ran her hands down his back and cupped his firm ass. He clenched and dropped his head into the nape of her neck. Crash loved to have his ass squeezed while he was inside her, and she had no issues with grabbing it.

"I want to taste you first." He slid his hard body down over her.

"Yes," Allyson hissed.

He spread her legs as he positioned himself between them and ran both his thumbs along the seam of her pussy. With a hum of approval, he slowly lowered his mouth between her legs.

"So damn wet," Crash dropped down as he spread her folds with his fingers.

His tongue leisurely slid against the opening of her sex before coming to a stop at her throbbing clitoris. He swirled around it several times before he went back to lick her opening again. She gasped when he plunged his long tongue inside her and pressed his thumb against her swollen nub.

"Oh, yes," she whimpered.

Crash fucked her with his tongue as he continued to strum her clit, until her body started to tremble. The orgasm hit her, and she had to bite down on her lip to keep from screaming in pleasure. The last thing she wanted to do was wake the kids.

When her body began to come down, he lifted his head and gave her a sexy grin as he climbed back up her body.

"That was the sexiest thing I've ever seen," he murmured against her breast.

She didn't get a chance to say anything because he slammed his cock into her in one quick thrust. The movement was quick, but something caused her to fall over the edge a second time so fast that she wasn't able to hold in the shout of pleasure.

"Shhh, baby." Crash pressed his lips to hers as he pumped in and out of her.

She grabbed his ass and dug her nails into his skin, causing him to whimper and begin to thrust faster and harder. Each time he drove into her, his pelvic bone kept in contact with her sensitive nub.

"Brent, yes. Don't stop," she sighed.

"You feel so fucking good, baby. Your pussy loves my dick, doesn't it," He whispered into her ear. "It was made for you, Ally."

"Your cock is so big inside me. Fuck me, Brent." Allyson loved dirty talk.

Those words coming from her seemed to drive him crazy, and he knelt up, pulling her hips up off the bed as he pumped into her over and over. The headboard started to thump against the wall, and she pressed her hands against it to keep it from making a noise.

"That's it, baby. Take every fucking inch of it." Crash groaned as he slammed into her.

"Yes," Allyson bit down on her lip as she clamped down, and her body shuddered with pleasure.

"Fuck, yeah," Crash groaned as he pushed into her and held himself there.

He grunted as his body convulsed as he emptied inside her. He pulled out a little and then pushed in once more, and she felt him jerk inside her. After a few seconds, he lowered himself on top of her.

"I love you," he cupped her face between his hands.

"I love you too," she whispered.

For several minutes, they held each other before cleaning themselves up. Crash kissed the top of her head when they snuggled in bed.

"I love you with all my heart, Allyson," Crash said.

Allyson lifted her head so she could see his face. His tone concerned her, and she saw it when she looked into his eyes—the fear.

"What's wrong?"

"I want to make sure you know how much I love you. I don't want you ever to doubt it because…" he stopped.

"Because what?" She touched his cheek.

"I may have to stay away from you and everyone else to keep you safe." Crash wouldn't look at her.

Allyson jumped up on her knees and grabbed his face between her hands. He seemed startled by the move at first but then cupped his large hands over hers.

"You're not pushing me away. After all the time we wasted, there is no way I'm ever letting you go. Do you hear me?" Allyson stared down at him.

"But this guy who's looking for Sidney is insane. He's killing people to find her, and I've never been afraid of dying, but I've finally got everything I wanted, and I'm terrified he could take it all away." He pulled her down on top of him and pressed his face into her neck.

"I'm not letting you go; I'm scared too, but don't let him break us apart. Plus, you can't leave those kids. They've lost enough," Allyson held him tightly.

"You're right. I can't let this piece of shit hurt anyone else." Crash hugged her tightly against him.

"You have the whole town of Hopedale protecting you, and nobody can hold a candle to the people of this town."

She prayed she was right and everyone would keep them safe until the threat against him was gone.

Chapter 23

Crash sat in the conference room of the office building inside the compound. Keith was taking no chances with the safety of anyone close to or related to Axel and Crash.

Titus sat at the other end of the long table, his hands folded on the table in front of him. Keith probably wanted to keep the man as far away from Crash and Axel as possible, especially since he now wore a bandage across his nose and two very black eyes.

Axel almost seemed pleased as he walked into the room earlier and saw the older man. To his credit, he didn't say a word out of the way. The last thing Crash wanted to do was take sides, but he wouldn't let Axel beat the older man, no matter what Titus did.

"What we know so far is this guy doesn't use a pseudonym twice," James O'Connor stated as he stood at one end of the table next to Keith and Aaron.

James was one of the oldest brothers and was Deputy Chief of the Newfoundland Police Department. His twin brother John was the Chief. They usually didn't get involved in investigations, but because of Crash, James asked if he could help. As far as Crash was concerned, they needed all the help they could get.

NES had over thirty employees, but only about twenty did actual security detail. Crash was also not the only one who was a former military member. Besides he and Elijah, there was Damon Bullet Blackwood, who was married to one of Keith's cousins, Justin Bish Bishop, who was also a nurse; Adrian Rock Hudson, who served with Damon and Elijah, and Caden Rex Dixon, who served in the United States military. Keith and Bull trained the rest of the men.

When Crash glanced around the room, more than half the men were there, and a couple joined the meeting virtually. All these men worked jobs but took time to be there for Crash. He was honored, but the man they wanted was a ghost.

"Also, we know that both the other brothers are dead. We're assuming Emir killed Nasir, and Akram died when he was a teenager," James continued.

"We don't know what he looks like, what name he's using, or who works for him, but all his siblings are dead. We're batting a thousand," Damon said from the corner of the room.

"Chill your undies there. I'm working with our friend Lyon Tu to see if he can age progress that photo we have. It's not a clear picture, so he said it could take some magic on his part." Smash looked up from behind his computer. "Colt is also looking for names connected to Nasir."

Colt Burke was the company's newest analyst, and his sister was engaged to Crunch. Keith hired him because, like Sandy, the guy knew what he was doing, and from what Crash knew, NES now had three of the top Analysts in the country.

"Nobody came up with a nickname for him yet?" Bish chuckled.

"I don't have one either," Elijah smirked.

"You haven't been in the province long enough for us to come up with one," Adrian responded. "But there's a few stories I could tell to make it easier to come up with one."

"Shut it." Elijah glared at his friend.

"Although I would love to hear all the stories of Mr. Fancy Pants over there, we have to focus," Keith interrupted the banter.

Axel's phone interrupted the meeting, and he glanced at the screen. His eyes narrowed, and he ignored the call, sending it to voicemail. A few seconds later, it started to ring again, but Axel ignored it. When it rang a third time, he jabbed the answer button.

"What do you want?" Axel was pissed.

Crash wasn't sure who was on the other line, but from the way his friend's face paled, he was sure it wasn't anything good that he was being told.

"Why are you here?" Axel glanced around the room.

Everyone quietly waited to see if the phone call had anything to do with the situation or if it was something else. Axel's only family was his dad, and Clint Wright was with Crash's parents until it was safe.

"I can't meet you right now. I'm busy," Axel said with disdain in his voice.

As the call went on, Axel seemed to get irritated. Crash knew his friend hadn't had a drink in a couple of days, so whoever was on the line easily ruffled Axel's feathers.

"If this is so damn important, why can't you tell me over the phone, Felicity," Axel practically seemed to choke on the name.

"Ex-girlfriend," Crash whispered as everyone listened to Axel's call.

"Jesus, give me a minute, and I'll call you back." Axel didn't even wait for a response.

"Everything, okay?" Keith asked.

"She says she needs to talk to me pronto, and it has to be in person. She says it's not something she wants to say over the phone." Axel stood up.

"Where does she want to meet you?" Crash asked.

"I didn't ask. I was hoping to get her to come here. Is that okay?" Axel asked Keith.

"I don't know if that's a smart idea, but tell her to meet you at Jack's place. That way, you're still in Hopedale, and I can send a couple of the guys with you." Keith pointed to Rex and Adrian.

"I can go with him too." Crash stood up.

"We don't need both of you out in the open," Keith said.

"He wants to go to make sure I don't drink," Axel rolled his eyes.

"Do you think you will?" Keith raised an eyebrow.

"I hope not, but this girl has a way of getting under my skin," Axel admitted.

"I can go with them." Damon offered.

"Fine. Make it a time when there aren't a lot of customers at the diner," Keith ordered.

"When exactly would that be? When it's closed?" Sandy chuckled. "That place is always full."

Keith sighed and ran his hand through his thick red hair. He scanned the room and then picked up his phone. He tapped the screen and then put the phone to his ear.

"Hey, Aunt Alice. What is the slowest time of the day at the diner?" Keith was going to make sure to control the situation.

"Never, I told you," Sandy interjected.

"Just a time when there is a lull in customers." Keith glared at Sandy.

"Am I wrong?" Sandy looked around the room.

"Nope," several of the men answered.

She wasn't wrong. Jack's Place was the most popular restaurant in the town. Since there were only two, and the other was a fine dining place, the diner tended to get all the other business.

"Okay, can you ensure the booth in the back is free around three?" Keith listened for a minute. "Thanks, Aunt Alice."

When he ended the call, he texted something and looked up again.

"Call her back and tell her to meet you at Jack's Place at three," Keith told Axel.

Crash glanced at his watch. It was a little after one, which meant Axel's ex had two hours to figure out how to find Hopedale. Since she wasn't from Newfoundland, Crash hoped she had GPS to find the town. It was only ten minutes from the city, but it was easy to take the wrong turn and get lost.

Axel made the call, and after a few minutes of arguing about whether it was then or not at all, she agreed to meet him. When he ended the call, he looked as if he had been given a death sentence.

"I take it wasn't a friendly breakup?" James asked.

"Let's say she enjoys fancy dinners, clothes, and cars but doesn't have the money for any of it. When I stopped catering to her whims, she made my life hell." Axel leaned back in the chair. "She's a lot."

For the next two hours, the people around him spent time going through documents on the deaths of Otto, Perry, Halima, and Nasir. The only thing found was whoever killed them was a sadistic bastard. They'd been tortured in ways no human being should ever have to suffer.

"I'm guessing this guy started with the beating before moving on to using the knife." James shook his head. "Sick bastard."

"According to Allyson, all the stab wounds wouldn't have killed. They were in spots that wouldn't be fatal." Sandy pointed to something on the report James held. "This was fatal."

"A bullet to the head would do that." James sighed. "Maybe we shouldn't set this meeting up at Jack's Place. If this guy is watching for Crash and Axel, we could endanger other people."

"We won't let that happen," Keith nodded toward the four men waiting to go with Crash and Axel to the diner.

"We'll check to see who's there and won't let anyone inside until we leave," Adrian promised.

"My sons are working today, and Aunt Alice is there. Nan and Tom are always there helping out," James told them.

"Do you think I want anything to happen to my nephews, Aunt Alice, Nan, or Tom?" Keith sounded hurt.

"Not intentionally," James replied.

Keith stared at his brother as if he'd slapped him. James' two oldest sons worked part-time at the diner. Mason was also working with Keith's construction company as a laborer because James told him if he took a year off before going to university, he wouldn't be sitting home on his ass. Danny worked at the diner after school a couple of days a week.

"The boys will be fine," Aaron stepped between his brothers. "They don't work until four."

Aaron held up his phone. Crash assumed he must have texted them or James' wife, Marina, to find out.

"Okay, fine. I'll stay here and work with the rest of you to see if we can get anywhere." James pulled out a chair and sat next to Titus. "Now, let's go over everything you know again."

Crash glanced at his watch for the third time. It was ten minutes after three, and Felicity had still not arrived. Axel had called her several times, but she didn't answer, and he got agitated.

"Do you want another cup of coffee?" Alice asked as she stepped up to the table.

"I want a shot of whiskey," Axel mumbled under his breath.

"I don't serve that here, young man, but I do have coffee and some blueberry pie," Alice said with a smile.

"He'll have both, and I'll just have coffee. Thanks, Alice." Crash answered before Axel said something stupid.

"I'll be right back." Alice turned and scurried away.

"You know we should've told her to be here at two. She might be here by now." Axel clasped his hands in front of him.

"We'll give her another ten minutes, then we're leaving," Adrian sat at the table behind Crash.

They only had to wait four minutes for Felicity to come rushing into the diner. She glanced around until she spotted Axel and headed toward the table. Crash met her a couple of times, but he couldn't say he knew her.

"On time as usual, Felicity," Axel griped.

"I'm sorry, but this place is like a maze. I don't know how you live in this province." She dropped down on the seat across from Crash and Axel.

"Get on with it," Axel waved his hand in the air.

"Jesus, let me catch my breath, for heaven's sake." Felicity pulled off her gloves and slipped out of her jacket.

"This will not be a long conversation, so no need to get comfortable." Axel's body tensed beside Crash.

Before Crash could say anything, Alice dropped off their coffee and pie. She glanced at Felicity and smiled.

"Can I get you something?" Alice asked.

"I'd love a latte, but I doubt you have that here," Felicity said.

"In fact, we do. Can I get you one?" Alice's tone didn't change, but Crash knew the woman well enough to see the aggravation in her face.

"Thank you. Extra hot, please." Felicity turned back to Axel without as much as a thank you to Alice.

"What's this all-important thing you needed to talk to me about in person?" Axel sipped his coffee.

"It's kind of private," Felicity whispered as she gave Crash a once over.

"Pretend he's stupid and doesn't understand English," Axel responded.

Crash lifted his cup to his lips to hide the smirk when he heard Adrian chuckle behind him. Axel wasn't giving this woman an inch.

"God, you're such a jerk," Felicity sighed.

"Always will be," Axel retorted.

She was about to speak but stopped when Alice dropped off the latte. Felicity took a small sip, and her eyes widened in surprise. She seemed shocked that it tasted good.

"Do you like it?" Alice asked.

"It's delicious, thanks."

Alice left with a little skip in her step. Crash enjoyed it when people underestimated the diner because seeing them eat their words was a pleasure.

"Axel, I came here to tell you..." Felicity sighed. "I'm pregnant."

Axel didn't move for a moment, but then he laughed as he slapped the table. He continued to chuckle for several minutes before Felicity got annoyed.

"It's not funny," she whined.

"Sure, it is. Who's the father because I know it isn't me?" Axel crossed his arms over his chest.

"Who else would it be?" Felicity whispered.

"Do you think I'm that stupid? We haven't slept together in four months, so unless you're over four months pregnant, there's no way it's mine." Axel leaned forward. "Why don't you try to con the other three guys you were screwing while you were living in my place?"

"Fine. It's not yours, but I was supposed to..." She dropped her head. "I don't feel well."

"Me either," Axel shook his head.

When Felicity started to fan herself, Crash turned to see the man at the next table having trouble getting to his feet. Crash tried to jump up to help, but everything around him started to spin, and he fell back on the chair.

Crash lifted his head and tried to focus on where Rex and Damon seemed to struggle to stand. The last thing he saw was Damon drop to the floor and Rex fall next to him. Crash went to his knees, and everything faded to black.

Chapter 24

Allyson got a call to come to the conference room in Keith's office complex. The building contained his offices for NES and his construction company. They wanted her to go over some of the autopsy reports with Keith's dad to make sure they didn't miss anything. Ian was not able to help because he was working at the clinic.

Surprised not to see Crash in the room, she frantically glanced around the room for him. She hadn't seen him heading to the bunkhouse, but he'd been to the gym that morning on the other side of the building.

"He's gone to Jack's place with Axel, Rex, Bullet, and Rock," Keith told her, using everyone's nicknames.

"Is that safe?"

Allyson probably shouldn't be questioning them, but she had a knot in her stomach since she woke up that morning, and he wasn't beside her. He'd texted to let her know where he was, but there was something in the back of her mind that she felt she should remember.

"We don't believe this man would be stupid enough to try anything during the day," Keith said, but something in his voice told her he wasn't entirely sure.

Her attention turned to the other side of the table where Sean sat, his reading glasses on the end of his nose and a mountain of papers in front of him. She sat next to him and dug into the documents before him.

"I've got a spreadsheet here to compare each of the victims, including the two friends Crash lost recently," Sean pointed to the laptop.

"Are we looking for a pattern?" She shivered when she thought about how much pain the poor people must have endured before their lives ended.

"This guy uses the same pattern with each victim. I'm assuming he probably does it all in the same order." Sean clicked a few keys on the computer, and the spreadsheet popped up on the large screen at the room's far end.

"He's a sick bastard," Keith said.

"You'll get no arguments from me on that one," Sean replied.

Crash and Axel had been gone for a while, but she wasn't worried since Keith didn't get any call about an issue. After all, they were in a public place. She hoped the sick feeling she was having didn't mean anything, but the last time she'd had it, someone had taken her son.

James reviewed all the research Titus had dug up and confirmed they hadn't missed anything. Nobody seemed to be getting anywhere, but everyone was doing something. James only glanced up when his phone vibrated on the table. He tapped the screen and the speaker on the phone.

"Danny, I'm kind of in the middle of something right now. Can this wait?" James asked.

"Dad, me and Mason are parked in the lot next to the diner. Mason wanted to see his girlfriend before we went to work." James' son whispered.

"Okay, buddy, make sure you get to work on time." James shook his head.

"Dad, there are two black SUVs parked right in front of the steps with no plates. Dad, two guys went inside with gas masks on," Danny went on.

"Get the hell out of there, Danny." James jumped to his feet.

"We can't. There's another guy at the bottom of the steps, and if we go, he'll know we're here." Danny didn't sound the least bit frightened

"Jesus, Fuck." James picked up the phone.

"Dad, we saw someone climb down off the roof of the diner a few minutes ago, but Aunt Alice has guys come check the ventilation system regularly. I don't think this guy is a repair guy. He's wearing a mask, too." Mason's voice sounded shaky.

"Wait," Danny didn't say anything for a few minutes. "Dad, they just dragged someone out of the door and threw him in one of the cars."

"We're on the way." James started to leave the room.

"Danny, what else do you see?" Keith asked.

"Shit, I think that's Crash." Mason gasped. "It is. They're throwing him in the other truck."

"They went back inside again," Danny interjected.

Allyson's heart almost stopped as she listened to the two boys give a play-by-play of what was happening. James had grabbed another phone and sent some cruisers to the diner.

"Hey, Mason, you still got that air tag on your backpack?" Danny asked.

"Yeah," Mason replied, and then there was some rustling.

"I'll be back," Danny said.

There was the click of a car door opening, and Mason said to be careful. Allyson held her breath while she waited to hear one of James' sons say something.

"Mason? Danny?" James shouted.

There was nothing, not even the sound of the boys breathing. Time seemed to stop before the sound of car doors again could be heard through the phone.

"Mason? Danny?" James shouted.

"He's getting in the car now," Mason said.

"Where the hell did he go?" James asked.

"Remember the air tags you gave us for our book bags because we kept forgetting where we left them?" Mason asked.

"Yes," James groaned.

"Danny stuck one on the back of one of those trucks," Mason told them. "Shit, they're coming out again."

"Where's your brother?" James yelled.

They heard the sound of the car door and Danny breathing hard.

"That was close," Danny panted.

"Didn't I fucking tell you to stay in that car?" James shouted.

"Dad, they got Crash," Danny responded. "We're going to follow them…"

"Do not follow them cars." James' words were lost because the call ended.

"They wouldn't follow them, would they?" Allyson asked.

"They're O'Connor males. Of course, they will," Sandy interjected.

"Shut it," Keith snapped.

"If they don't get killed by those men, I'm going to kill them myself." James was out the door with everyone behind him.

"We better go. There's no way someone got Crash and Axel out of there without hurting someone. I better call Kurt, too."

Kurt O'Connor was Alice's husband; if anyone did anything to hurt her, he would make them wish they were never born. Allyson followed Sean out of the room, leaving Titus with Sandy and Colt.

"Let me know what's going on," Sandy shouted as Allyson left the conference room.

"I will," Allyson ran to catch up with Sean.

Fire trucks, police cars, and ambulances surrounded the diner. First responders continued to carry people out of the building and bring them to where they'd set up a triage area. Allyson scanned the area as she tried to keep her emotions under control. From the looks of things, they needed all the help they could get.

She was checking one of the servers when she overheard an officer say a container was found near the ventilation system. It pumped gas into the building and knocked everyone unconscious.

Allyson kept herself busy examining people as they arrived. So far, nobody was seriously hurt, but some of the older people were taken to the hospital for safety. Alice, Nanny Betty, and Tom were three of them. They'd been in the back of the diner helping the cook prepare for the supper rush.

"If anything happens to Aunt Alice, Nan, or Tom…" Keith pressed his lips together.

"Their vitals were stable when they left. Your dad's gone with them; they'll get the best care. They were all awake when they left." Allyson assured him.

"This was set up. I think that girl was part of it." James walked next to them.

"Did you get hold of Danny and Mason?" Keith asked.

"They're not answering. Marina is going…" James' words stopped when his wife came running across the parking lot.

"Where are they?" Marina shouted.

"They won't answer."

James' phone rang as he pulled his wife into his arms. When he looked at the screen, he blew a breath as he tapped it.

"Where the hell are you two?" James bellowed.

"Dad, they pulled into that old warehouse off the highway. Remember that place Poppy Tom said would be a perfect place to set up a training center for service dogs," Danny whispered.

"Yeah, out by Indian Meal Line," James waved to a couple of officers.

"Yes, they drove right in there. Hang on," Mason said quietly.

"Dad, I sent a picture. Another car just drove up, and a guy got out. He pulled another man out of the back of the car. He looks pissed," Danny said.

"You two need to get the hell out of there," Marina ordered.

"Mom, they won't see us. Trust me. We both have an air pod so we can hear you guys and keep our voices down. Nobody will see where we parked the car." Mason assured his mother.

"You got out of the car?" Marina gasped.

James pulled up the picture, and Allyson leaned over to see the screen. James used his fingers to zoom in closer, and Allyson gasped.

"I think that's Witt Davenport," Allyson said.

"Who's he?" Marina asked.

"He's a plastic surgeon. I worked with him at the Health Science." Allyson shivered.

Was he involved in this? Was this why he'd been at her house that day? Maybe there wasn't anyone at her home, and he was there to do something.

"That's the guy who helped with the intruder at your house, right?" James asked.

Allyson nodded.

"Boys, I need you both to get out of there," Marina begged.

"Mom, we can stay here to make sure they don't leave," Mason said.

"I don't want you two in danger," Marina sobbed.

"We're both going to be police officers. Isn't that what we're going to be doing every day?" Danny responded.

"Yes, but you're not trained right now. Get your asses out of there," James ordered.

"We wanted to help." Mason sounded defeated.

"I know, and we appreciate it, but those guys are dangerous. We have people on the way," James assured his sons.

Allyson knew these people had Crash and Axel. The question was, what were they doing to them?

"Ahh, Dad?" Danny whispered.

"What?"

"We aren't going anywhere?" Mason sounded nervous.

"What the hell do you mean?" James snapped at his sons.

"I think we may have tripped a booby trap because someone is coming through the trees.

"Get out of there." James and Marina said together.

There was the sound of rustling and the boys breathing heavily. They seemed to be moving but weren't speaking. They could probably hear their parents, but they were smart enough not to talk if someone was close by.

"False alarm." Mason chuckled.

"What?" James looked as if he wanted to strangle his sons.

"It was a moose," Danny laughed.

A loud pop echoed through the phone, and Allyson gasped.

"Did you hear that?" Mason whispered.

"That was a gunshot," Danny replied.

"Get out of there now," James ordered.

"We're getting in the car now but you guys better hurry. Someone is yelling inside like they're in pain," Danny told them.

With that, James took off in a sprint toward where his car was. Allyson watched as several cars sped out of the lot.

"God, please let him come home," Allyson prayed to herself.

Chapter 25

Crash could hear echoes of conversations around him, but it wasn't easy to lift his head. When he tried to move, he realized his arms were above his head, and his feet barely touched the ground. He tried to move, but it was as if he weighed a thousand pounds. When icy cold water hit his body, it made him jolt and fight against his restraints.

"There he is."

Whoever spoke sounded familiar, but the accent didn't. Crash shouted as another spray of icy water covered him. He shook his head and lifted his eyes to look at his surroundings.

Someone hung in front of him, and he had to blink several times to clear his vision. When he finally did, he realized it was Axel, and he was black and blue with blood streaking his face and body.

"He's still alive, don't worry." The man spoke again.

"Who the hell are you?" Crash tried to yell, but his voice became raspy.

"I'm wounded that you forgot me so easily," the man said.

Crash watched as two men stepped beside him and spun him around to face the man speaking. They kept a tight grasp on him, even with his restraints.

"It's okay, my buddy B won't hurt me." The accent was gone, and the face clear.

"Snapper?" Crash growled through his teeth.

"That is one of my names, but my true name is Emir Hasan, and you stole Aya from me." Snapper stepped closer, and his accent was back.

"I didn't steal anyone." Crash tried to lunge toward the man.

"Do you see these men? They are trained in several torture techniques I could think of." Snapper crossed his arms over his chest.

Crash scanned the four men behind him. He recognized one of them as Snapper's left-hand man when he was in Alberta. The guy was a mean bastard with a massive scar on his face. It looked like he'd been burned, and the scar pulled his left eye and mouth down.

"You remember Torch, don't you?" Snapper or Emir motioned to the scarred man.

"What are you going to do, beat us to death the way you did, Otto and Perry, or drive us over a cliff like you did with Wyatt?" Crash pulled on the restraints over his head.

"Maybe," Emir glanced at Axel. "This guy has a very foul mouth. He called me some nasty things."

Crash looked at Axel. His friend was still breathing, but he wasn't moving. Crash didn't like the way his head was hanging at an odd angle. He wanted to call out to his friend but wasn't sure if the man could respond.

"Now, help me get Aya, and I'll ensure you don't suffer." Emir picked up a long stick.

"Why would I know where she is? Titus was the one who put them in hiding," Crash lied.

He wasn't sure exactly what happened, but a stick poked into his ribs, and his whole body convulsed. The guy stuck him with a cattle prod. Crash had seen them in Alberta because he'd spent time on a ranch for a couple of months while he was sobering up.

"Hurts, doesn't it?" Emir pulled it back. "Titus will die a painful death when I find him, but I know you know where she is. Tell me, and I'll let Torch kill you humanly."

"Why would I tell you when you're going to kill me anyway? Fuck you," Crash spat.

Emir pulled out a gun from the back of his pants and turned toward the back of the room. Crash held his breath as another man dragged someone across the floor. He clenched his teeth when he saw the plastic surgeon come forward.

"Where can I shoot him that will be painful, but he won't die right away?" Emir asked Witt as if it was no big deal.

To his credit, Witt looked mortified by the question. Clearly, he wasn't there to hurt anyone, and from the way Torch shoved the man toward Crash, he wasn't there of his own free will. Still, he seemed familiar with Emir.

"Julian, what the hell are you doing?" Witt asked Emir.

"Julian?" Crash was confused.

"Yes, another of my names. Julian is my hard-working pharmaceutical salesman. He is calm and tries to be a friend. He even took out that woman you care about so much," Emir smirked. "She's a little too, shall we say, seasoned for my taste, but I knew you spent a lot of time with her. I thought maybe she would lead me to Aya, but she knows nothing."

Crash stiffened. The guy at the hospital the day Wyatt and Ellie died talking to Allyson. He seemed familiar, but Crash didn't get a look at him with so much going on.

"So, where can I shoot him?" Emir turned back to Witt.

"You're insane. I'm not going to tell you where to shoot someone." Witt started to back away, but one of the men stopped him.

"Would you rather I shoot one of your hands off?" Emir aimed the gun at Witt.

"You're fucking nuts," Witt shook his head. "I was brought here against my will, and now you want me to help you torture someone? I'm a doctor, for Christ's sake."

"You won't be if I shoot your hands off," Emir glared at Witt.

"Why do you want her?" Crash tried to distract Emir.

"Since my sister wouldn't fulfill her obligation to our family. It will be Aya's job to marry in her mother's place ." Emir sounded sadistic.

"This is not the eighteen hundreds. If she was raised in Canada, she probably has a mind of her own." Crash knew she did.

"I will train her." Emir stepped toward him and, without another word, lifted the gun and shot Witt in the chest.

Witt staggered backward and dropped to his knees with his hand against his chest. His eyes were wide with fear as he looked down to where his blue shirt was slowly turning red with his blood.

"If you're not going to help, you're useless." Emir placed the gun on the table next to Axel.

Emir slipped off his suit jacket and started to roll up his sleeves. The guy was large, and Crash had seen him hurt people, so he knew the guy could pack a punch. Emir whispered something to Torch, and the large guy dragged Witt out of the large warehouse.

"Now, you're going to see exactly what I did to your friends because even though I have men who do this for me, I wanted to be the one to hurt each one of you." Emir pulled his fist back and slammed in right into Crash's gut.

Punch after punch, Crash was held in place while Emir continued to inflict his punishment. He was sure at least two ribs were broken because it was hard to get air into his lungs. When a fist connected with his jaw, his head flew back.

It was difficult not to shout out in pain, but he wasn't giving this asshole the satisfaction of seeing he was winning, but he was. Crash wasn't sure he could take anymore and could feel himself lose consciousness, but Emir stopped and stared at him.

"Are all of you stubborn or stupid?" Emir punched him again.

Crash wasn't sure how long he'd been out, but he jolted awake when icy water hit his body. He cried out as he tried to move away from the spray. He was feeling the beating he'd received, but when he opened his eyes, Axel was gone.

"Where… is… he?" Crash grunted out the words.

"He's in the corner," Torch smirked and turned Crash to where he could see Axel tied to a metal table.

Emir was pulling a knife from Axel's stomach, and his friend cursed out in pain. Crash winced as Emir drove the knife back into Axel. He was going to kill them, but they couldn't let him get his hands on Sidney. No matter what, she needed to remain safe from this lunatic.

"Dear God help us," Crash whispered.

Chapter 26

Allyson did her best to keep from panicking. There were still people who needed her. She glanced behind her as Keith headed to the other side of the parking lot. He looked pissed, but who could blame him. Not only were three of his family affected by what happened, but four of his employees as well. Not to mention, there were friends of the O'Connors who had been inside.

Luckily, it wasn't a busy time of the day, or things would've been worse. Rex sat on the ground holding his head, and Allyson crouched to make sure he was okay.

"Are you feeling okay? You should've gone to the hospital," Allyson asked, checking his pulse.

"I'll be okay, sugar. I have a bit of a headache." Rex's Georgia accent was in full force.

"Can I at least recheck your vitals?" Allyson pushed.

"Sure, but I don't think I got as bad as the rest. When I felt off, I opened the window next to my booth," Rex assured her.

"Still, I'd feel a lot better."

"I think Rusty is about to pop a blood vessel," Adrian said from beside Rex.

Allyson turned when she heard Keith's voice boom from about ten feet away. It would've been comical if the situation wasn't so serious, but when a man well over six feet is towering over a young girl that barely reaches his chest, and she's yelling back, it was a funny picture.

Sidney and her parents arrived shortly after the situation at Jack's Place, and the girl was pissed. She did what she could for the victims and then ranted about how she needed to help fix this.

"This is all because of me. These people got hurt because of me," Sidney shouted.

"This is not on you," Keith told the young girl.

"If he weren't trying to find me, he wouldn't be killing and hurting people." Sidney shook her head. "They saved me from a life nobody wants to live only to be tortured and lose their lives."

"Sweetheart, you can't think that way." Roger wrapped his arm around her shoulder.

"You taught me everything to protect myself. I can knock a man out with one hand, but you never taught me how to deal with people dying because of me." Sidney covered her face with her hands.

Allyson wasn't sure what kind of training Roger could give her. As far as she knew, he was a foster father who had retired from his job.

"She could probably kill someone with one finger if he taught her what he knows," Adrian said.

"What do you mean?" Allyson asked as she tucked her stethoscope into her medical bag.

"Sandy found out he was part of the Canadian Special Forces. When he retired, he and his wife were recruited to take in children rescued from dangerous situations. His wife was with Canadian Intelligence," Adrian explained.

"From all over the world?" Allyson asked.

Adrian nodded and tried to stand up. When he staggered, he sat back down.

"There is an ambulance there. Please, both of you, go to the hospital and make sure everything is okay. I can only do so much here," Allyson begged.

"I think that's a good idea." Ian walked behind the men.

When they both nodded, Ian motioned for the paramedic to come over. Allyson turned her attention to where Sidney faced down Keith.

"If you don't let me go with you, I'll get my car and find this place myself." Sidney poked Keith in the chest.

"Are you trying to get yourself killed?" Keith glared at the young girl.

"I know how to use a gun, probably better than you. I want to face this asshole." Sidney wasn't backing down.

Allyson could see by the look on Roger and Ethel's faces they knew Sidney wasn't giving in. They looked concerned but proud at the same time.

"I don't care if you can use a gun. I don't want to have to worry about you getting yourself killed while I help my brothers and the rest of the cops bring home my friends. Do you get it? This guy is not like the bullies you face in school," Keith shouted.

"I'm not stupid. Remember, he killed people I care about to get to me. He murdered my mother," Sidney shouted right back.

"I don't have time for this. You're not going, and that's final," Keith didn't have a chance to turn when Sidney jumped in front of him.

"I'm not a child. I'm a grown woman. So either you let me go with you, or I follow you in my car." Sidney narrowed her eyes.

Keith tried to step around her and, at one point, picked her up and moved her aside. By the time he pulled open the door to his jeep, she had already jumped into the back seat.

"I'm coming too," Allyson jumped in next to the girl.

"What the hell is wrong with you both?" Keith yelled.

"I'll stay in the jeep, but I'll be there in case anyone needs medical attention," Allyson explained, praying nobody would need it.

She wanted everyone to be safe, but from what she'd heard when James spoke with his sons, she was worried. Crash was strong, but she'd also seen what this man did to his friends. She didn't want to think about what he was doing to Crash and Axel.

"For fuck's sake," Keith grumbled as he got into his jeep.

Trunk got in next to him, and both men checked their guns before Keith shoved the jeep into drive and sped out of the parking lot. He was silent for about five minutes and then locked eyes with Allyson in the rearview mirror.

"You know if you get hurt, Crash will have my balls in a vice?" Keith said.

"I'll stay in the Jeep and keep out of sight," Allyson assured him.

"You don't need your balls anymore anyway. Emily told Abbie you're getting neutered," Trunk chuckled.

"Fuck off, asshole," Keith grumbled.

The tension in the truck was thick, and Allyson glanced over at Sidney. The girl looked scared, but there was a determination in her eyes. She wasn't about to let the situation get to her. Allyson reached across the seat and took Sidney's hand.

"It's going to be okay," Allyson whispered.

Fifteen minutes later, Allyson wasn't sure any of them would be okay as Keith's jeep bounced over the uneven road leading to where several police cars were parked.

"Stay in the jeep," Keith ordered as he and Trunk exited the vehicle.

"I…" Sidney stopped as soon as Allyson squeezed her hand.

"We need to stay here. You don't want to endanger any of them, do you?" Allyson asked.

"No, I already did that." Sidney moved closer to Allyson.

"You didn't do anything, Sidney." Allyson wrapped her arm around the young girl.

She watched the men and women slowly surround the large building a few yards away. She couldn't hear much but made sure they crouched in the jeep. She could feel Sidney tremble as they clung to each other.

"I'm not as brave as I first thought," Sidney whispered.

"You're braver than you think." Allyson didn't know what else to say to her.

A few seconds later, shouting and the sound of guns going off startled them. Allyson wasn't sure who was shooting, but it didn't matter. Someone was going to be hurt or killed if the police didn't get the situation under control.

"He's running," a police officer shouted.

Allyson looked up as several police officers ran toward the trees. She barely got a glimpse of someone disappearing into the woods. He wouldn't make it easy for the authorities to put him away.

"Do you think Brent and Axel are okay?" Sidney whispered.

"I hope so." Allyson swallowed down the lump in her throat.

The jeep door was yanked open, making Allyson and Sidney scream. Ready to fight for her life, she lifted her feet to kick whoever scared them.

"Ally, we need a doctor. Quick," James said as he held up his hands.

"I'm a med student. I can help, too," Sidney offered.

"We can use all the help we can get," James told them.

Allyson was glad she'd had her medical bag with her when she jumped into the jeep, but her heart was thundering in her chest. Crash was in that building, and he'd been there for hours. Was it possible he was still alive? Her eyes filled with tears as she ran behind James toward the large opening of the warehouse.

The police escorted several men out of the building in handcuffs. One stopped and glared at her. The scar down the side of his face was horrific, and she almost missed it when he tried to lunge in her direction. Allyson stepped back, but the guy never got close.

"Do that again, and I'll handcuff your legs to your hands." Nick shoved the man roughly.

"In here, Allyson," James shouted.

On the floor, inside the door, someone lay on their side in a pool of blood. She knew it wasn't Crash because the guy wasn't large enough, but she gasped when she turned the man over.

"Witt?" Allyson whispered.

"He was shot because he refused to help with torturing Crash and Axel," James explained.

"He's lost a lot of blood, but I've got a pulse. It's weak, but it's there," Allyson said as she and Sidney worked on the doctor.

"Ambulance is here," someone shouted from the doorway.

When the paramedics came running in, Allyson stepped back as she told them what she'd done. Before she could finish, one of the guys shouted that Witt's heart had stopped.

They worked on him for twenty minutes, but it was too late. He was gone. Allyson tried to keep her composure as they covered him up, but the sob broke, and she covered her mouth with her hands.

"Where's Brent?" Allyson choked out the words as James pulled her into his side.

"He's over in the other section," James guided her deeper into the warehouse.

Allyson pulled in a shaky breath when she finally saw him. He sat against the wall, and his body was black and blue, but he was looking up at a police officer and talking. He was alive.

"Where's Axel?" Allyson asked.

"He's refusing to go to the hospital until we catch Emir," James told her. "But he needs to go. Both of them do."

When Crash looked up, his eyes locked with Allyson's, and she sprinted toward him.

Chapter 27

Crash wasn't sure what happened, but Emir bolted past him and out through the back of the building. The sound of gunshots echoed through the building, and he lifted his head in time to see dozens of police swarm around him.

"He ran outside," Crash told an officer who'd started to release the restraints.

The officer shouted at someone, and several ran out the back. Crash winced as someone lowered him to the ground, where he could lean against the cool concrete wall. He glanced over to Axel. He'd managed to push up against the wall but seemed to struggle for a deep breath.

"Jesus, I'm still alive," Axel huffed.

"We need to get you to the hospital," Aaron crouched in front of them.

"Not until... you get that son of a bitch in cuffs." Axel lifted his hand from his stomach.

"You're bleeding. Badly," Aaron pressed something against Axel's stomach.

A police officer stepped beside Aaron and Crash holding a first aid kit. Aaron worked to stop Axel's bleeding, but he was right. Axel was going to bleed to death if he didn't get to a hospital.

"Did you get him?" Crash asked.

"He took off into the woods and had an ATV waiting for him. He's in the wind," the officer looked pissed.

"Fuck," Axel groaned.

Crash was about to ask where the paramedics were when he looked up and saw her. Allyson walked into the opening of the room, and her eyes widened. He was probably a frightful sight if he looked as bad as he felt.

"What is she doing here?" Crash asked Aaron when he saw Allyson.

"Talk to Keith. She came with him." Aaron waved for Allyson to come closer.

She dropped next to Crash and gently cupped his cheek. A tear ran down her cheek as she slowly turned his head and examined his face. He tried not to wince when she touched the swelling across his cheek.

"I don't think anything in your face is broken," she said softly.

"I'm fine," Crash told her, trying to smile.

The movement of his lips was painful, and from the look on her face, he didn't fool her for a minute. He was about to ask her to check on Axel, but he saw Sidney beside him.

"Jesus. Is Rusty out of his fucking mind?" Crash looked up at Aaron.

"Rusty didn't have a choice." Keith walked in from the back of the building. "It was either let them come or run them over."

"We kind of hijacked his back seat." Allyson smirked sheepishly.

"He needs to get to a hospital." Sidney stood up and waved for the paramedics rushing toward them.

"They both do," Allyson agreed.

"I'm…" Crash stopped when she narrowed her eyes. "I'm going to the hospital."

An hour later, he sat in a hospital bed, regretting coming to the place. The doctors poked, prodded, x-rayed, and poked again, but considering the pounding he received from that bastard, he only ended up with a couple of broken ribs and some stitches above his eye.

Axel was in surgery because of three stab wounds. There was some internal damage, but they were lucky because they could be dead. Crash wasn't a fan of the the man, but he didn't deserve to die.

They needed to catch Emir soon because while he was free, nobody was safe. Although, he didn't have his men since they'd been arrested. The guy had no loyalty to his people because he ran and left them to face the music. Crash wanted two minutes alone with Torch to give him a taste of what was done to Axel.

"Are you having any pain?" Allyson asked where she sat next to him.

"Not much," he lied.

"You know there are medications that don't have narcotics in them," Allyson smiled.

She'd obviously picked up on his concern about taking anything that may cause him to relapse. He'd had a harder time kicking the pills than the alcohol all those years ago. He didn't want to go back there again.

"I know, but I'll take something if it gets too bad. I promise." He lifted her hand to his lips.

"I was so worried about you," she admitted.

"I'm sorry, but we didn't know… wait… did they find Felicity?" Crash asked.

"I don't know. Everyone in the diner was either brought to the hospital or treated in the parking lot." Allyson stood up. "Let me go check."

She was out the door before he could stop her, but since Hulk was outside the room, Crash knew he wouldn't let her get too far. He lay his head back against the pillow and tried to take a deep breath. There was nothing worse than rib injuries.

A few minutes later, Allyson returned with an iPad. She tapped the screen several times and seemed to spend forever scrolling through it.

"Nobody brought in with the first name Felicity," Allyson said as she continued to tap the screen. "I'll check the other hospital."

"She was at the table with us," Crash told her.

"No, she wasn't at St. Clare's Hospital either," Allyson held the iPad against her chest.

"They must have taken her too," Crash muttered to himself. "She had to be in on it."

"Wasn't she Axel's ex?" Allyson asked.

"Yes, but I'm pretty sure it didn't end well. He was pretty cold to her. Especially when she told him she was pregnant."

Crash closed his eyes to try and remember if he saw anything. He did have a fuzzy memory of being dragged down over the steps of the pub, but he couldn't lift his head. That was it until he woke up in restraints.

"Let's not worry about it now. Get some rest, and we'll deal with it tomorrow. A.J. said they were going to leave you alone until tomorrow. Mostly because I threatened him." Allyson smirked.

"Afraid of his sister-in-law, huh?" Crash smiled as he opened his eyes.

"I can be pretty scary when I want to be," Allyson sat next to him.

She placed the iPad on the side table and linked her fingers with his. It was as if her touch helped ease his discomfort.

"Try to sleep," she whispered as he let his eyes close again.

He wasn't sure how long he'd been asleep but woke to voices outside his room. He looked around the room and saw Allyson curled up in the small chair near the window. Her eyes were closed, but there was no way she could be comfortable.

"I need to know if he is okay," a female voice said.

"I'm sorry. I can't disclose any information on any patient." Hulk's voice echoed through the room.

"Are you a doctor?" the woman shouted.

"Nope," Hulk answered.

"Then you can't keep me from going in there." the woman didn't know who she was dealing with.

"Actually, I can. If you want information, go talk to the police." Hulk's body blocked the doorway.

"Who is that?" Allyson whispered.

"I have no idea." Crash shrugged.

Allyson uncurled herself from the chair and fixed her hair into a messy bun. She walked out through the door and stepped around Hulk.

"Keep your voice down. There are ill people here who don't need someone shouting and disturbing them," Allyson said.

"Who are you?" the woman asked.

"I'm Dr. Allyson Sullivan, and who would you be?" Allyson asked.

"I'm Felicity MacLeod. I need to speak to Axel or his friend. I didn't know what he was going to do. He said he was an old friend of Axel's and wanted to surprise him." Felicity started to sob.

"Why don't you come in here and we can talk?" Allyson guided the woman into Crash's room.

Hulk stepped inside, looking less than happy that the woman was getting her way. She didn't look the same as she had at the restaurant. Her hair was a mess, and her makeup smeared.

"I didn't know. I got Axel to the diner and then... I woke up in a motel room. I don't know how I got there." Felicity dropped down on the chair Allyson had been sleeping in.

"How did you meet him?" Crash asked.

Felicity looked up and gasped when she saw him. Her face paled, and for a second, he thought she was going to pass out, but she sat up straight and shook her head.

"Did he do this to you?" Felicity whispered.

"Depends on who you're talking about. Can you describe him?" Crash asked.

"He wasn't as tall as you or Axel. He had dark hair, and his eyes were almost black. He said he served with you both. He showed up on my step about two weeks ago. At first, I told him to go to hell because I didn't know where Axel was, but… he's charming. He asked what happened with us, and he seemed so interested." Felicity pulled her hands down over her face.

"But you live in Nova Scotia. Why are you here?" Crash knew she was the reason Axel left that province.

"When I found out where Axel was living. I told Titus," she said.

"Wait, did you say Titus?" Crash sat up.

"Yes, that's his name. Titus Gibson," Felicity told him.

Crash asked Hulk for his phone and searched for Titus Gibson because there had to be a picture of the man somewhere online. After all, he was a high-ranking officer at one time. It only took a few minutes, and he found a picture taken before they were sent overseas. Titus aged a bit, but there wasn't much of a difference.

"Is this the guy?" Crash held up the phone.

Felicity stood up and approached him, staring at the phone. When she looked up at him, she shook her head.

"No, this guy has a darker complexion." She sat back down.

That meant Emir was also using Titus' name to get information. How many identities was he using? Hulk stepped out of the room with his phone to his ear. Chances were he was calling either the police or Keith or both.

"Where is Axel?" Felicity asked.

"He had to have surgery, but he should be out by now," Allyson glanced at her watch.

"Can you check to see if he's out?" Crash asked her.

She glanced from him to Felicity and then back to him again. When Crash gave her a nod, Allyson headed out of the room, but Hulk stepped inside right away. Were they really worried that Felicity was going to hurt him? The woman was barely a hundred pounds and looked ready to fall apart if she moved too fast.

"A.J. is on the way to talk to her," Hulk informed him.

"Who's A.J.?" Felicity suddenly seemed very nervous.

"He's a police officer," Hulk said.

"Okay." she seemed to relax.

Allyson returned a few minutes later with Keith behind her. Clearly, he hadn't gone too far when Crash came to the hospital. Then again, Alice, Nanny Betty, Tom, Adrian, Rex, and Damon were brought in from the diner, not to mention the other patrons.

"Axel is out of surgery and in recovery. Everything went fine, but he'll be in hospital for a few days." Allyson sat next to Crash.

"I'd ask to see him, but I doubt he will want to see me. I can't blame him. We weren't a good match to begin with." Felicity sighed. "But I'd never wanted anything to happen to him."

"I'm sure he understands that, and once you talk to A.J., maybe I'll see if he is taking visitors." Allyson smiled at the woman.

Crash wasn't sure Axel would be so forgiving, but the woman seemed genuinely remorseful. Maybe she knew something that could help find Emir and end all this.

Chapter 28

"I'm telling you, these guys are fucking robots." Aaron sat back on the chair.

Allyson listened while Aaron, Crash, Keith, Nick, and James discussed the men arrested at the warehouse. They'd had several charges placed against them, but not one asked for a lawyer or responded to any questions from the police.

"That guy they called Torch, we had him in the room for six hours, and all he did was stare at the wall." Aaron went on.

"The other three are not much better. I'm starting to wonder if they speak English at all," Nick interjected.

"They're well trained. I remember Torch when I was in Alberta. He didn't speak very much, but he does speak English." Crash sighed.

He'd told Allyson that Emir had been the guy he bought the pills from back in Alberta, but he'd known him as Snapper. Evidently, the guy is good at hiding his accent or faking one. He was a Chameleon.

"Did you know any of the other guys?" James asked.

"I don't think so, but I didn't get a good look at the others. The only reason I remembered Torch was because of the scar." Crash shifted in the chair and winced.

His face was bruised, but most of the swelling was gone. His body was still black and blue, and it would take a while for his ribs to heal completely. He'd slept in the recliner since he was released from the hospital because he said it was easier to get up and down. Allyson wished she could help him more, but he refused to take anything stronger than Advil.

"I wonder how he got that scar," Keith said.

"He was definitely burned," Allyson remembered the guy who glared at her.

"You saw him?" Crash didn't look happy.

"They were taking him out when I was going in to help..." she stopped before saying Witt's name.

She still couldn't believe he was gone. The guy was an arrogant ass, but he didn't deserve to die. She still didn't know why he was there, but that was for the police to figure out. She shivered when she thought about what could've happened to Crash.

"I'm still not finished with you for letting her and Sidney come there," Crash said, pointing a finger at Keith.

"Like I said, I had to take them or run them over. Would you rather I did that?" Keith smirked.

Crash glared at him, but Allyson knew he wasn't mad at his boss. Neither she nor Sidney gave the man a choice, and Keith was not about to waste time trying to drag them out of the jeep.

"Did Felicity help at all?" Crash asked.

"She said he'd taken her to the warehouse and told her it would be turned into a place to help veterans. What a crock of shit he gave her. She did say he'd been looking at other property, too, but wasn't sure where it was located. Other than that, she wasn't much help." Aaron sipped from the cup in his hand. "She did say she was surprised he'd come looking for Axel because, from what she knew, Axel hated Titus. Of course, she didn't know he wasn't Titus."

"Axel hated the man. He and Dale were close," Crash told them.

"How is he doing, by the way?" Nick asked.

"They're releasing him tomorrow. He's been quiet, but he knows Felicity wasn't involved." Crash had talked to him after she'd dropped in to see him.

"So, no chance of them reconnecting?" Allyson asked.

"Not a chance. As far as I know, she left this morning to go back to Nova Scotia." Crash shifted in the chair.

"We should let you get some rest." Keith stood up.

"I'm fine," Crash said.

"Yeah. Sure." James chuckled. "Broken ribs are not painful at all."

Allyson was about to walk the men out of the bunkhouse, but her phone rang. She didn't recognize the number but answered it anyway since she was still waiting for some calls about transferring her insurance to the clinic.

"Hello," Allyson answered.

"Hi, Allyson. It's Julian Burgess. How are you?"

"I'm good. How have you been?" Allyson walked into the bedroom because the men were getting louder as they left.

"Great,but I haven't seen you around the hospital lately. One of the nurses said you're going into private practice," Julian said.

"Yes, here in Hopedale. I'm taking over for Sean O'Connor because he's retiring," Allyson explained.

"Wonderful. I'm calling to talk to you about that. I wanted to get you some samples to put in your clinic. Could we meet somewhere?"

Allyson wasn't in the mood to deal with his energy, but she'd never sat down with him to talk about what he sold. Usually, if she had questions on different drugs, she'd call her sister, but maybe going into private practice would give her a heads-up on new medications coming out.

"I'm actually not available right now, but let me take your number and get back to you. I've got some personal things going on," Allyson explained.

"Oh, no. Nothing serious, I hope," Julian said.

"Nothing I want to discuss right now, but let me get your number."

Allyson walked back into the living room, grabbed a notepad from her purse, and wrote down his name and number.

"Give me a couple of days, and I'll call you." Allyson dropped the pad and pen on the table.

"I'll look forward to it. Don't forget now, but if I don't hear from you in a few days, I'll touch base with you again," Julian pushed.

Allyson rolled her eyes—typical salesman.

"Sure," Allyson said.

When she ended the call, she turned. Crash sat on the edge of the recliner, trying to use the coffee table to get to his feet. He was trying to push himself so the kids could come back to the bunkhouse with him, but his family insisted he get well before he tried to take care of two babies.

"Caleb called me earlier," Crash told her as she sat down on the couch.

"What did he say?" Allyson reached across to hold his hand.

"He wanted to make sure I didn't go to heaven," Crash shook his head. "Said he missed me."

"I'm sure he does. Maybe we can get them to come over for a little while tomorrow. At least he can see you are okay," Allyson suggested.

"I don't want to scare him with all this." Crash pointed to his injuries.

"We can explain it's just a booboo." Allyson linked her fingers with his.

That night, Allyson tossed and turned. She couldn't get her mind to shut off because she kept going back to the day she'd gotten home, and her patio door was open. It had been weeks ago, but it had to be connected. When she finally drifted off to sleep, she was woken by shouting.

"She's got to know about this." Aaron's voice drifted in from the living room.

"I'll tell her, for Christ's sake, but I'm not waking her," Crash returned.

"Too late." Allyson stepped into the room.

"Shit. I'm sorry." Both men looked apologetic.

Allyson crossed her arms over her chest as she waited for one of them to fill her in on what was so vital. They glanced at each other, and each one motioned for the other to say something.

"I don't care which one it is. Tell me." Allyson sighed.

"Allyson, your house is on fire," Aaron told her.

"What?" She gasped and grabbed the wall to steady herself.

"I got the call, and I came right over here." Aaron stepped closer to her. "It's pretty bad."

"Why wouldn't you wake me right away?" Allyson looked around her brother-in-law to lock eyes with Crash.

"Because I heard you tossing and turning all night and know you didn't sleep much. The fire department is there, and there's nothing you can do until the fire is out." Crash pulled out a chair for her.

Allyson eased into the seat and tried to slow her heart. Everything she owned was in that house, not to mention things from her and Bethany's childhood. There were things she couldn't replace. Her mother's homemade quilts and the things she'd kept for Cameron that belonged to Trent were irreplaceable.

"I want to go see it," Allyson rasped as she stood up.

"There's really…" Aaron began, but she held up her hand.

"I need to see if anything will be salvageable."

She didn't wait for an answer as she made her way to the bedroom to get dressed. Now, she was convinced everything going on with Crash and the patio door incident were connected.

Her entire street was blocked off from one end to the other. Thankfully, the houses were not close together, so there was less danger to the other residences. Allyson covered her gasp with her hand when she saw the black soot rising from the place where her house was. Flames flicked out of windows, and streams of water from the firehoses caused heavy steam to fill the air.

"They aren't going to save anything, are they?" Allyson whispered as Crash wrapped his arm around her.

"I don't know, sweetheart." He kissed the top of her head.

"You shouldn't be here. You're still…" she began, but he pressed his finger to her lips.

"I wouldn't be anywhere else," he replied.

"Mom," Cameron shouted from the other side of the street.

He ran toward her, his eyes huge as he watched his childhood home burn. Allyson wrapped her arms around him and tried to hold back the tears.

"What happened?" Cameron asked.

"We don't know." Crash glanced around.

Something in the way he was scanning the spectators told her he was looking for something suspicious. She didn't know what it was, but he seemed to think it was all related as well.

For over an hour, the firefighters fought to douse the flames and make sure to extinguish the fire completely. By the time it was out, her house was gone. A shell of the former dwelling remained, steam still swirling from inside as firefighters sprayed water over what Crash called the hot spots.

"It's all gone," she sobbed.

"It's only stuff, Mom. Nobody was hurt. That's what's important." Cameron wrapped her in another hug.

"He's right, sweetheart. It could've been so much worse." Crash ran his hand up and down her back.

"I know you're right, but there are things I'll never be able to replace. My mom's quilts and pictures and that stupid bat were valuable to me," Allyson said with a snort.

"Mom, I have one of Nanny's quilts, and I'm sure there are copies of pictures with Aunt Bethany and Pop. Hell, Uncle Oliver probably has a ton."

Leave it to her son to always find the silver lining. He was right, though. It was just a house and things. She could replace it all, but the people she loved could never be.

Crash and Cameron finally convinced her to head back to the compound. It was getting close to supper time, but she couldn't feel any less hungry. The only thing she could smell was smoke, and she was desperate to shower away the smell. Cameron headed to the other bunkhouse to get cleaned up while everyone else headed home.

She stood and let the hot spray flow over her. Her body shook as the sobbing began, and when the shower door opened, she was on the floor with her arms wrapped around her legs.

"Baby, come here." Crash helped her to her feet.

The slight wince made her feel worse because he was still injured, but he simply turned her away from him. At first, she didn't know what he was doing until she felt his hands in her hair, and the scent of her shampoo filled the enclosure.

Crash gently massaged her scalp as he washed her hair. Allyson closed her eyes and let her mind try to shut out the past week's events. It was all too much, Crash's abduction and the fire, not to mention still having to worry about some psycho who wanted Crash dead because he couldn't get his hands on Sidney.

Crash rinsed and conditioned her hair and then washed her from head to toe. When she tried to stop him, he pushed her hands away and continued to clean away the horrible day.

When he finished, he quickly washed himself, and then they stepped out, and he wrapped a towel around her. Allyson found Crash in the kitchen, smiling when she finished dressing. Two plates sat on the table covered with stainless steel domes.

"Isabelle dropped off supper for us and Cameron. Cam took his food with him," Crash explained.

Isabelle O'Connor-Young was Keith's cousin and owned A Taste of Hopedale, one of the top fine-dining restaurants in the province. The food was incredible, and since the diner had been closed for a few days, she'd taken over sending the food to the compound. According to the O'Connors, if someone needed to be there, they shouldn't have to worry about cooking, even though there was a fully functional kitchen in each bunkhouse.

"That family is so wonderful." Allyson sat down at the table.

She wasn't hungry, but when Crash lifted the lids, the smell of the food made her stomach suddenly decided food was a good thing. The plate contained fresh steamed vegetables with pan-fried cod fish covered with a special sauce known as drawn butter.

"You're not wrong."

Crash poured them both a glass of wine from the bottle Isabelle had obviously left. It was chilled and opened so they could drink it with their meal. Chardonnay was one of her favorites, but that probably wasn't the reason she chose it. Isabelle prided herself on pairing the proper wine with a meal.

"That food was amazing," Allyson said when she finished.

"So was the company." Crash smiled.

"The company was exceptional." She reached across the table and placed her hand in his.

"I wish I could take you in that room and end the night making love to you," Crash whispered.

"I'd be happy being in your arms. I know you're still having pain." Allyson lifted his fingers to her lips.

"That I can do." He stood up and tugged her to her feet.

"Are you sure you can lay flat now?"

She didn't want him to be uncomfortable because of her, but he nodded and shut off the lights. He was careful with the way he crawled into the bed, but once settled, he motioned for her to come closer. They lay in silence, and she let out a contented sigh.

"I shouldn't feel this relaxed after losing everything," she whispered.

"You still have me." He kissed her temple.

"That's better than anything in that house." Allyson placed a kiss on his cheek.

Chapter 29

It took more than a week for Allyson to get answers about her house, and it wasn't good news. The fire was arson, and to make matters worse, they found a body inside the structure. Crash knew it was playing on her because they didn't know who the person was. From what Aaron found out, they used the body to start the fire.

Crash was feeling much better, and except for the slight twinge, if he moved too fast, he was mostly back to himself. Axel was healing but having a rough time keeping away from the bottle. He hadn't had a drink, but Crash could see he was struggling.

Allyson was finally going to the clinic to get things ready to start the following Monday. She had meetings with Sean and Ian and later someone from the hospital. He was glad to see that Leah would join Allyson as her nurse at the clinic.

He had finished changing Mila's diaper when his phone rang. He picked up the baby as he glanced at the screen. It was from the clinic, and he figured Allyson was calling.

"Hello, sweetheart," Crash answered.

"Hello, babycakes." Ian chuckled.

"Sorry, I thought you were Ally," Crash laughed.

"Didn't mean to disappoint you," Ian replied.

"No problem. What can I do for you?" Crash bounced the baby on his hip.

"Allyson said she left the number of the rep from the pharmaceutical supply company on a notepad there. I'd need to speak with him too," Ian said.

"Sure, let me check."

Crash glanced around the living room and kitchen and saw the small notepad on the counter. Trying to juggle Mila and the phone, he picked up the notepad.

"I think this is it. Julian Burgess?" Crash read the name.

"That's him," Ian replied.

Crash told him the number and dropped the notepad back on the counter. He was about to ask for Allyson, but Mila knocked the phone out of his hand, and before he could catch it, it dropped into the sink filled with the dishes he'd put in there to soak.

"Fuck," Crash yelled.

Mila jumped in his arms and stared up at him as if he'd slapped her. Her eyes filled with tears, and within seconds, she let out a loud wail. Caleb came running from the bedroom where he was playing and looked up at Crash, trying to soothe the crying baby.

"It's okay, buddy. She just got a bit of a scare." Crash assured the little boy.

"You yelled," Caleb said.

"I know, buddy. I'm sorry, but I dropped my phone in the water. I didn't mean to scare you or Mila."

The baby cuddled into his shoulder as she calmed to a soft sob. Crash felt horrible, but now he had no way to call anyone if he needed them. He swayed back and forth with Mila as Caleb sat on the floor and went back to playing with his car.

When Mila finally settled down, she fell asleep, and he placed her in her portable crib. He stepped out on the porch to see if anyone was around to call Keith about the phone. Not that he needed it for work cause he'd been placed on leave until this was all over.

Of course, the place looked abandoned, and he blew out a frustrated breath. He made his way back into the bunkhouse and sat down on the couch. Someone would drop by if they couldn't get hold of him.

Over an hour later, he did everything to dry out his phone, but it wasn't working, which pissed him off. Allyson told him she'd be home around supper time, and she probably hadn't had a chance to eat all day. A little after four, he tossed the phone on the counter and pulled out the stew that Keith's grandmother dropped off the day before.

The woman almost died a week earlier, but she was back, making sure everyone got fed. Alice reopened the diner, and everything there was back to normal. He stood next to the stove, stirring the thick stew, when his eyes fell on the notepad.

"Julian Burgess? Why does that name sound familiar?" Crash muttered to himself.

A flash of Witt shouting at Emir caused Crash to drop the spoon on the counter and pick up the notepad again.

"Julian, what the hell are you doing?" Witt asked Emir.

"Julian?" Crash was confused.

"Yes, another of my names. Julian is my hard-working pharmaceutical salesman. He is calm and tries to be a good friend. He even took out that woman you care about so much," Emir smirked. "She's a little too, shall we say, seasoned for my taste, but I knew you spent a lot of time with her. I thought maybe she would lead me to Aya, but she knows nothing."

"Fuck," Crash turned off the stove and ran to the front door.

He blew out a breath when he saw Keith heading toward the bunkhouse. He didn't look happy, and Crash hoped he wasn't right about this guy.

"Why is your fucking phone off?" Keith snapped.

"Rusty, you need to send someone to the clinic. I think Emir is heading there." Crash tried to keep his voice low.

Caleb was inside, and the last thing he wanted to do was scare the child again. Crash was surprised that the little boy was adjusting so well, especially with all the changes over the last several weeks.

"Why didn't you call me?" Keith pulled out his phone.

"I dropped my phone in the sink when I was talking to Ian." Crash explained. "Get someone over there."

Crash glanced over his shoulder at Caleb. The little boy stared at him, and Crash forced a little smile. He wasn't sure if the kid was fooled, but he went back to playing with his toys.

"What's the guy's name?" Keith asked him.

"Julian Burgess, but when Emir had us, Witt called him by that name. I didn't put it together until now." Crash wanted to run and jump in his car, but he couldn't leave the kids.

When Keith finished the call, he looked up at Crash.

"Go on. I'll get Trunk and Hulk to meet you at the gate. They're in the gym." Keith stepped inside the bunkhouse.

"What?" Crash stared at his boss.

"I know you want to go get this guy. I shouldn't be letting you go, but if it were me, nothing would stop me." Keith pulled his weapon from inside his jacket. "Don't let this prick get away."

Crash didn't hesitate as he ran down the steps; his ribs objected, but he didn't care. He needed to get to Allyson and make sure the feeling in the pit of his stomach was wrong. Something told him it wasn't.

As promised, Hulk and Trunk were waiting by the gate, and they jumped in his car when he pulled up next to them. The gate opened, and Crash practically put the vehicle on two wheels as he sped around the corner toward the clinic.

"Call Ian and see if he answers," Crash told Trunk.

"Do you want me to try Allyson?" Hulk asked.

Crash nodded because he couldn't get the words out. He hated speeding through the small town, but he needed to get to her.

"Ian said he left the clinic an hour ago. The guy didn't show up by the time he left." Trunk pulled out his gun from the back of his pants.

"Allyson isn't answering." Hulk met his eyes in the rearview mirror.

"Fuck," Crash shouted as he pounded the steering wheel with his fist.

"She may be caught up with something." Trunk pointed to the parking lot outside the clinic. "Isn't that her car?"

Crash saw the small SUV parked next to the entrance, but it was the vehicle next to hers that had the hair on the back of his neck standing up on end.

"Who's car is that?" Crash asked.

"I think that's Leah's car." Trunk leaned between the seats.

"It is. See the sticker on her car. That's the one the fire department gave out to the kids. Her dad is the chief." Hulk pointed to the back of the car.

Crash blew out a breath when he saw Aaron and two other police cruisers pull into the parking lot ahead of him. They may have been worrying for nothing, but he wasn't taking any chances.

He didn't even bother to turn off the car as he jumped out and ran toward the clinic. Aaron stopped him from running inside. He motioned for one of the other officers to go around the back of the building, and he headed into the front with the rest.

"Stay behind us," Aaron ordered Crash.

They stepped into the empty reception area and quietly moved together toward the hallway leading to the exam rooms. Aaron pulled open the door when Leah stepped out of one of the offices and shrieked when she saw them.

"Holy shit balls. What are you guys doing?" She pressed her hand against her chest.

"Where's Allyson?" Crash whispered.

"In her office with Julian." Leah pointed to the room down the hall.

"Are you sure?" Aaron asked.

"Yeah, I've been in the file room, but I would've heard them come back up the hallway. What's going on?" Leah looked concerned.

"Take her outside," Aaron ordered one of his officers.

They continued down the corridor toward the closed office door. The name still said Dr. Sean O'Connor, but this would eventually be her office when he retired. Aaron knocked on the door. Nobody answered.

"Allyson, it's A.J.. Are you there?" Aaron glanced back at Crash.

Aaron slowly turned the knob and pushed open the door. The room was empty, but papers covered the floor, and one of Allyson's shoes lay in the middle of the office.

"He's got her." Crash shook with rage.

Aaron pushed him out the door and guided him out of the building. Leah was next to her car, her hands clasped in front of her.

"Where's Allyson?" Leah ran toward them.

"He took her out the back." An officer ran toward them.

"How do you know?" Crash asked.

The officer held up her stethoscope. Crash's head began to spin, and he bent over with his hands on his knees. He was finding it hard to catch his breath when he thought about what this guy was capable of and what he could do to Allyson.

"He may call your phone." Aaron crouched in front of Crash.

"Well, that's fucking lovely because my phone is crap. I dropped it in the sink."

"I'm on it," Trunk said as he put his phone to his ear.

Keith would get his phone replaced, but would it be before Emir called him, or would this guy call at all? Was he after Allyson the whole time?

"I'm sorry, Crash. I was in the file room. I didn't…" Leah covered her mouth. "I should've…"

"He wouldn't hesitate to take you too," Crash pulled the woman in a hug.

"He's been coming to the hospital for months. He seemed so nice." Leah sobbed.

Of course, he did. The man was a master of manipulation and could fool anyone. What had he brought into her life? If anything happened to her, he'd never get over it.

"Keith has a phone being sent here as we speak," Trunk told him.

"With my number?" Crash asked.

"Yes, Sandy has multiple phones put aside for us. I don't know what she does, but she sets them up pretty fast," Trunk explained.

"Where the fuck did he take her?" Crash muttered to himself.

"We'll find her." Aaron sounded confident, but would they find her in time?

Chapter 30

Allyson sat across the desk from Julian and skimmed through the pamphlets he'd handed her. Leah stood next to her, chatting with Julian about Allyson's house fire.

"Do they know who the woman was?" Julian asked.

"No, the body was too badly burned. I think they're trying to match dental records." Leah sighed.

"Leah, you don't have to wait around." Allyson loved the woman, but she didn't want to talk about the fire.

"No can do. Dr. Ian said to wait for you." Leah smiled. "But I'll go do some filing if that's okay?"

"That's fine," Allyson told her.

"Nice to see you again, Julian," Leah said as she left the office.

Allyson sat back in her chair, and something hit her. Julian asked if they knew who the woman was. The police had not said whether the body was a man or a woman. She glanced at him for a moment and then shook her head. She was paranoid.

"Something wrong, Allyson?" Julian leaned forward.

"No, you asked if we knew who the woman was, but we don't know…" Allyson stopped when he pulled his hand from behind his back.

"I was hoping you didn't pick up on that," Julian said as he pointed a gun at her.

His voice completely changed, and he suddenly had an accent she'd never heard before. She looked at the door behind him, wondering if she should shout out to Leah, but she couldn't do that. Leah had been through enough in her life.

"I wouldn't do that if I were you." Julian stood up and locked the door.

"Call your man," he practically growled the words.

Allyson reached for her phone.

"Put it on the desk so I can see you are calling him," Julian tapped the desk with the gun.

She pushed the phone in the middle of the desk and unlocked it. She tapped Crash's number and hit speaker. The phone went right to voicemail. She tried again but got the same result.

"You must have another way to contact him," Julian snapped.

"It's his only number. Maybe he's charging his phone." Allyson went to stand, and Julian grabbed her arm.

"Well, we will have to call him later, but we won't be staying here." Julian unlocked the door. "If you make one sound, I will kill your friend. Do you hear me?"

Allyson nodded and tripped over her sneakers next to her desk. She kicked one under her desk and the other in the middle of the office.

Hopefully, someone would see it and know something was wrong, but to be sure, she purposely pushed a pile of papers on the floor when she tripped.

"Quiet," Julian whispered.

Allyson tried not to stumble again as he dragged her to the back of the clinic where the staff entrance was. She was relieved that they weren't going to pass the file room because Leah might see them.

Julian very quietly pushed open the door and held her against him as they let it close. Allyson almost fell over the narrow steps as he pushed her ahead of him, knocking her stethoscope off her neck. He looked down at it but didn't bother to pick it up. She thought he was going to put her in the back of the car, and she ran through ways she could get out, but he popped the trunk and pointed to it.

Allyson wasn't going to anger this man. He'd already killed several people, and she was sure he wouldn't hesitate to put a bullet in her if she did anything.

"We'll call him again when we are in a safe place," Julian said and then closed the trunk with her inside.

Allyson's heart pounded, and in the darkness of the trunk, she felt claustrophobic. She needed to keep from panicking and hyperventilating because that wouldn't help her at all. She closed her eyes, took several deep breaths, and tried to calm her racing heart.

The car jolted forward, and she shifted in the trunk. She couldn't hear anything except the engine and the sound of the road as they drove. She wasn't sure how long or how far they had driven, but the car took a sharp turn, and then she started to bounce as they went over an uneven road. It reminded her of the gravel road that led to the warehouse.

He wouldn't be stupid enough to go back there. Would he? This man had managed to stay under the radar for years. He fooled a lot of people, including her, because she'd never have guessed he had a Middle Eastern accent in all the times she spoke to him. They'd even had drinks together. Was he watching her all this time because of Crash?

The car slowed, and she opened her eyes. Should she try to escape when he let her out of the trunk or go along with him until someone found her? After all, he had taken her phone, and she knew Sandy could track it. Surely, he wasn't arrogant enough to think he could use her phone and not have it traced.

The trunk popped open, and he was there holding the gun. She awkwardly climbed out. It was hard to move with her hands bound, and she stumbled when he pushed her toward a small shack.

"Nobody would ever think of looking for me here. I've been under his nose for so long, and he never even noticed." Julian pushed her toward the door.

She pulled it open and cringed at the musty smell that hit her as soon as she walked into the small place. There was a propane heater and a rollaway bed in the corner. She wasn't sure of his plan but prayed he wasn't going to do anything to her.

He pushed her toward a kitchen chair and shoved her down on it. Before she knew what he was doing, he'd zip-tied her hands behind her and her legs to the chair.

"I'm going to call him again." Julian pulled her phone from his pocket and held it up to her face.

It unlocked, and he brought up Crash's number. When he tapped it, the call went straight to voicemail again. It wasn't usual for him to have his phone off, and she was concerned.

"How long does it take to charge a phone?" He shouted.

"I don't know. His phone is never off." Allyson wasn't lying.

Julian began to pace the small shack and mumble to himself. Allyson worried that he was becoming unhinged and wasn't sure he wouldn't kill her anyway.

"He will bring me my Aya if he wants you returned safely. If he stalls, you will suffer." He pressed the gun against her forehead.

Allyson swallowed the bile that came up in her throat and tried to keep the tears from falling, but they ran down her cheeks. It didn't seem to affect him in the least.

"Stupid women always think tears will bring a man to his knees. Not me. I don't care. I love to see a woman's tears." Julian ran the gun down her cheek.

She pulled away as much as she could, but he grabbed her face with his other hands and pushed the gun between her lips.

"I could pull this trigger now and wouldn't blink an eye. You are only a woman." He pulled the gun away and left her in the shack to step outside.

Allyson panted as she tried to compose herself. The man was insane, and there was no other word for it. There was no doubt in her mind that he was going to kill her no matter what.

"Brent, please find me," she whispered to herself.

Her phone began to ring, and the sound caused her to jump. She struggled to get to the phone before he heard it, but it was too late. He rushed in, and when he saw Crash's name on the screen, he grinned and answered the call.

"B, my man," Julian said with his accent gone again.

"Where is she, you, son of a bitch?" Crash's voice came through the speaker.

"Is that the way to talk to an old friend?" Julian smirked.

"You're no friend of mine. Where is Allyson?" Crash sounded as if he was about to explode.

"She's right here with me. Tell him, Allyson," Julian said and held the phone in front of her.

"I'm here, Brent," Allyson tried to cover her fear.

"Are you okay?" Crash asked.

"She is. For now, but if you want to see her again, you'll bring me Aya, or you'll get Allyson back in pieces." Julian pushed the gun to her temple, and Allyson whimpered.

"If you hurt her, I'll make you wish you were never born," Crash yelled.

"Tsk tsk, is that any way to negotiate with someone who can take away the woman you love? You do love her, don't you, Brent? Or should I start calling you? What was that name your friends called you?" Emir smirked. "Yes, Crash. Kind of ironic considering the way your friend Wyatt and his lovely wife lost their lives."

"You're the reason they're dead." Crash sounded as if he was going to explode.

"And I'll be the reason she dies if you don't bring me what I want. You have two hours, and I'll call you back with directions. Remember, I've got no issues with making this pretty lady suffer."

Allyson gasped as he dropped her phone on the table and shot a bullet through it. He wasn't going to call Crash back. He was going to kill her.

Chapter 31

"You can't bring Sidney to him." Roger practically lept out of the chair.

Again, they were gathered in the conference room with a timer on the monitor to let them know how long they had to put a plan together. They weren't even sure if he had any other men or women helping him.

Crash sat with his hand tangled in his hair as his head dropped down. Allyson was his world, and he would do anything for her, but he couldn't risk Sidney's life, and nobody would let him.

"He's not getting her," Titus said with his hands placed flat on the table.

"You don't have any say in what we do here. Don't forget, you're the reason we're all in this fucking mess." Axel glared at the man.

Keith, James, Nick, Aaron, Crash, Roger, Sandy, Axel, and Rex sat around the conference table trying to put a plan together that wouldn't put Sidney in danger and get Allyson home safely.

Elijah paced behind Crash, his hands linked, resting on top of his head. Allyson was his family, but he agreed Sidney couldn't be put in danger.

They were discussing different plans, but Crash only half listened as he watched Titus at the end of the table. There was something he wasn't telling them, and Crash was about to ask when the door of the room slammed open.

"I want to help," Sidney said through heavy pants.

"How did you find out about this?" Roger jumped up to his feet.

"Mom told me what was going on, but you should've been the one to tell me. Allyson is in trouble because he wants me, and I'm not going to let her get hurt." Sidney glared up at Roger.

"You're not doing this," Roger raised his voice.

"I'm a grown woman with as much tactical training as most military personnel. I can do this." Sidney wasn't backing down.

"You're not going near that psychopath," Titus shouted as he shot to his feet.

The room went completely silent as all eyes turned to Titus, who was practically vibrating at the end of the table. Crash never saw the man lose his cool, ever.

"Who the hell do you think you are?" Sidney scoffed.

"I'm your father. That's who I am, and that man isn't getting close to you." Titus stopped as if he realized what he'd said.

Roger's eyes narrowed, and Sidney's mouth opened and closed several times, but nothing came out. The rest of the room was dumbfounded. How did nobody know about this?

"You're her father?" Axel said slowly.

Titus fell back into the chair and let out a string of curses. He clearly didn't want this secret revealed at all. He pulled his hands down over his face, and Crash saw the tears in the man's eyes.

"You were never supposed to know," Titus whispered.

"You'd rather I believe my father abandoned me and my mother and left us with a murderer?" Sidney finally spoke.

"It was what your mother wanted." Titus's pained expression told Crash this wasn't easy for the man.

"Why?" Sidney asked.

"Because Emir would've killed her and you. I met your mother when she came to visit a friend in Canada. Emir brought her with him, but he allowed her to stay with her friend. He'd given orders that Halima wasn't to leave the house without an escort." Titus blew out a slow, shaky breath.

"The friend didn't listen," Sidney said.

"No, her friend was married to Virgil. She was also from Syria, but she'd moved here with her parents when she was a teenager. It's why Virgil could speak the language," Titus said as he glanced between Crash and Axel.

"He knew about this too?" Crash asked.

"He didn't know Sidney was my daughter, but he knew Halima and I were in love." Titus looked back to Sidney. "Emir had arranged for her to marry a man in Syria, but I think somehow he figured it out."

"Why would you say that?" Roger asked.

"Nasir said he was suspicious. He was the one who planned the extraction to make it look as if he wasn't involved. He wasn't the monster I led you to believe. The name on the papers you received was changed from Emir to Nasir, but everything went wrong when Emir suspected his brother of helping me."

Titus picked up a folder and held up a picture of a man. He looked familiar, but Crash couldn't place him.

"This man double-crossed Nasir and told Emir about the plan, but it ended up biting him in the ass because he ended up very badly burned in the fire after the explosion. They arrived the same time you did, and his men were the ones who killed Virgil and Dale."

"Torch was the man who went to Emir," Keith muttered.

"Yes, he's been Emir's right hand, and if what Nasir told me was true, the guy would die before he crosses Emir," Titus said.

James was on the phone right away, calling someone to make sure the men arrested were put on suicide watch. The last thing they wanted was these guys taking the easy way out.

"Why the fuck do you have to keep countless secrets?" Crash shot to his feet. "If we'd known this…"

"What? You could've been extra careful? This guy won't stop until he gets what he wants or someone takes him out." Titus stood up. "We have less than an hour to put a plan together, but you," he pointed at Sidney. "Are not getting involved."

Sidney slowly stood up and rested her tiny fists on the table. She leaned closer to Titus and looked him straight in the eyes.

"You don't and won't tell me what to do. You may be my biological father, but you don't own me. Isn't the reason I'm in danger because my uncle wants to run my life. No. Nobody is doing that. If I have to become the bait to get Allyson back to her family, I'll do it, and you can sit down and shut your mouth." Sidney's body shook with rage.

There was no way out of it. She wasn't going to back down, and from what Roger told them, she was very well trained. As the plan was put together, Crash watched the time tick down, waiting for the call. Titus looked as if he'd been chewing glass, and Sidney didn't even flinch as they set out the plan before her.

"We'll have you in view the whole time. We'll make a better plan when we know where this is happening," Keith explained.

"I trust you guys. Plus, I'll be armed, too." Sidney pulled a black box out of her backpack.

She pressed her thumb against the top of it, and there was a soft click. When she pulled out a Walther PDP F-Series and proceeded to take it apart and put it back together again, the whole room watched with wide eyes.

"That's a nice piece." Nick whistled.

"It's my favorite. I have a Sig Sauer P365, too," she said proudly.

"They're registered," Roger answered James before he could ask the question.

"Good," James replied.

Crash's phone rang, and everyone turned toward him. He glanced at the number, but it wasn't Allyson. Sandy tried to ping her phone after the call, but she had no luck. He tapped the screen and waited a second before he spoke.

"Hello," Crash stared at the phone.

"Hello, my friend. Are we ready for the exchange?" Crash looked up at Sidney, and she nodded confidently.

"Yes," Crash replied.

"Really? That seems almost too easy," Emir said with a sinister chuckle.

"Where do we make the exchange?" Crash snapped.

"Oh, there won't be an exchange…"

"You son of a bitch, you said if I brought her to you, Allyson would be returned." Crash fisted his hands on either side of the phone, which sat on the table.

"Such nasty language, but I did say you'll get her back when I have Aya, and you will, but I'll send her your location when Aya and I are free."

"How do I know we can trust that Allyson will be safe?" Crash didn't trust the man for a second.

"I'll give you my word," Emir promised.

"And I'm supposed to take the word of a killer?" Crash probably shouldn't be provoking him.

"If you want her back, yes." Emir sounded annoyed.

"Fine. Where am I meeting you?" Crash asked.

"Oh no, B, my friend. Aya will receive instructions once you send me her number. I'll instruct her where to meet me and when I have her with no tricks. I'll send Allyson's location."

This guy was nuts if he thought they were sending Sidney by herself, but he had to think he was winning. Crash gave him the number of the phone Keith issued to Sidney when the whole thing started.

"She's to come alone, or my men will make sure nobody leaves this location alive. She's to be there first thing in the morning," Emir said before the call ended.

Sandy had Sidney's phone up on the large screen, waiting for the text from Emir. Minutes seemed to tick by like hours, and when Crash thought the bastard tricked them, a message appeared on the screen from an unknown number.

Sandy immediately started to let her fingers fly over the keyboard of her laptop, bringing up a map of the large area about twenty minutes. It was a large area of woods between Hopedale and Summerbrook. Hunters used shacks during moose season, but Crash wasn't familiar with the area himself.

"That's a pretty big area," Axel said.

"I'm assuming that red pin is where he wants her to meet him," Sandy pointed to the flag.

"How the hell is she supposed to get in there? That's a lot of thick woods and brush." Crash could see there wasn't a whole lot of open space.

"I know that area." Elijah moved to the map. "My dad and Uncle Lewis used to take me there hunting."

Elijah turned around with a huge smile on his face.

"I know that place like the back of my hand," Elijah slapped his hand against the screen.

"Are you sure? You've been away for years. That could've grown in a lot since then." Keith scanned the map.

"I'm sure. Uncle Lewis still hunts with Dad, and they go there all the time. The only problem is, with the snow, it's going to be a hard hike to that clearing."

Crash didn't care what it took; he was getting to Allyson, and if what Elijah said was true, she was in one of those shacks. Hopefully, the ones showing on the aerial shot of the area were the only ones there.

"He wants me there by morning so we can go scope out the place before it gets dark." Sidney pulled her backpack on, but her gun was tucked in the waist of her jeans.

"Let's go," Crash shot to his feet."

Chapter 32

Allyson felt colder than she had ever been before. Julian turned on the small propane heater, but it did little to warm up the drafty structure. She was not dressed for the cold, and the wind seemed to howl through every little open crevice of the shack.

With her hands restrained behind her, she couldn't even warm them up, and they were painfully cold. Her fingertips were stinging, and she was sure they were near frostbite.

"Can you please release my hands so I can warm them?" Allyson begged.

"It is colder than I'd expected it to be today. I can't wait to get out of this damn Canadian weather." He lifted the heater and brought it closer to her.

"I'll be leaving soon, but don't worry. When I'm safely away from here, I'll send your location to Brent. There should be enough propane to last until morning." Julian glanced around the shack and then headed to the door. "It was nice to meet you."

With those words, he opened the door and slammed it behind him. Allyson sat wide-eyed, expecting him to come back, but when seconds turned into minutes, she realized she was there alone.

He hadn't released her restraints, and although the heater was closer, she was still cold. She struggled with the zip ties, but she didn't have the strength in her icy hands to break the plastic. She tried to kick her legs free, but again, no luck.

"Damn it," she shouted into the quiet of the shack.

She shifted in the chair to see if she could move closer to the heater. Maybe there was some way to use the heat to weaken the zip ties. Moving the heavy chair was a struggle, but after shifting several times and once catching herself from tipping over, she was closer to the heater but not enough to touch the plastic restraint against it.

She couldn't give up. The heat did start to warm her icy fingers, and she flexed them several times to get circulation back in them. She began to tug and pull at the ties to the point she knew they'd bitten through her skin. Still, she didn't stop. It was so quiet, with only the sound of her grunts as she struggled to escape and the wind outside.

She didn't know how long Emir had been gone, but she was sure it was enough time for her to escape without him knowing, although he didn't say he wasn't coming back.

She'd been struggling forever to get her hands free, but it worked, and she was able to slip her hand out of the bond. When she looked at her wrists, she cringed. The blood was probably the reason she was free.

She looked down at her legs, and her only idea was to stand up and slam the old wooden chair against the side of the shack. It had seen better days, and she was sure it wouldn't take much to break the legs.

It took three tries before the chair shattered, and she managed to pull her legs free. For a few minutes, she stood by the heater to warm up before she attempted to leave, but what if she got lost? She didn't even know where she was.

As she warmed herself, she glanced around the sparse shack. There wasn't much in it, but it did seem familiar. It was as if she'd been there before or somewhere similar. The one window in the structure was boarded up, and she wasn't keen on opening the door until she knew for sure Julian was gone.

She should probably stop thinking about him as Julian because it wasn't his name. He was Emir Hasan, the man who'd murdered more people than they probably knew about. She could understand why Titus wanted to keep Sidney away from the man.

"Brent, what do I do? Leave or stay and hope you find me?" Allyson whispered.

As she took a second glance around the shack, she saw a wooden box at the end of the bed. She didn't expect to find anything, but maybe there was a blanket to use when she hurried across the small area and dropped down to her knees.

The box creaked as she pulled open the top. She pulled the items out one by one and placed them on the floor next to her. Inside were binoculars, a first aid kit, zip ties, game bags, a flashlight, a lighter, and several other things that a hunter would use. She'd seen her dad and uncle pack for their moose hunting trips and had gone with them once, but it wasn't for her.

If she was right, the large bag at the bottom probably contained rain gear. She ripped open the bag and started to cry. It was exactly what she needed. Under the bag was also a knife and a backpack with protein bars.

She also found a map with the area number on it. As she scanned the map, she knew exactly where she was. This was the same area her dad had hunted, and although it had been a long time since she'd been there, she had a map and could find her way out.

It had turned dark, and heading out into the deep brush of the woods was a stupid idea. She hoped the propane would last all night, so she pulled the heater close to the bed. The mattress wasn't the cleanest thing, but she needed to try to get some sleep before she made her way out.

Allyson got little to no sleep, but she finally gave up when dawn came around. The heater had shut off before daylight, and she was starting to feel cold, but that wasn't going to stop her.

She pulled on the gear from the bag she'd found and tucked it in as much as possible. Her boots weren't meant for deep snow, but at that moment, it was all she had. She shoved the first aid kit, binoculars, lighter, and flashlight into the backpack and pulled it on her back. The knife she kept in her hand in case she needed to use it.

She slowly opened the door and looked out, making sure nobody was there. She was sure Julian or Emir wouldn't have waited outside all night in the cold, so she felt somewhat confident he was gone. As she closed the shack door, she glanced down at the map at the x. She assumed it was where she was and started to follow the path on the map.

She'd been trudging through the woods for what seemed like hours when there were three loud pops, and someone screamed. Allyson stopped for a moment but continued to make her way along the path. She'd taken three steps when her foot landed in a hole, and she toppled to the ground. The pain surged through her ankle, and she cried out. When she tried to lift her foot, she found it was broken. Now, what was she going to do?

Chapter 33

Crash and Axel hid in the trees next to the open area where Emir wanted Sidney to meet him. She wasn't there yet, but she was in the car waiting for the time to come closer. There was no sign of Emir, and Crash was anxious that the man had already done something to Allyson.

"She's fine," Crash muttered to himself.

"She fucking well better be." Elijah's voice crackled in Crash's ear.

"Any movement yet?" Keith asked through the earpiece.

"Nothing," Axel answered.

"I'm soon going to have to come in there." Sidney sounded nervous.

"We got you," Roger told her.

Before they left the compound, there were several discussions on who would be going, and Roger didn't give anyone an option. Titus wanted to join them, too, but he was outvoted. He was left standing outside the building as they all pulled away in the vehicles.

Keith had called Sandy to see if Titus had returned to the conference room, but she said he had headed toward the safe house.

Crash wasn't sure if he would ever trust the man again, but he was pretty sure Titus would do anything to protect his daughter.

"Alright, I'm heading in through the path," Sidney whispered; then there was the sound of a car door.

The only sound around them was the rustling of the trees and the wind whistling through the brush. It was cold, but Crash and Axel kept their weapons aimed at the open field. He was confident that Keith, James, Nick, Aaron, and Roger were in similar stances. Elijah was still in the SUV, keeping an eye for anyone coming in behind Sidney.

"I think he was bullshitting about having more men here," Axel whispered.

"I think you're right." Crash stiffened as Sidney appeared from the trees.

She searched the area as she ambled to the center of the field. Crash scanned the trees to see Emir's appearance but found nothing. Sidney threw her hands up in the air and spun around.

"I'm here. Where are you?" Sidney shouted.

The next thing Crash saw was her digging into her pocket to pull out her phone. She tapped the screen and put it to her ear.

"Hello," Sidney answered.

"Hello, Aya," Emir's voice crackled through Crash's earpiece.

"Smart girl to put that on speaker," Keith chuckled.

"My name is Sidney. Now, where are you?"

"I named you Aya, but maybe Sidney suits you better because of your parentage." Emir chuckled.

"What is that supposed to mean? I'm here now. Come out so Allyson can go home," Sidney shouted into the phone.

"Look up." Emir stepped out from the other side of the field

Sidney put the phone back in her pocket and started to walk towards him. She held her hands in her pockets, where she'd put her gun. Crash could hear her muttering something to herself, but they couldn't figure out what she was saying.

"Stop," Emir yelled when she was in the middle of the field.

"Can we stop with the dramatics?" Sidney snapped.

"You think I'm here to take you away, don't you?" Emir walked toward her.

"Isn't that what you wanted?" Sidney didn't seem the least bit scared of him.

"I did until I found out the truth." Emir stopped.

"The truth?" Sidney's voice cracked.

"Yes, how your whore of a mother allowed herself to be used while she was promised to another man. One *I* chose for her." Emir's eyes narrowed.

"We need to get her out of there," Roger whispered.

"That's not my fault," Sidney continued.

"No, but you must pay the price," Emir lifted his gun, but someone stepped out of the trees and shouted.

"It's me that should pay the price." Titus stalked toward Emir.

"You," Emir practically growled the word. "I'll be happy to end you too."

Emir turned the gun toward Titus and shot, but Titus had a weapon himself, and before Crash blinked, there was a bullet-sized hole in the middle of Emir's forehead. Sidney screamed and dropped to her knees. Crash and Axel jumped up and ran toward where Emir lay on the ground.

"It's over." Axel kicked the gun away from Emir's hand.

"He's been shot," Roger yelled from where Titus was on his knees.

Crash was frantic as he searched Emir for something that told him where Allyson was, but the only thing he found was a phone. He called Sandy to see if she could find something to tell them where the phone had been.

"We'll find her," Axel assured him.

In less than an hour, the field was filled with police and more of the NES staff. Elijah called his father and uncle to get an idea of where they could look for Allyson in the area. Lewis told them there were four hunting shacks in the area.

"What if he didn't even keep her here?" Crash blew out a breath.

"She's smart, and she'll find a way to get in touch if she's not here," Aaron told him, but Crash wasn't convinced the man believed it.

Sandy sent them all maps of the area with the cabins marked. Crash, Trunk, and Axel headed to one while the others were divided among the rest of the searchers.

Sidney wanted to help, but Keith convinced her to go to the hospital with Titus and Roger. She went reluctantly, but she was pretty shaken.

"These woods are so fucking dense," Trunk grumbled.

"It's why it's a good hunting ground," Elijah said from behind them.

"I thought you went to check one of the other ones." Crash asked.

"I'm not familiar with the other ones, but I've been to this one." Elijah pointed to an opening in the path. "If we go that way, we'll get there faster."

Crash thought they were going in circles until he heard someone crying. Axel must have heard it, too, because he put a finger to his lips. They tried to be as quiet as possible. Crash was in front as he turned onto another path, all the air whooshed out of his lungs.

"Allyson," he practically screamed.

She sat on the ground with her leg wrapped in gauze and sticks on both sides of her ankle. Somehow, she'd managed to position herself in the shelter of some trees, and when she looked up, he wanted to find Emir and kill him again. Her lips were practically blue, and her face red from the cold. Ice had formed on her lashes and hair, but she lifted a hand to reach for Crash, and he dropped to his knees.

"I...I tried... my ankle..." Allyson whispered through chattering teeth.

"We'll get you out of here."

Crash couldn't hold back the sob that erupted from his throat as he picked her up in his arms. They'd found her, and she was alive. That's all that mattered.

The hospital waiting room was full by the time they arrived. In true Hopedale fashion, the news of Allyson's rescue had flown through the town. Crash never left her side until they wheeled her into the trauma room.

He was now pacing the waiting room with her dad, sister, and son, as well as his family. Sandy had brought Lily to watch Caleb and Mila so Crash's family could be with him at the hospital. Sidney had joined them and let them know Titus was okay. He'd been shot in the shoulder but would make a full recovery.

"She's a tough cookie, Vera," Lewis said where he sat rubbing his hands together.

It sounded as if Allyson's father needed to say the words to convince himself everything would be okay. Thankfully, he wasn't alone, and Vera sat next to him, rubbing his back gently.

"You're right, dear. She's tough," Vera agreed.

It seemed as if they'd been there for hours and probably had been. Several people had brought coffee, and he'd lost count of how many cups he'd had. When he looked up to see Cameron leaning against the wall, Crash walked toward him.

"I'm sorry, Cam," Crash said as he stood next to the young man.

"Why are you sorry?" Cameron looked confused.

"None of this…" Crash stopped when Cameron raised his hand.

"Unless you're about to say none of this is your fault, I don't want to hear it because it's not. Let's be glad the asshole is dead, and Mom is safe." Cameron held out his hand. "You're good for her, and I don't know why it took you guys so long to get together, but I'm glad she found you."

Crash took Cameron's hand, shook it, and then pulled him into a hug. He had his mother's forgiving nature and willingness to help. When Crash pulled back, Cameron smiled at him.

"Just don't break her heart," Cameron said.

"I won't," Crash promised.

Chapter 34

Allyson wasn't sure if she'd ever be warm again, but the heated blankets the nurses brought her were undoubtedly the best thing in the world. She was slightly hypothermic when she arrived at the hospital, and she'd broken the ankle, which sucked, but she was alive and safe.

She looked next to her and smiled at Crash as he softly snored in the chair, his arms crossed and his head hung down. He hadn't left her since she was admitted, and no matter how often she told him to go, he refused.

Even with two days' worth of stubble and mussed hair, he was still the most handsome man in the world to her. She lay her head back on the bed and sighed. The doctor wanted her to stay for a couple of days to make sure there were no issues with being out in the cold weather for so long.

She'd only been out there for maybe two or three hours, but thankfully, she had managed to move into the trees to keep from being out in the wind.

"I've come baring food from Jack's place for the winter princess," Cameron walked into the room with several bags.

Crash's head popped up, and for a second, he looked dazed. He shook his head and went to relieve Cameron of some of the bags. She was starving because the food in the hospital sucked.

"Winter princess? Really?" Allyson rolled her eyes.

"According to Elijah, you had icicles on your eyelashes." Cameron chuckled.

"He is full of it," Allyson shook her head.

When she took the first bite of the thick, delicious burger, she hummed with delight. It was the most amazing thing she'd ever tasted at that moment. When she moved to sit up, she grimaced.

"Do you want me to get the nurse?" Crash quickly dropped his food on the table.

"No, I'm fine. I moved too fast," Allyson assured him.

"If you need something for…" Crash stopped when she glared at him.

"Says the man who refused pain medication not too long ago," Allyson retorted.

"She's not wrong," Cameron said, then took a huge bite of his burger.

By the following day, Allyson wanted to go home and was in the middle of telling the doctor when she realized she didn't have a home anymore. Her house was gone.

"What am I going to do?" She sighed.

"I think your issue is taken care of," Bethany smiled from the doorway of the room. "Hi, Adam."

"Hello, Bethany," Dr. Adam Cramer replied.

Adam was a colleague and knew most of the same people Allyson knew since he practically treated most of them at one point or another.

"Well, I'll get the nurse to bring in your release papers, and well, you know the drill." Adam smiled and left the room.

"Is he married yet?" Bethany chuckled as she sat next to Allyson.

"No, I don't think he'll ever settle down. He's married to the hospital, I think," Allyson threw back the blankets and frowned at the cast. "This is going to be inconvenient."

"It's only for a few weeks. It could've been a lot worse." Bethany's voice hitched.

"I know," Allyson didn't have to be told.

"Brent finally left your side, I see," Bethany teased.

"He's not far. Went to get a wheelchair." Allyson chuckled. "What did you mean when you said my issue had been taken care of?"

"You'll find out." Bethany grinned as she helped Allyson dress.

The drive back to Hopedale was relaxing, and she managed to sit so that her leg didn't get jostled. Crash held her hand most of the way and brought it to his lips to kiss her knuckles. When they passed her street and headed toward his home, she wasn't sure what was happening.

"Before you protest, hear me out," Crash said as they stopped in his driveway.

"Okay?" Allyson said, dragging out the word.

Crash turned in his seat and took both her hands in his. She wasn't sure where this was going, but from the expression on his face, he seemed determined.

"Your house is not livable right now, and I'm sure you'll want to rebuild it, but until you do, I want you to stay with me and the kids." He cupped her cheek. "I love you, Ally, and I want you to live with me for the rest of our lives, but that's up to you. Right now, this can be temporary if that's what you want. No pressure."

Allyson glanced up at his house and smiled at Caleb waving from the large living room window. Megan was behind him, holding little Mila and helping the baby wave as well. Was this what she wanted? She turned back to Crash and smiled at the hopeful glint in his eyes.

"I'll stay," she whispered as she leaned forward and kissed his lips.

Over the next several weeks, Allyson's family and friends did what they could to salvage anything from her burned-down home. They found her safe, which contained all her papers and thankfully was fireproof. Most of everything else was either damaged or trashed.

Her dad did bring her copies of any pictures he had of her mom and photos of her as a kid. Thankfully, she'd been smart enough to save all her photographs of Cameron on a thumb drive that was also kept in the safe.

She managed to still see patients at the clinic with the help of a knee scooter that Crash had gotten for her because the crutches were not working for her. She only had another couple of weeks left with the cast, and she couldn't wait to get it off.

Axel had been struggling a lot, especially when the medical examiner identified that the remains found in Allyson's house was Felicity. She had been dead before the fire, but that didn't make things easier for Axel. He may not have wanted to be with the woman anymore, but nobody wished that on her.

She'd talked to her father about the property where her house once stood and asked if he wanted to keep it or if they should sell it. Her dad came up with the idea of turning it over to Cameron so that he could build his own place there someday.

Crash was having nightmares but had been seeing the therapist to work through them. With everything that happened, it was a wonder they all weren't in a psychiatric hospital. The men who were arrested from the warehouse were finally answering questions since they all knew about Emir's death. They admitted to breaking into Allyson's home to plant cameras. They said Emir was convinced Allyson knew Sidney because of her relationship with Crash.

Titus was recovering from his gunshot and rented an apartment in St. John's. He wanted to get to know his daughter, but it was going to be a gigantic ask for Sidney. Still, the man was trying.

"I'm convinced it would be easier to throw the food over Mila," Crash grumbled as he tried to feed the little girl.

"Pretty sure that wouldn't help." Allyson laughed.

Crash sighed as Mila giggled and grabbed the spoon, knocking it all over the tray of the highchair. Some of it flicked up and hit him in the middle of the chest, making Allyson stifle her laughter.

"Both of you think this is funny, huh?" Crash narrowed his eyes and scooped up a heaping spoonful of baby food.

"Don't even think about it," Allyson cautioned.

"Why? You can't run away now," Crash teased and pulled the spoon back as if he were going to flick it.

"Brent," Allyson said with a warning tone.

"Allyson." Brent smirked.

Allyson struggled to stand up and pull her scooter closer. Caleb was on the other side of the table staring at the standoff, and when Crash released the tip of the spoon, the food hit her right in the chest.

"Uh oh," Caleb giggled. "You're in trouble now, Uncle B."

Before Allyson could retaliate, Mila squealed and slammed her hands down on her tray. Crash turned in time to see the bowl of food completely flip over and cover his pants.

"Karma," Allyson laughed.

"Are you taking her side, little girl?" Crash crouched in front of the baby.

"Da.. da," Mila said with a giggle.

Crash stopped and stared at the baby. They had been calling him Brent in front of Mila, and he never discussed what they would call him in the long term. He'd already had Mike O'Connor put in the legal adoption papers since his specialty was family law.

"Did she…" Crash stared at Mila.

"She called you Dada." Caleb sat up excitedly.

"I don't… I never…" Crash locked eyes with Allyson.

"To her, that's what you are." Allyson smiled.

Crash dropped down on the chair in front of the baby, and Allyson could see he was struggling to keep his composure. Between the loss of his friends and everything that had happened over the last couple of weeks, he didn't have time to grieve.

"Don't cry, Uncle B." Caleb stood next to Crash.

"I'm okay, buddy." Crash hugged the little boy.

"I miss Mommy and Daddy." Caleb rested his head on Crash's shoulder.

"Me too." Crash's voice cracked.

Allyson wished she could do something to take away the pain of the loss for both Crash and Caleb, but the truth was that they needed to go through the stages.

"Mommy and Daddy will always be in here," Crash whispered and pointed to Caleb's chest.

"In my heart," Caleb smiled.

"That's right, buddy." Crash kissed the top of his head.

"You and Ally are our other mommy and daddy, right?" Caleb looked up with hopeful eyes.

Crash met Allyson's gaze across the table, and she swallowed down the lump in her throat. She wanted lots of children and never thought she would get the chance again.

"Is that what you want?" Crash asked, but he was still watching Allyson.

"Yes," Caleb said without hesitation.

Crash didn't say anything, as if he was waiting for her response. What could she say? There was nothing she wanted more than to be with Crash and help raise Mila and Caleb. She nodded.

"Then let's see what we can do about putting that plan into action." Crash's face lit up.

Chapter 35

It had been almost six months since Wyatt and Ellie died, and Crash stood beside their graves, holding Allyson's hand. He'd left the kids with his mother while they went to visit. They were heading to Mike's office as well to finalize the adoption papers.

He never expected the whole thing to take so long, but Mike told him it wasn't unusual. Since he'd been named the legal guardian in the will, it would make things easier, but they also wanted to have Allyson on the papers.

"You shouldn't be here." Crash crouched in front of the headstone.

He didn't know why Wyatt had hidden what he knew from Crash and Axel. They probably would never find out, but the one thing they did know was that because of him, Crash was going to be the father he always wanted to be. It was bittersweet.

"We're going to adopt them today. I debated about changing their last names, but Ally gave me the idea to put both your names as the kids' middle names. So, they'll have two middle names now." Crash smiled up at Allyson.

"I'll never let them forget either of you or the sacrifice you made to keep Sidney safe." Crash stood up. "When they're older, I'll bring them here to visit."

He stood quietly with his arm wrapped around Allyson for a few minutes, and then they slowly left the cemetery.

"It would be easier if you were married, but it will still work," Mike told them as they sat across from him.

"But it can still be done?" Crash asked.

"Yes," Mike smiled.

"Good," Crash glanced at Allyson.

She looked uncomfortable with the conversation, and he wondered if she thought he didn't want to marry her. The truth was, he had planned to ask her that evening. They might only be together a few months, and it had been one thing after the other, but the one thing he knew was that she was it for him.

"I'll file this with family court, and it should be settled in a day or two." Mike shook Crash's hand. "If I haven't told you, I'm sorry about your friends."

"Thanks," Crash nodded.

His mom called as he arrived home. She was so excited that he was going to propose to Allyson that she practically squealed on the phone. He was glad Allyson had not stayed close to him because his mother was loud.

"So, she has no idea?" his mom asked.

"I don't think so," Crash whispered.

"I'm so happy for you, Brent. I know you've loved her for such a long time."

"Thanks, Mom. Are you sure you don't mind keeping Mila and Caleb all night?" He knew her answer before she said it.

"Are you kidding? I love having them here."

By the time Crash ended the call, he found Allyson in the living room curled up on the couch, the fireplace lit, lights off, and a blanket over her legs. He turned on the sound system, playing some soft country music, and joined her on the sofa.

"Are Mila and Caleb okay?" Allyson asked as she leaned back against him.

"Yeah, Mom is in her glee," Crash kissed her cheek.

"So, we have the whole house to ourselves all night. Whatever will we do?"

Allyson dropped her head back and looked up into his face with a huge smile. It faded when she saw the expression on his face. His face was probably green because he was scared shitless to ask her. He hadn't planned any big, elaborate romantic gesture. He wanted to make it simple and tell her how he felt.

"What's wrong?"

"Absolutely nothing." He smiled and cupped her cheek.

"Why do you look ready to vomit?" She could read him better than anyone.

"Ally, I promise you there is nothing wrong." He stood up and took her hands.

When she stood up, he pulled her into his arms and stared at her beautiful face. It was as if everything he was so scared about disappeared, and the words flowed.

"I don't know what I would've done without you over the last few months. I've loved you for so long that I don't remember when it started, but I know it's only grown so much that you are my reason for breathing. I did some pretty shitty things, but I must have done something good to have you come into my life." Crash stepped back and took her hands. "I know this is fast, but the truth is, you're all I've ever wanted."

"Brent, what are you…" Allyson stopped when he dropped to his knee.

"I love you, and I want to be a family to you, Caleb, and Mila. I want you to be my wife. Allyson, will you marry me?" Crash pulled the ring from his pocket and held it up to her.

Allyson stared at the ring with tears in her eyes and her hands clasped in front of her chest. He smiled when she giggled and dropped down to her knees next to him.

"Brent, I love you too." Allyson cupped his cheek. "Are you asking this because you think it will make the adoption easier?"

"Absolutely not. I planned this before Mike told us that. I promise this has nothing to do with the adoption. I love you, and I want to spend the rest of my life showing you how much I love you."

Allyson gazed into his eyes, and he held his breath. Seconds ticked by, and his heart felt as if it was going to jump out of his chest if she didn't say something. Then she smiled.

"Yes. Yes, I'll marry you." Allyson flung herself into his arms, and they tumbled to the floor.

"Jesus, woman. You had me worried there for a minute." Crash took her hand and slipped the ring onto her finger as they lay on the floor.

"I love you, but I'll always keep you on your toes." She kissed him hard on the mouth and then jumped to her feet.

"What are you doing?" Crash lay flat on the floor and stared up at her.

"You'll have to follow me to the bedroom to find out." She winked and backed out of the room.

This was the woman he loved, and he was damn well sure going to meet her in the bedroom because, from that point forward, she'd be by his side until the day he took his last breath.

Epilogue

His head felt as if someone had hit him with a bat, and it wasn't easy to lift it off the pillow. The bed felt different, and he forced his eyes open to glance around the room. The light streaming in from the large window caused him to slam his eyes shut.

Gage 'Smash' Hodder groaned as he rolled over away from the window. He hadn't felt this hungover in years because he'd stopped drinking excessively ten years ago. Before that, he would get wasted every Friday and not sober up until Monday morning.

He met his boss at a club in Alberta the week after getting arrested for hacking into a government website to see if he could do it. Keith 'Rusty' O'Connor found Gage at the bar and offered him a job, but only if he cut down the partying.

"If you stop getting smashed every weekend, I'll guarantee you a job you'll love and pay you what you're worth," Keith said to him that night.

It was also how he got the nickname Smash, but only a few people knew that. He always told people he got it because of the way he could smash the computer keys, and most people believed him.

However, now he lay in a strange bed, definitely hung over but couldn't remember drinking. As a matter of fact, he didn't remember anything about how he got where he was. He sat up in the bed and lifted the blanket.

"I'm fucking naked," Smash muttered to himself.

He ran his hands down his face and scanned the room. It was definitely a hotel and not a cheap one. As he stretched to glance out the window, he heard the door of the room open. Smash pulled the sheet up as a woman came into the room.

"Oh, look who finally woke up." She smiled as she held out a large cup. "I figured you'd want coffee."

Smash took the drink and sipped carefully. He held back the moan as the rich, dark liquid slid down his throat. He couldn't remember coffee ever tasting so good; after another sip, he placed the paper cup on the nightstand and looked around for his clothes.

"Ummm… I'm pretty sure I wasn't naked when I came in here," Smash asked the woman as she sat on the foot of the bed.

She went to the closet and pulled out a hanger with a dark suit and tie hanging around the collar of the jacket. Smash never wore suits unless it was a formal function, but he hadn't been to one in over a month when one of his co-workers got married.

"I hung it up so it wouldn't be all wrinkled." She lay the suit next to him on the bed.

"Thanks," Smash said.

"You seem confused." The woman walked into the bathroom.

"Yeah, a little. I don't remember anything about last night," Smash admitted.

"I believe that. You were quite intoxicated by the time you got here. I managed to get you in bed before you fell over," she said from the bathroom while Smash searched the pockets of his suit for his phone.

"Where exactly are we?" Smash asked.

"The Fairmount Hotel," she replied.

Well, at least he knew he was in St. John's, but how and why, he had no idea. He also had no clue who the woman was in the bathroom. That was something he never experienced before. He didn't do one-night stands and only slept with women he'd dated seriously.

"You have a late checkout, so we'll get breakfast first."

The woman didn't seem to know he was drawing a complete blank from the previous night. Would he be an asshole if he asked for her name because his mind was a complete blank?

"I could eat," Smash told her.

"Good, it's already ordered and should be here in a few minutes. You have enough time to shower." She walked out of the bathroom and smiled.

He had to admit she was beautiful, and the dress she wore hugged her body in all the right places. She had ample curves, which was what he liked, but there wasn't a spark of recognition when he looked into her eyes.

"Is there a robe I can pull on?" He asked.

He didn't care what happened the night before. Smash didn't feel comfortable walking around naked in front of a stranger. She raised an eyebrow at the request and then chuckled as she tossed a white terry cloth robe to him.

"You seem a lot more modest this morning." She smiled.

"I'm sorry. I don't normally do this, but last night is a blank." Smash struggled to pull on the robe.

"You don't remember anything?" Her eyes widened.

Smash felt horrible. He wasn't sure if she was hurt or angry that he didn't remember her. He had never used a woman in his life, but Smash had a feeling he'd done something.

"I'm sorry, no," Smash admitted. "Who are you, by the way?"

"You really don't remember," she walked around the bed and sat next to him.

"No." Smash shook his head.

"My name is Yvette, and I'm your wife."

About the Author

What does someone say to describe themselves? You could start by saying what others say about you. Scratch that. It doesn't matter what others think about you. So here we go.

First of all, I'm a wife and mother. I'm also a grandmother. That alone would fulfill any woman's life, and to be honest, it does. But.....

I'm also a writer, someone who loves to tell stories of love, suspense, heartache, and, of course, happily ever after. For most of my life, I've written those stories for myself. It's a type of therapy, I suppose. I love the characters I create. They become part of who I am because there's part of me in them.

So... Now that you know this about me. I hope when you read my books, you fall in love with them.

You should also know that I'm a Newfoundlander. What is that, you ask? We're a proud people who live on an island off the east coast of Canada. Some people believe Canada ends with Nova Scotia. It doesn't. If you keep going east, you will see a beautiful island full of amazing people and magnificent scenery. That is where my stories are set because, let's face it, the greatest stories always come from the places you know and love.

Rhonda Brewer Books

NES Series

O'Connor Brothers Series

O'Connor Girls

O'Connor Prequel

Where to find me

Rhonda Brewer

Keep up to date on all things new.

Follow me on

Rhonda Brewer Webpage
Facebook
Twitter
Instagram
Amazon
All Author
Bookbub
TikTok

Sign up for my newsletter and never miss another release!

http://www.rhondabrewerauthor.com/talk-to-me

www.ingramcontent.com/pod-product-compliance
Lightning Source LLC
Chambersburg PA
CBHW071043250626
47159CB00002B/353